LOVE
in the time of the
DEAD

Tera Shanley

OMNIFIC PUBLISHING
LOS ANGELES

Omnific Publishing
1901 Avenue of the Stars, 2nd floor
Los Angeles, CA 90067
www.omnificpublishing.com

First Omnific eBook edition, October 2013
First Omnific trade paperback edition, October 2013

The characters and events in this book are fictitious.
Any similarity to real persons, living or dead,
is coincidental and not intended by the author.

Library of Congress Cataloguing-in-Publication Data

Shanley, Tera.
    Love in the Time of the Dead / Tera Shanley – 1st ed.
    ISBN: 978-1-623420-58-1
    1. Contemporary Romance — Fiction. 2. Zombies — Fiction.
    3. Apocalypse — Fiction. 4. Urban Fantasy — Fiction. I. Title

10 9 8 7 6 5 4 3 2 1

Cover Design by Micha Stone and Amy Brokaw
Interior Book Design by Coreen Montagna

Printed in the United States of America

For Anthony, my Beautiful Boy in English.

Chapter One

The earth had been conquered by darkness, and the dead didn't remain so for long. The streets had been paved with destruction, and the stubborn searched for the light because they had hope. They searched for the light because they must; because giving in to death wouldn't relieve the gnawing ache of hunger for something more. There were whispers of a place where the Deads gathered at the water's edge in the mountains of old. A place where peace could still be found in simple acts of valor and happiness, achieved by the lucky and the determined. The world hadn't come to an end, just an end as man knew it. But there had to be a balance for the chaos. There had to be asylum from the damned.

The words were written on a mirror in an old, abandoned gas station bathroom in what Laney Landry fervently hoped was bright red lipstick. The last sentence was hurried and scribbled, the letters fusing together to snake into one monstrous word, like the writer had run out of time. Run out of life. At least that was what the pile of bones to the right of the sink suggested. They were picked so clean they didn't even have an odor. She read it again, and loss clenched inside of her. It was the first page of a book, and it had been so desperately long since she had read one. Since she had read anything with an ounce of hope in the spaces between the lines.

A shadow covered the dusty evening light that filtered through the ceiling-length frosted window beside the bathroom stalls. A lone figure shuffled slowly across the span of it. The man looked huge, but maybe it was just the shadow playing tricks on her. Not one of her team.

She cursed softly and grabbed her backpack. Where there was one, there would soon be others, and she'd be damned if she was dying in some Quickie Mart bathroom out in the middle of nowhere. She sprinted for the door but hesitated as she opened it. The words were stark against the dirty mirror and they stirred in her…something. It had been a while.

"Jarren," she hissed to her older brother. He and the others rifled through the storage room in search of supplies that had long been picked dry, like the bones in the bathroom. "Time to go. We've got Deads, at least one, on the west side of the building."

"Let's move," he whispered, and Mitchell and Guist headed for the door without hesitation. She got stuck behind Mitchell on the way out, which wasn't all bad. His backside was lovely, but she wouldn't tell him that in a million years. It would inflate his barely-controlled ego to the size of the gas station in two cocks of a pistol. She allowed a private smile. Best to look and not touch with that one.

The east side of the building was clear for the moment, but the Deads would catch their scent fast enough. Jarren led them to the edge of the woods at a full sprint.

Finding the perfect sleeping tree was an art form many had not had the chance, or time, to master. The deeper they hiked into Colorado territory, the more important it became to track down the clusters of pine trees big enough to hold them. Pines weren't like oaks or Bradford pears. They offered strong, sturdy trunks that grew straight up into the sky. Their branches were thick and plenty and so thinly spaced on the large ones that they acted as a ladder to safety. For a four-man team of tree climbers, finding a sizeable pine was right up there with finding snickerdoodles. The trick was finding one old enough to hold them in pairs, and young enough to grow branches within reaching distance of the ground. *There.* She pointed silently to the same one Jarren was already eyeing. Mitchell and Guist scurried up a nearby evergreen with the grace and agility of a pair of jungle cats. No doubt she didn't look like that when she climbed, but they all had a foot of height on her. Valid excuse.

Her fear of heights had ebbed with the appearance of a new, much more debilitating fear, which was waking up to breakfast. *Being* someone else's breakfast. She gripped the lowest branch while Jarren kept watch. Her brother didn't offer her a boost, but that was his way. He'd said it a million times before: coddling her wouldn't turn her into a survivor. As she strapped her harness around the tree trunk and cinched the straps around her torso, Jarren chose a branch in close proximity to hers. Home sweet home and family dinnertime had changed so terribly much in the past few years.

"Let me see it again," Jarren ordered as he pulled a roll of semi-sanitary bandages from his rough first aid kit.

"It's fine," she said around a bite of Spam.

He arched his eyebrows and waited. There really was no use in arguing with him when he got like this. Stubborn ran in the family. She sighed dramatically and lifted her shirt to reveal the day-old stained bandages that hid an impressive wound.

The gauze stuck on each lap, but determined and gentle, he removed it slowly and tucked it into a crevice in the bark. He whistled, long and low.

"Well, it seems to be healing, so there's that." Her brother had never been one for flattery.

He shook his head in disbelief for probably the thousandth time in the week since she'd been bitten. This bite from a Dead was the second one she'd received and lived through, and it seemed to be exactly two bites more than any other human soul on the planet had ever survived. Jarren had been right in his childhood taunts. She was a freak.

She winced in pain as he poked and prodded, searching for infection. Deads didn't just bite. They ripped flesh.

"Well, at least now we know for sure," he said with a significant look.

Immune. Other than a brutal healing time, she was otherwise unaffected by the bite of a Dead and the rapid infection that tenaciously turned its victims into slobbering, depraved, hunger-crazed zombies.

Her first bite had happened in the year of the outbreak. She and Jarren had been hunting for a small colony and taken by surprise when they ran into a large group of Deads. They got away by the skin of their teeth, but Laney had been bitten on the leg after she lagged behind and fell. The implications of that day would stick with her for as long (or short) as she lived. The Dead had spit out her flesh as if it tasted like hell-fire and then keeled over, convulsing. Jarren had dragged her off to escape, but they both watched in shock as the Dead died his final death.

And then they waited. It only took minutes for a human to turn. So she and Jarren had said their tearful goodbyes and waited for the Dead's infection to spread through her bloodstream and to her brain. He would kill her after she turned. It was their promise to each other. But minutes turned to hours and then to days, and other than a fever and an impressive scar, she suffered no ill effects.

The bite the week before was only different in that it was on her side instead of her leg. Just as with the last one, the Dead that bit her had perished and she had remained utterly human.

"I keep trying to think of a reason that Dead bit you," Jarren said. "I mean, no Dead has tried to bite you in two years. They try to kill you, yeah, but they never show any interest in eating or turning you. It's like you smell bad to them. I swear, it's like Deads can smell that you're dangerous or something."

She scanned the open field in front of them out of habit. The moon wasn't full, but it offered enough light. A wary fighter was a living fighter. "Well, they smell pretty awful to me, too. It's like a shrimp in a dirty diaper when they're close."

Her brother chuckled. "Thank the powers that be for that over-sensitive schnoz of yours. It's gotten us out of more than a few jams. So I was thinking. I'm pretty sure that Dead couldn't smell you because his nose had been bitten off."

Gross. "Makes sense. I can't see how I could look different to them. Their sight is terrible, so it has to be the way I smell."

Jarren finished his first aid, and she handed him the other half of the canned meat, the food of champions when they were out in the open and between colonies.

"You know it's going to be a battle tomorrow, right?" he asked.

The stars above them twinkled through the thick needles of their sleeping tree. A rare, beautiful sight. "I know, but what choice do we have?"

"What's your average looking like this week?"

"This week? Let me see." She ticked off bodies on her fingers. "Seven Deads a day."

"Has to mean we're getting close. Really close."

"Hmmm," she said noncommittally. It was pointless to grow excited about anything when every day was likely to be your last.

Deads seemed to hover around the colonies that housed the remaining humans. They could be kept out with high walls, since Deads were terrible climbers, but they still lingered, walking slowly in circles and waiting for a mistake that would grant them a meal of human flesh on the go. Generally speaking, the denser the Dead population, the closer a colony. And a colony was exactly what the team sought.

Nerves before battles kept her up at night. On regular Dead killing days, she slept like a felled log, but fear crept in the nights before big fights. She drew a long breath to calm the shakes. "Great, now I'll never get to sleep," she grumbled, adjusting her position on the tree branch.

"You want me to tell you a story?" Jarren offered.

Laney snorted. "I think twenty-three is getting a little old for bedtime stories, don't you?"

Jarren leaned forward and lowered his voice. "The boys won't hear. I'll be quiet. Come on, Laney. Everyone knows you're a badass during the day. But I know you. You are allowed to have a hard time at night."

The offer was tempting. Jarren was an excellent storyteller, ever careful to mention only make-believe things. It had been a hard lesson early on that stories of their unfortunate reality or people they had lost only made them too emotionally charged. With this lifestyle, it was best to leave emotions off the table.

She opened her mouth to tell him to start the story already when the wind shifted and the tell-tale stench of a Dead filled her nostrils. She brought her fingers to her lips and then pointed to her nose. He would get it.

He turned and made quick, jerky motions to the tree behind them, where Mitchell and Guist had already grown still. With her unusual Dead warning system, the boys wisely tended to keep one eye on the woods and one eye on her.

Ten minutes of bone-chilling silence later, a lone Dead shuffled slowly through the woods below them. The sheer mass of him said he was the hunter from the gas station, but he was alone. Odd. The Dead stopped and swiveled his head, scenting the air before he moved in the direction of their trees.

She froze. The last thing she wanted was to attract the thing. The Dead was one big son-of-a-gun, and she eyed the thin branches above for an escape. If she could add another fifteen feet to their distance from the monster, she would.

Jarren smirked and made a calming gesture with his hand. How was he always so unruffled by zombies?

Laney took a deep breath as the Dead shuffled closer to their trees. Bad idea. She nearly gagged. The stench of a Dead at that proximity was overwhelming. She needed to settle down. Deads never looked up for danger. She was safe in the tree. Safe, safe, safe.

The monster shuffled ever closer and stopped just at the base of the pine tree they were frozen into. He swiveled his head back and forth, back and forth, snuffling the air noisily. What did it tell him? Could he smell them from down below? He turned his head slowly toward the trunk of the tree and snapped his face upward to look directly at her. She stifled a shriek. His filmy, searching eyes scoured the moonlight-soaked branches, and she dared not even breathe. Her heart hammered like a stampede of horses with the fear that he would see her move and come scurrying up the tree as best he could.

The Dead shifted his weight, and the moon-deprived shadows compensated. His face was cut and bitten, and strips of decaying flesh hung loosely around his neck. His clothes were shredded, and the tatters of camouflage garb that were visible were covered with stains in various stages of drying.

Monroe.

Jarren gave her a wide-eyed glance as recognition lit his face. It quickly dissipated to subdued acceptance. They would have to kill him. It was their promise.

Monroe had fallen the week before, on the same day she was bitten. Undermanned and outnumbered, he hadn't made it out of the fight.

She strained her eyes in the dark. *Something* had to be left after humans were turned. Shades of memories, perhaps. Time and time again she had witnessed Deads instinctively stay close to friends, family, old homes, and haunts. Most would argue that when they were turned, they became something entirely different, forsaking anything that had ever made them human. She couldn't help but question that line of thinking. If there was no human mental capacity left, then why had Monroe been following them for a week? Alone. And how had he known to look for them up in the tree when no other Dead had figured it out?

Not seeing his quarry, Monroe the Dead shuffled off toward Mitchell and Guist's tree. Jarren motioned for her to stay put. He pulled a machete out of the front strings of his pack, as slowly and quietly as a sigh of wind. A gun would be much easier, but too loud. It would draw other Deads.

Monroe turned as Jarren hit the ground. A loud and inhuman bellow belched forth from his decaying vocal cords as he charged her brother. Laney gripped the tree bark until the pads of her fingers screamed. It would have been easier if they were battling together, as a team. Fighting for her own life left no time to panic over his safety.

The Dead tried to encircle Jarren with his arms, but he easily ducked and hit Monroe hard from behind. Decayed muscle tone made Deads clumsy. They didn't possess superhuman strength or speed, but what they did have were very few kill zones, making them extremely difficult to put down. They were also completely unaffected by pain. Their nerve endings died with their humanity.

Monroe stumbled from the blow but righted himself and turned just in time to watch Jarren's machete make its final arc toward his face.

"Sorry, old friend," he murmured as Monroe crumpled in on himself and fell like a sack of stones to the pine needle blanketed earth.

Laney tossed a rope down to her brother, and he tied it around Monroe's exposed leg bone. He disappeared into the night, dragging the Dead's body behind him. The last thing they needed was for her nose to become desensitized by sleeping near a Dead's carcass all night. He was back in half an hour, though it felt like much longer. Her imagination could be downright cruel sometimes, and it didn't help that dragging a large Dead's body through a carpet of leaves and dried grass wasn't exactly quiet work.

Surely she would never get to sleep with the vision of her old friend's face on a Dead. It was so fresh and raw, but the weight of being followed had lifted with his death. Slumber finally found her in the wee hours of the night.

Laney woke with a start as a Dead's guttural moan echoed in her ear. Her body was pressed into the creaking branch under a great weight, and she instinctively pulled a knife from a sheath under the cuff of her pants and screamed a battle cry as she thrust it at her attacker.

Jarren blocked the knife easily right before the point of it pierced the skin over his temple.

"Good," he said, sounding satisfied.

She panted from the adrenaline jolt. Mitchell and Guist were chuckling below her, and the sound filled her veins with liquid fury.

"Jerk!" she exclaimed, pushing her remorseless brother hard in the chest.

He flipped off of her with a shocked yelp, and his harness tensed as he dangled harmlessly under his sleeping branch. She spared the harness a dirty look and started to unhook her own.

"Don't be mad," he said. "You know I have to test you sometimes. It's for your own good."

He sure made ignoring a half-assed apology easy. She scrambled down the tree with her pack thrown over her shoulder. She understood the need for his tests. Jarren had to reassure himself that she would be okay if anything ever happened to him. She got it, but she didn't have to like it, and she sure as hell wasn't obligated to take the tests graciously.

On the ground, she checked her pack. She refolded the harness and put it in place, re-tied her hiking boots, and made sure her knife was secured at her ankle. The weapons at her waist were checked and tucked safely into a Teflon holster over her thick, forest green cargo pants. A simple black tank top hugged her not-so-womanly curves and served as a barrier between her skin and the short green vest that housed her handguns. How many hundreds of times she had done this exact ritual? By the time she retied her dark brown locks so they were out of her face, Mitchell was headed her way. Great.

He stopped in front of her and reached slowly and unnecessarily around to set his pack beside hers.

"It's so hot watching you brain a Dead first thing in the morning," Mitchell said as he leaned forward, forcing her to look up to meet his eyes.

He was tall and trim, filling out his tight black cotton shirt and cargo pants impressively. And with warm caramel brown eyes to highlight his dark hair, she understood why all of the women at the colonies threw their hearts at him. To a wiser woman, he was obnoxious the majority of the time and borderline unbearable the rest.

"Still not interested, Mitchell," she ground out.

"Can't blame a man for trying," he said through an amused grin.

She sighed impatiently and rested her hands on her hips, which only seemed to amuse him. "I wish I could still file for sexual harassment in the workplace."

"Oh yeah? Who would you file with? And besides, you need me. You just don't want to admit how much."

"What I need is a minute," she grumbled. She grabbed her pack and headed off to find a menial, though vital, amount of privacy.

"Not too far," Jarren called after her. "Leave her alone, Mitchell."

She smiled to herself at Mitchell getting reprimanded. It wouldn't help, as that man was incorrigible, but it was nice to hear nonetheless.

She checked her surroundings once, then twice. The Colorado mountain breeze held a clean, earthy scent. Mitchell and Jarren were still in view, arguing quietly, and Guist checked and re-checked his weapons. That man was even more thorough than she was.

She turned to the task of relieving her full bladder, then washed her face with water from her canteen and brushed her teeth. She bent all the way forward, feeling the pull of relief in every vertebrae down her spine as she stretched aching muscles. She didn't have to worry about Mitchell and Guist watching her. They had been together long enough to know each other's routines, and they at least respected her enough not to spy. She hoped.

Laney returned to the group more composed and ready to move. Mitchell tossed her a rough biscuit and mumbled a half-hearted apology. She nodded and picked off the moldy bits before inhaling the small breakfast. Jarren and Guist poured over a map as she washed the modest meal down with canteen water.

Mitchell and Guist had been Jarren's childhood friends. They had all enrolled in the Army right out of school and had gone their separate ways after being stationed in different places. They had hung out through the years if and when they were lucky enough to have leave at the same time. Their training made them a force to be reckoned with when fighting Deads. Those men meant safety.

She begrudgingly did, in fact, need Mitchell for survival against the Deads. She needed all of them. She didn't have to inflate their egos any more than necessary by telling them that, though. And besides, they needed her too.

"Looks like we're going to have to go through a couple of smaller towns just outside of Denver to get to the road we need. It's that or tack on another day," Jarren said, looking up from his map.

Laney groaned internally. She hated towns. Too many places for Deads to hide, plus the buildings all stank of zombies so her nose was basically rendered useless.

"Well, I'm all for not prolonging this mission," Mitchell reasoned. He winked. "I'm tired of Laney's cooking."

"Har, har. Questionable cooking for questionable company," she said through a sweet smile.

Jarren folded the map and secured it into his backpack. "Head 'em up and move 'em out."

A quote borrowed from Dad. Her chest hurt with the effort to compose herself. Thoughts of the lost rattling around in her mind wouldn't help anything. It wouldn't keep her alive, and survivors knew that was all that mattered. Laney viciously stomped out the pain.

She was a survivor.

Chapter Two

Laney ignored the impulse to check her mag for the hundredth time. It was a comforting habit, and a good one to have, but the boys tended to go on high alert if she checked it too often. She had a full mag at hand and plenty of back-ups. She just had to settle down and get through the day.

They were all settling into the new formation they had been forced to adopt since Monroe was lost. They had been five pair of eyes instead of four for so long that it still felt odd at the beginning of every hike. Mitchell's gaze was glued to her every time she checked her tactical rifle.

"I still think it's a shame what you did to that gun," he told Jarren, likely trying to lighten the somber mood.

Jarren shrugged unapologetically. "Never get them mixed up now, do we?"

Laney smiled at her Mini-14. Jarren had come back from deployment to find her in all the sports he didn't approve of. And yes, ballet was a sport. Or, at the very least, it required a great deal of athleticism. Jarren bought her the gun as a joke. He'd even gone one step further and taken it to a friend of a friend who added all sorts of modifications to customize it for her, including a glossy blue custom paint job and switching it from semi-automatic to automatic. So maybe it wasn't the most legal gun. Who was worried about legality now?

"You know that color makes you a target," Mitchell pushed.

"Please," she grumbled. "Deads are color blind. The only person it bothers is you."

"She's got a point, man," Guist spoke up. "And anyway, I think it suits her."

"Thanks, Guist," she said with a satisfied nod. "It's good to know someone else appreciates my baby." She kissed the stock and kept moving forward. "And besides, she's never misfired on me and that's what counts."

Edging to the outskirts of North Table Mountain Park gave her a first glimpse of civilization. Or what would've been civilization had it existed anymore. She took a draw of the air and hesitated at the sickly sweet smell. Her pause was enough to stop the others. Jarren arched an eyebrow, and she nodded. They were coming.

The metal click of weaponry and footfall against dry twigs were the only noises in the clearing as she slunk forward beside the others. Thick, once protected forest gave way to a scattering of small houses, and around one of these abandoned homes sauntered the first wave of Deads. It was likely their very human scent that attracted them, and when the filmy, rolling eyes of the zombies landed on them, the creatures galloped toward them. Buckled knees and rotted flesh didn't seem to slow them down in the least.

There were five of the monsters: two females and three males. The sound of gunfire cracked against the clearing as she pulled the trigger at almost the exact moment the others unloaded their weapons. There was no panic or fear. Only a single-minded need for survival, and the Deads stood in the way of that. She'd pulled too many triggers to get scared easily. All were downed by direct hits to the brain before they were even a real threat. The noise would attract other Deads in the area, but that was fine. They'd be on the move before more arrived. She ran behind Guist, guns at the ready, fingers beside their triggers. Just one easy motion away from trigger ready. The team moved as one in front of her, eyes trained in a full circle around them.

"Smell is getting stronger," Laney informed them breathily.

Jarren grunted and spoke up. "All right boys, town is close, and if we can get through it today we'll be to the colony by dark. Stay calm, stay collected, stay focused. Stick to the roofs when possible."

She pulled them to a stop when they came to a road polluted with abandoned cars. The smell of the Deads that moved between and around the rusting automobiles was atrocious. She held her breath for relief. "How many, you think?"

"Too hard to get a head count," Jarren whispered. "Cars are blocking them too bad. We'll stick to the woods near the road. We can follow it into West Pleasant View and hit 1-70 from there. It'll be the easiest path through the mountains."

The group melted silently back into the woods to pick their way through the forest at a jog. Everyone seemed rushed by both the need to escape the unusually large herd of Deads and to get what promised to be a treacherous day over with.

"Remember," Jarren hissed, "no matter what, we get Laney to the colony." He met Mitchell's and Guist's eyes seriously.

They nodded. Everyone knew how imperative it was that she lived. The reminder of the importance of her survival left a bitter taste in her mouth, but she couldn't quite put a finger on why.

The massive ghost town left a deep ache in her gut. So much suffering had happened there that it was like a dark, stifling cloud was filling every shadow, every building, every air molecule. Trash and debris littered the streets, and bodies and bones lay in haphazard heaps. Fat flies buzzed lazily around Laney's face, and she nearly went mad swatting at them. Even Guist, immovable, impenetrable Guist, gagged at the smell. Adjacent to a small highway, a green sign contrasted against the blue of the sky. It had an arrow that pointed in the opposite direction and read "This way to Denver." She could only imagine the sheer number of Deads in a city that size. Jarren, thankfully, had the good sense not to drag them through the middle of it.

As if he read her charitable thoughts, Jarren gifted her with a "Let's rest here."

She sat on the gnarled root of a tree and squinted at the dilapidated exit sign. "I always wanted to visit the mountains in the spring," Laney said with a small grin.

Jarren tossed her an apple from his pack. "Well, I don't think it will be quite as picturesque as you imagined. Anyway, it's fall."

"Party pooper. So why is it so important to get to *this* colony?"

Mitchell dug through his pack noisily in search of food. "It's the biggest?"

"Well, that's part of it," Jarren admitted. "The bigger the colony, the better chance we have of finding someone who can help us figure Laney out."

"Plus," she said, "I'm dangerously low on tracer ammo. I'll have a better chance of finding someone who can remedy that little problem in a bigger colony, right?"

"One-track mind," Mitchell said, watching her like she was an exotic bug that had done something interesting.

She bit into her apple, a rare treat during missions. The last colony they stopped at had a small orchard and gave them apples as part of the payment for the group's freelance work. There were at least a hundred small bands of fighters just like them that lived outside of the colonies for various reasons. Some were brawlers, unable to live a subdued and defensive life. Some were adventure seekers, and some simply didn't fit well into the social atmosphere that the colonies offered. Whatever the reasons, all came to colonies to trade, regroup, or to fulfill a simple need such as getting a safe night's sleep or socializing after a long run. Or, more importantly, to find the bed of a lover that would give a moment of relief from the nightmares they'd lived. In return, the fighters worked various jobs around the colony to trade for supplies. The most common work included thinning the crowds, so to speak. They cut down the numbers of ravenous Deads that hovered around the colonies, and then they moved on to their next self-inflicted mission. She and the boys had been nomads for two solid years.

"So who is the leader?" Laney asked, checking their surroundings again.

"Name's Sean Daniels," Jarren said as he tossed his apple core away.

Laney snorted in a definitively unladylike fashion. "Sean Daniels? What a douchey name. Never trust a man with two first names."

"Hey!" Mitchell pointed to his chest. "Derek Mitchell?"

She arched an eyebrow. "I rest my case."

"Come on, Laney. Don't get judgey before you meet the guy," Jarren cut in defensively. "I've heard good things about him."

"Like what?" Guist asked.

"Like he is leading the biggest colony in America successfully, and he has been for three years. He has minimal losses under him, and he is fair. That's what I hear, at least."

Laney rocked her head back, snoring softly, and Jarren punched her in the arm. He was chronically optimistic about the different colony leaders, and they always turned out to be pricks. Colonies' defensive agendas were so radically different from their offensive ones. The two groups very rarely saw eye to eye on anything. More often than not the leaders were hard pressed to even let fighter teams into their colonies for fear they would rile up the masses and deplete their numbers. They needn't worry though, she thought as she caught a putrid whiff of rotting Deads. This life was far too glamorous for most colony dwellers.

"Time to do some work," she whispered as she hooked her Mini back onto the strap laced from shoulder to ribcage.

The men didn't hesitate behind her. Her nose had never been wrong.

It was their longest day in recent memory. Jarren, having never been to Denver before, had grossly underestimated how large it was, even in the border towns. They kept a breakneck pace, but even at this clip they'd be lucky to make it into the mountains by dark, much less to the colony nestled miles inside of them.

Traveling the bridges and overpasses that led around the edge of the city had started out the trip with an eerie feeling Laney couldn't manage to shake. Two small bands of Deads were on one of the bridges, but they were easy to dispose of. Well, easier than the rest of the fights had been. There weren't necessarily more Deads in cities than any other place on the planet. The creatures tended to stay where food was, and since humans were a rare find, the zombies in cities habitually migrated. That's not to say humans didn't exist at all in cities. Some stubborn fighters cleaved to their homes and eked out a hidden existence amongst the predators. They were probably all gristle. A Dead would likely choke on those leather-tough old buzzards.

The hours after they crossed the bridges brought too many skirmishes to count and had the group treed up fire escapes twice in as many hours. Laney had fallen over some rubble as they were being backed into a stairwell and had cut her hand badly trying to catch herself on the glass riddled floor. Jarren had wrapped it tightly the moment he felt they were safe enough to administer first aid, but that had been hours before and her trigger hand was now throbbing in rhythm with her racing heart. She'd had worse, though, so what was the point in complaining?

They had about forty-five minutes of daylight left, and the team was trapped in a housing development on the edge of town. Deads were more active at night, and the action had definitely started picking up.

Laney checked the lock on the front door again. Pictures of a young family lined the hallways, and two small gap-toothed children grinned from within dark wooden frames. She couldn't help but imagine that the children who once played in these rooms were presently in the horde of zombies banging on the door and groaning for a taste of their flesh. She pried her gaze from the happy pictures and swallowed a lump in her throat. Houses like this one felt haunted by the ghosts of the unresting souls of the families that once lived in them.

"What's the plan, boss man?" Mitchell asked. "We going to try for the colony tonight or are we bunkering down?"

Jarren shook his head. "Can't bunker down here. The windows and doors won't hold under the growing numbers, and they are making enough noise to attract all of the Denver Deads."

"We go up then," Guist said as he flew into action and ran downstairs. They didn't have to discuss it. They had been in this exact same situation before. Their first order of business would be to search for something to get through the ceiling.

The houses were attached in that neighborhood, which would make it easier to travel by roof. The problem would be getting outside from the upper floor. There were windows they could climb out of, but the Deads would see them and follow, which would make it impossible to get down and escape.

"I'll cover the front door in case they get in before Guist makes it back," Laney said. She braced herself in front of the banging entry.

Jarren and Mitchell took the stairs behind them two at a time. Furniture scraped across wooden floors as it was stacked and dragged around the room above her. Window glass broke and tinkled across the floor. *Bang, bang, bang.* The noise grew louder as the Deads became more frantic outside the door and the outer walls of the house. She wiped sweat off her brow to keep it from her eyes.

"Guist? Guist!" she yelled as the frame of the door splintered loudly. Deads were coming in sooner rather than later, and the team was low on ammo. All hell was about to come barreling through that door and she only had half a clip left before she got to her last mag of tracer bullets. Those she would desperately need after dark.

"Guist, we got company!" Where the hell was he?

The door gave way, halting only momentarily as the small chain creaked and tensed before it snapped, illuminating the entryway with waning daylight and a mob of walking Deads. Guist appeared and sprinted for the stairway behind Laney. He held an ax in a white knuckled grip, and slid into the stairwell just as the first wave of monsters poured through the front door.

She checked out. She always did in battle. It was necessary for survival. No fear, no thought, just her instincts guiding her body.

Shot to the head.

Next Dead.

Aim.

Shot to the head.

Next Dead.

Guist's strong grip dug into her shoulder, dragging her up the stairs while she kept the Deads at bay. It was all he could do. Guist had been out of ammo before they even made it to the house. Other than blades, he was weaponless. He yelled something behind her, but she couldn't understand him over the sheer volume of the gunfire and the roaring Deads who stumbled and crawled over the bodies she felled. At the top of the stairs, Guist pulled her into a bedroom just as the zombies clawed at her clothing and gnashed their rotting teeth inches away from her skin. The door slammed behind her, and Mitchell pushed a dresser in front of it so fast it almost hit her in the hip.

She slid her rifle to her back and reached around to help steady the pile of furniture under Guist. He was already hacking away at the drywall in the ceiling with the heavy blade.

The dresser in front of the door was rocking steadily by the time the hole in the ceiling was wide enough for a man, and between shouted orders, Jarren and Guist were through to the attic to try to tear through roofing wood and layers of shingle.

"Up you go, sweetheart," Mitchell yelled over the noise of the banging door.

She hesitated. They hadn't had time to balance the furniture properly, and Mitchell would never make it up without falling. She didn't have the upper body strength to lift him through the hole behind her.

"You first, then lift me up!" she yelled.

"No way, Laney. I—"

"Don't argue, Mitchell. I'm going to need you to lift me up. Now go!"

Mitchell cursed under his breath and grabbed the back of her head, sliding his fingers into her hair. The pressure from his grip brought their lips together. His kiss was as unexpected as it was violent, and it left her wide-eyed and panicked.

Mitchell held her gaze a moment longer. "Don't be long."

He scrambled up the makeshift ladder and Laney lunged to hold it steady. The dresser that held back the Deads fell over as Mitchell made it to the attic, and with one fear-filled glance at the splintering door behind her, Laney scrambled clumsily up the unbalanced load. It rocked and swayed dangerously, starting to topple. She wouldn't make it. She screamed, a frantic and terrified sound, arms flailing and reaching desperately for the hole in the ceiling that meant salvation.

A strong hand caught her at the wrist and pulled. Mitchell grunted with the effort, and the attic beams strained and creaked under the new weight. A Dead caught her leg. It clawed and pulled and she kicked her feet frantically. Another pair of hands grabbed her arm and lifted her away from the rotting fingernails that scrabbled at her ankles. The furniture fell in a pile below her as Deads crawled on top of the pieces and jumped clumsily for the hole in the ceiling.

Mitchell pulled her onto his chest and held her so tightly she couldn't drag air into her lungs. Jarren covered the hole with a large piece of particle board. Guist hacked tirelessly through the final layer between them and sunset as a sheen of sweat trickled down the side of his neck.

"It's okay. You're all right. You're safe," Mitchell cooed as Jarren screamed at them both for her being the last one up. She had scared him badly, but it couldn't be helped. Mitchell would have been taken if they'd reversed the order.

"Let me go!" Laney yelled, feeling weak.

Hurt flashed in Mitchell's eyes, but the look was quickly replaced by a sneer. "Sorry, Landry. I've just never heard you scream like a girl before. Made me think you were one for a second."

She punched him in the face. Hard. She didn't know why. He always said stuff like that, but a combination of confusion over his kiss, fear, embarrassment, and a very near death experience had her desperate for an outlet for all of the roiling emotion consuming her. Mitchell's sneering face made a fantastic outlet for it all.

"What the hell, Landry?" Mitchell yelled as he rubbed his jaw.

She turned before he could see her eyes water. Light seeped into the attic as a Dead got his fingers through the hole under the board and the weight ripped a piece of drywall off. Mitchell stomped at the decaying fingers that found purchase, and Laney balanced on attic beams to help with the hole for the roof access. Guist had the hole big enough for her small frame to fit, and he and Jarren hoisted her through. The ax was shoved through the escape hole so she could widen it for them at a more efficient angle. She checked her surroundings and then went to work. The ax swung its violent arc as she threw her entire body into every blow, chopping through the roof as fast as her injured hand would allow. She ignored the nagging pain completely until the boys were through the hole minutes later. As Jarren jumped through, she dropped the ax and held her bleeding hand tightly to her abdomen. It didn't help the pain, but she didn't want anyone to see how badly she had damaged it—herself included.

Guist retrieved the ax and the team ran in a low and careful lope, easily making the small leap from roof to attached roof in an attempt to avoid the attention of the impressive numbers of Deads trying to get into the house they had escaped. When they reached the end of the row, they hunched down quietly so Jarren could check the map. He pointed to their left toward a thick pine forest, and they silently climbed down a fire escape on the last house. Darkness was falling fast, but they could still see small groups of Deads coming in, attracted to the noise. The team jogged carefully to a playground behind the houses, and when the coast was clear enough, they ran for the safety of the woods.

Six miles of dark and piney forest stood between the small band of fighters and the borders of the colony. Even if it would be the longest distance they had ever traveled by dark, it would be too risky to bed down in a tree with their scent so fresh and so close to such a large number of frenzied man eaters. Getting treed with no ammo would mean a slow death. They would have to try to make it to the colony that night.

A couple of fast paced miles later, Laney's body threatened to give out. They had been going all day on truly meager rations, and the last adrenaline crash left her shaking and weak. That and she couldn't see a damned thing. The eyelash moon was less than helpful and she had to stop to dig her night glasses out of her pack. Her terrible night vision was also an excellent excuse to catch her breath. She hated lagging behind.

"What's the hold up?" Mitchell demanded, panting. "Let's go."

"I can't see where I'm going and I need to get my mag of tracer ammo, too."

"I've seen you load on the run a hundred times."

Yep. He was still mad.

Jarren doubled back for them. "Let her be, Mitchell. We're all winded."

Mitchell growled in frustration. "We're four miles from the colony and losing precious Dead-free moments."

She pulled her glasses on and tossed her pack over her shoulder. "Okay, I'm ready." Her stomach rumbled loudly, despite the terrible timing.

"No time for that, Landry," Mitchell snapped and jogged off.

"Didn't say there was," she grumbled.

Jarren ran beside her, relying on his impeccable night vision instead of his night glasses. "You smell any?" he asked.

Breathlessly, she replied, "The smell hasn't gone away. They're around us—we've just been lucky to miss them so far. I bet they'll be gathered around the colony for sure, though. We won't be able to avoid them there."

Two Deads came crashing through the trees in front of them, and Guist and Mitchell offed them with blades. They had to save the remainder of the ammo to give them a chance at getting through the gates of the colony.

The hours that followed were long, treacherous, and exhausting. The stream of Deads that came for them was endless. What should have been four miles turned into many more as they got turned around in skirmishes time and time again, like a cruel pinball game in the forest. It wasn't as if they had time to check a compass, either. They finally had a chance to check their position near dawn when they were out of ammo and hopelessly and utterly treed. Their blades would never be enough against the number of Deads that gathered around the bases of the three trees they had managed to scurry up.

Now what? No one knew where they were, and in a cruel twist of fate, the map said they were no more than a quarter mile from the colony border. Such a short distance from safety, but the team would starve months before the Deads would give up on them and leave in search of another meal.

A Dead came much too close to grabbing her ankle, and Jarren nodded for her to go up to the next branch. It groaned its discontent under her weight. The branches were already thinning that far up. The tree wasn't big enough for one of them, much less both her and Jarren, who had refused to leave her side. The Deads were clumsily clawing their way up the tree and there was no more room for Jarren to move up. Dead after Dead fell as they lost purchase on the bark. If they had any sense, they would use their numbers to push on one side and knock down the tree. As it was, they were so frenzied for a meal that they ended up pushing evenly against the trunk from all sides, keeping it upright. Thank goodness for a Dead's bad sense.

The tree rocked dangerously, and she held on for dear life. A quick look at Mitchell's and Guist's bigger trees proved they were having trouble as well.

"If we have to go down—" Jarren started.

"No! Don't even start talking like that. We'll figure something out."

The tree rocked to the side again, and Jarren's eyes held a sadness so deep, it seemed to pool in their green depths. Straining his voice over the flesh-hungry moans of the Deads, Jarren started again. "If we go down, I'm going to jump to my left. I'll fight as long as I can and draw the bulk of them to me."

"Jarren, please," she begged through a tightening throat.

"I don't see another way. It's still important you make it to that colony. Don't give up. Don't let thoughts of me cloud your judgment." Jarren kicked one of the better-climbing Deads in the head and sent him sprawling back down to earth. "Get your knives ready. Here, take my machete."

"No, you'll have nothing to fight them off with!"

"That isn't the point, Laney. The point is to distract. You jump as far right as possible and run for the colony. It's right through there." He pointed with his machete and then tossed it up in the air and caught it dexterously. He handed it to her, hilt first. "I love you, little sister. And I'm proud of you. You wouldn't even believe how proud I am of you."

She nodded tightly. If she opened her mouth to say anything, a sob would come out. She understood her importance, but at the moment it was hard to care. Her brother was the single most important thing in her life. He was her connection to everything that was good, the light that made her small existence livable.

"I can't do it," she whispered raggedly.

"You can and you will, Landry. I'd never forgive you if you didn't survive, do you hear me? You have to try."

The tree rocked dangerously to the side again, and Jarren sidled farther down the branch.

Her heart hammered so fast she felt faint. She'd lose him. She'd lose him. She'd lose him. Sure, she'd die soon after, but at the moment, that wasn't so important.

Mitchell and Guist seemed to be taking Jarren's lead. They readied themselves to jump.

Laney stifled a scream as she watched Jarren scoot to the edge of where the branch would hold his weight. He took a quick, deep breath and glanced at her one last time to make sure she was ready.

And then he jumped.

Chapter Three

At first, the engines couldn't be heard over the groaning of the Deads. Some unexpected movement made Jarren yell and reach around to catch the branch before he fell. Two brown Hummers barreled through the masses of Deads and skidded to a stop under Laney's tree, just as a Dead grabbed onto Jarren's dangling legs. The Hummer hit the Dead squarely, but the force of it pulled Jarren's arms free of the branch and flipped him onto the hood. All upright Deads lurched toward him as he struggled to right himself and grab his blades. The doors to the Hummer opened and three men jump out with assault rifles. They cleared out an area, and one of them pulled Jarren into the open door by the scruff of his shirt. The other Hummer was attempting to rescue Mitchell and Guist. It was then or never.

With her heart hammering into her throat, she jumped but landed farther away from the rescue vehicles than she had intended. The man in the Hummer screamed at her, but she couldn't make out a single word he was saying over the rushing sound in her ears. She had fallen hard and rolled to the side, and when she came up, the machete was already poised. Not her weapon of choice, but it would be efficient enough. She spun and sliced, and when the huge blade found itself stuck in a Dead, she pulled out the next knife, spinning low to avoid being grabbed. So many Deads were closing in on her that progress toward the Hummer slowed to a halt. She turned to hit a Dead on the side of his face with a hidden blade in the butt of her rifle when she stopped suddenly, barely avoiding a direct hit to a set of the most vivid and angry blue eyes she'd ever seen.

"This way!" the man yelled.

The massive truck was close, and had been inching closer under the weight of the bodies that had thrown themselves on top of it. The man shoved a hand gun into her palm, and she took out the closest attackers while he unloaded clips into the crowd to clear a path.

The man yanked her through the door and slammed it behind them, clipping off a few Dead digits that held on to the door frame stubbornly. The driver hit the gas immediately while her rescuer pushed her roughly into the back seat where Jarren had been waiting. Jarren pulled her to him and hugged her until she couldn't breathe.

"Where is Reynolds?" the man in the passenger seat asked as he looked around.

"Didn't make it, sir," came the sullen reply.

"What do you mean he didn't make it? He was just here. Go back!"

The driver shook his head. "Sir, I saw them get him. He's gone."

The man with the blue eyes cursed and threw his helmet hard onto the console. He hadn't purposefully thrown it at Laney, but the helmet ricocheted off the plastic and flew up to cut her across the temple.

She didn't expect the sudden pain and gasped in shock.

"What the hell, man?" Jarren mumbled and pulled her back to get a look at the gash.

The passenger's unapologetic eyes found hers. "Reynolds was a good man and he's dead now because of you. You better be worth it."

"She is," Jarren said quietly.

The Hummer jerked and strained for every foot of ground. Laney had no idea if Mitchell and Guist had made it, or where their Hummer was in relation to theirs. Rotting corpses blocked all views outside of the tinted windows.

A box toppled on top of her at a sharp jerk of the truck, spilling tin cans and bottled waters. So the men hadn't come from the colony gates. They must have happened upon them while they were heading back from a supply run. She frowned thoughtfully at the man in the passenger seat. He was giving hushed instructions, void of hesitation or fear. Every so often he would turn his head just enough for her to get another look at his breathtakingly blue eyes. She had never seen eyes more pure, furious, animated, or glorious. She found her gaze transfixed on a thin scar that ran from his hairline down the side of his jaw. It added to his mystery. He had a masculine profile and straight nose. His jawline was chiseled, and his high cheekbones added a feline quality to his eyes, which slanted at an angle ever so slightly. Not the *here kitty, kitty* kind of feline quality, but the *lion that ate the ringmaster* kind. His brown hair was cropped short, and the darker color played up the intense blue in his eyes. Before the end of the world, he was exactly the type of guy who would have ignored her completely in school. Current times found her not easily intimidated by anybody. Still, the man inspired awe.

A glint of gold caught her eye. How disappointing. He was married. Of course he was married! A man like him probably had every eligible female falling at his feet. Look at her. He had probably just given her a concussion, didn't care in the least, and she was still spontaneously ovulating for him.

A concussion. That had to be it because men didn't affect her like that. She shook her head to rid herself of the last of the dizziness. Her cheeks flushed with angry heat at her curiosity about such a rude and brash man. Shock was the only explanation for the fluttering in her stomach.

"You okay?" Jarren asked with a worried look.

"Yeah, I'm fine. Just shocked we're still breathing," she lied.

The man with the blue eyes pulled a walkie talkie up to his lips. "We're at the first gate," he said into it.

If she looked directly through a small opening created by an armpit and a shinbone of two Deads, a tiny window of sight was created. Laney strained her eyes. A huge cinder-block wall that stretched as far as she could see towered toward the sky. The gate in front of them was made of heavy layers of wood and was lifting slowly to reveal an opening for them to pass through.

"Are we bringing the Deads in with us?" Jarren asked in alarm as they inched through the entrance to the colony.

He didn't receive an answer, but he did get a very dirty look from the man with the radio.

When they were through the imposing gate, they were met with another wall identical to the one behind them. The Hummer turned and the driver hit the gas and raced alongside the wall. Her stomach lurched, and she dug her fingers into the seat cushion like a startled cat. The bulk of Deads that still held onto their vehicle lost their grip under the speed and fell off. The rattle of gunfire sounded all around them, and the corpses started to fall. The other Hummer pulled up at the rear, and the gate to the colony slammed closed, squishing several Deads in its wake. Another huge door on the inside wall appeared some three hundred yards later and the Hummer stopped, idling. They waited.

"What happens now?" Jarren asked after a few minutes of stillness.

The man in the passenger seat continued to ignore them, but the driver spoke up. "Every Dead has to be killed and removed before we can open the next gate. Can't take any chances."

She got that. All it took was one missed Dead to kill off an entire colony.

One uncomfortable and impossibly quiet hour later, the second gate finally opened for them. She had wanted to ask what they did with all of the Deads' bodies, but the annoyed look on the blue-eyed man's face had kept her curiosity silent.

The open door revealed yet another wall, and the Hummers pulled in and stopped.

"Get out," her rescuer demanded curtly.

Mitchell and Guist exited the Hummer behind them, and an intangible weight lifted from her shoulders. A group of heavily armed men descended upon them and searched the undercarriages of the Hummers immediately. Laney and Jarren were pinned against the wall, and after a shocked moment, Mitchell and Guist received similar treatment. The rescue team from the Hummers removed articles of their clothing, and Laney's rescuer glared at her team with annoyance written on every one of his features.

"Take your clothes off," he barked.

Panic rose in her throat. "What?"

He sighed in obvious frustration. "Have to check for bites. You don't get through that last gate until we make sure you aren't turning Dead on us."

"Surely you can cut her a break though," Mitchell said in a dangerous tone. "She's a woman. She shouldn't have to strip down in front of everyone."

She turned a panicked look on Jarren. What about the healing bite on her side? They'd kill her when they saw it.

The angry leader narrowed his eyes and stepped closer. He was stripped down to his cargo pants, and she tried to keep her gaze professionally on his face and not on his sculpted physique.

"Are you afraid we'll want to look at your body? Is that the problem? Because if so I can assure you, you don't have to flatter yourself. I think I can speak for all of the men here when I say we like our women softer. A little more…" He hesitated, as if he were searching for the right word. "Womanly," he finished. "Take your clothes off."

Burning heat crept into her cheeks. She had never been so embarrassed in all of her life. To make matters worse, all of these strange men were laughing cruelly at her, and the man she found so intimidatingly attractive had just hit squarely onto her biggest insecurity.

Jarren started toward the man with a dangerous look in his eyes, but she caught his arm and shook her head. It wouldn't solve anything. She unbuckled her vest of weapons and shrugged out of it. Her team turned away and started undressing.

Turning her back to the waiting crowd of men, she faced the wall to finish removing her clothes. When her shirt was in the pile beside her, the men started murmuring to each other. It could have been the huge peacock tattoo that snaked from her shoulder blade to her opposite hip, the plume of bright green and blue feathers snaking around her hipbone that could have caused their reaction. More likely it was the crusty bandage that wrapped around her waist.

Vulnerable, Laney crossed her arms over her chest in an attempt to cover up. She chose to focus on the grout between two cinder blocks in front of her face. The subtle click of a gun and cold metal that pushed through the gathered hair in the back of her head created the most terrifying sensation.

"What is this?" the blue-eyed man demanded.

His lips were so close she could feel his warm breath tickle the fine hairs on the back of her neck when he spoke.

"A tattoo."

"Don't be a smart ass. You know what I mean."

Jarren stared at the cinder blocks beside her as if they held the answer they needed. Mitchell was resting his head on the wall, watching her with intense brown eyes. She could see the fear in them.

"I shot her," Mitchell spoke up, never taking his eyes from hers.

The gun stayed its position on the back of her head. "Why would you shoot her?"

"It was an accident. It happened last week while we were fighting Deads."

"Take the bandage off."

Laney hesitated. She didn't want to remove her arms from her chest.

"Do it!" the man yelled so loudly that she jumped.

Her lip trembled embarrassingly as she removed the bandage with shaking hands. The steady hum of murmured questions picked up again as she painfully pried the clingy bandage off the healing wound.

The man shoved her head into the cinder block wall with the barrel of the gun. The rough surface scraped painfully on the gash at her temple.

"Looks like a bite to me. In fact it looks *exactly* like a Dead bite. I've seen them a hundred times."

Jarren jumped into action. "Wait, wait, wait! Think about it!" He held his hands up in surrender as he sidled closer to Laney. Ten guns trained on him instantly. "Look at all of the scabbing. Look at it! That wound is a week old and a quarter healed. She would be turned by now."

"I've seen people stall before turning," the man argued.

"But how long?"

"An hour."

"Okay. We've been with you for well over an hour and she is still human."

The man hesitated. Laney could almost hear him grinding his teeth. He loosened his grip and kneeled down to look closely at the wound. "What kind of gun?" he asked Mitchell.

Mitchell spoke up, void of hesitation. "Shotgun, sir."

"I didn't see a shotgun in your weapons pile."

"Lost it, sir. Right after I shot her."

"Shotgun seems inefficient for a fighter's weapon. You have to reload too often."

"It was my father's, sir," Mitchell lied smoothly. "Had sentimental value to me."

"Must have been tragic to lose it then," the man said sarcastically. His instincts were spot on. No doubt he smelled a rat but he was unable to argue with facts. And the fact was, she was still human, which should have been impossible if she had been bitten so long before.

"Put her in quarantine for a few hours to be safe. I want two guns on her at all times."

She was allowed to dress again but was denied all of her weapons. They were led through the final gate and greeted with the chaos and jovial exclamations that came with a returning supply run team. How long had their rescuers been gone and how far had they been forced to travel to fill the Hummers?

She was flanked by two guards who dragged her unnecessarily to an outlying set of buildings. She stumbled, trying to get a better view of the homecoming. The happiness and relief that radiated from the masses was infectious, and she yearned for more of it like a drug. It seemed the blue-eyed man was very well-liked and his face transformed as he spoke to friends and received "welcome homes" and pats on the back. He went out of his way to greet every person and even stopped to ruffle the hair on a few little boys. The children positively glowed under his attention. His face only changed back to a mask of unhappiness when he came to one searching woman. He became serious, a blanket of sadness seeming to settle over him as he took her gently by the arm to find privacy. She must have been Reynolds's woman.

Laney lost sight of them as she was led to a medical building. The biting sadness nagged at her. She didn't have to imagine what the woman was going through as the men broke the news to her. She'd been through it before. Laney had survived, as the woman would, but she hadn't wanted to.

A middle-aged man with glasses and a receding hairline greeted them. He was tall and skinny as a rail, but his easy smile, clear eyes, and relaxed nature screamed health and vitality.

"Got orders to quarantine her for a few hours," one of her guards explained.

"Heavens, why on earth is she to be quarantined?" the doctor asked, concern growing on his countenance.

"Show him," the guard ordered.

Laney lifted her shirt, and the doctor's face went pale. "Why would you let her into the colony?"

"Relax, Doc. She passed gate inspection. The wound is old. The quarantine is just a precaution. Besides, if she even looks at you wrong, we'll shoot her."

The guard sounded a little too eager for comfort, but Doc had already recovered and was poking around the wound.

"This could use some antibiotics."

"You have antibiotics?" she asked.

"Nope, not since the first year," he said through a grin. "I was just pointing out that you could use them. What happened?"

"I was shot," she rushed.

"All right, and what about the hand?"

Laney looked down at her un-bandaged hand, which had never had the chance to close with all of the action the past couple of days had brought. "Cut it on glass."

"And your head?"

"One of your welcoming committee threw a helmet."

"Ah, yes. Some of our boys have a bit of a temper around outsiders."

She remembered her rescuer's furious eyes. Temper was a colossal understatement.

"Well, you boys can take a seat over there." Doc motioned toward a row of chairs near the back wall. "This young lady needs some stitches." He pulled out some antiseptic wipes and looked at her critically. "Maybe a shower first."

The shower was glorious. Granted, it was a blue tarp with tiny pinholes poked into it that dribbled depressingly slow streams of mountain-cold water when a bucket was poured over it, but she couldn't remember the last time she'd felt so relaxed. Well, when she could ignore the guards who watched her like hawks on a rat. The thin curtains around the shower area surely didn't hide much. They had already seen her goods at the gate, though, so she tried her best to ignore them and enjoy the clean, fresh water sprinkling over her like a spring rain. Doc even graced her with a healthy dollop of what smelled like homemade shampoo.

Stitches were an unpleasant follow-up to her ten minutes of pure bliss.

Doc was close to being finished with stitching her hand when an older woman came in. Laney liked her right away. The woman's laugh was infectious, and she didn't glare at Laney as if she were a tarantula. The woman had long gray hair and laughing blue eyes that looked like they would crinkle in the corners when she was amused.

"I'm Mona," the woman said. She handed Laney a pair of cotton pants and an old, comfortable shirt. "I'll have your other clothes washed and dried before your quarantine is over," she promised. She turned to leave, but paused. "What's your name?"

Laney hesitated. Reactions to revealing who she was always varied, and she wanted Mona to like her.

The woman smiled knowingly. "I already know who you are, dear. I just want you to confirm it."

She sighed. "Laney. Laney Landry."

"Nice to finally meet you, Laney."

Doc offered her a cot, and she fell asleep almost immediately, only barely able to resist the urge to zombie moan at her guards who scowled at her as she made herself comfortable. She wouldn't miss them when her quarantine was over.

Just as Mona promised, she came through with the newly laundered clothing, along with the news that Laney could leave the medical building, on grounds that she hadn't tried to eat anyone as of yet. "You have to keep one of your guards, though," Mona informed her as she scurried to get redressed.

Laney grumbled but conceded. Every leader was different and every colony followed different rules. Apparently rule number one for Denver was don't trust outsiders as far as you can throw them. And when one gets the chance…throw them.

"Can I at least pick who I get?"

"I don't see why not," Mona said, smiling.

Laney squinted her eyes and treated her pick every bit like the beginnings of a terrible schoolyard kickball team.

"I'll take Chuckles over there." She pointed to the stone-faced man who hadn't said a word.

"Thank God," the other guard said and left without preamble.

Laney glared after him in annoyance.

"I think it's time you met our fearless leader properly," Mona said, opening the door for her.

"Fantastic. I can't wait," Laney said sarcastically. She squinted into the bright sunlight. Damn, she wished she could have slept awhile longer. The exhaustion still pulled heavily at her injured and sleep-deprived body. She was so hungry that her stomach had finally given up on being fed, and now felt queasy instead of famished. If she knew her team, though, they were already trading and working for food and supplies for their next run. They always refilled quickly in case they needed to bolt. She just had to find one of them and mooch a meal.

"Come on, then," Mona said, no doubt seeing the look of escape on Laney's face. "He doesn't want to meet with you, so we will have to be clever about it."

"Great!" Laney said. "Neither one of us wants to meet, so let's just not."

Mona gave her a patient look. "I think it's important you two talk."

Laney bit her lip and held her tongue. She had a feeling Mona might be nice about it, but in the end this woman would still get what she wanted. Laney recognized a stubborn streak when she saw one.

She followed Mona down a gravel path between buildings. People were gathered in small groups, talking and throwing unhappy looks in her direction. Laney sped to catch up to the fast-paced older woman. She wouldn't be much good in a fight, but one warning glance from Mona was keeping the lynch mob at bay.

They came to a tall, stone-bricked building in the middle of the colony, and Mona stopped so abruptly that Laney ran into her. "Sorry," she murmured.

Mona glanced at her with a hint of worry overshadowing her bravado. "Do try to act normal, dear."

"Oh, you mean like—" Laney waved her arms slowly in front of her and moaned "—*braaaaaaaains.*"

Mona stifled a giggle and swatted her hands down. "Do that in here and you'll likely get yourself shot. Again."

"Right. Best behavior. Got it."

Mona arched an eyebrow skeptically but turned to nod at the guards posted on either side of a thick wooden door. "She's with me. She's here to talk to Sean."

To Laney's surprise, the guards let them pass without delay, and she looked at Mona with a renewed curiosity as they went down a long hall that boasted several closed doors. They walked until they came to one with another set of guards posted in front. The armed men quickly opened the door for Mona and stepped aside to let them pass.

Laney straightened her shirt and steeled herself. She could probably teach a class in bad first impressions. Sean Daniels had better be ready.

Chapter Four

Whatever Laney had expected to be behind that door, it wasn't what she in fact encountered. The entire room was filled with jungle gyms, miniature art tables, and brightly colored bins of toys scattered all over the floor. There were strings of finger-painted pictures hung up to dry and an entire wall devoted to drawings created by children. And right smack dab in the middle of that room was a dark-headed little girl with the biggest and most compelling brown eyes Laney had ever seen on a three-year-old.

"Mona!" the child cried when she noticed the older woman. She flew up from the table where she'd been sitting with a man in military garb, and charged Mona for a hug.

The man stood and nodded respectfully to Mona before he took his post in the corner of the room.

"Thank you for watching her while I was away, Brian."

"Anytime," the man replied with a smile.

"Look, Mona," the child said excitedly. "Look what Brian drawed."

Mona examined the paper. "Oh, good. He's teaching you how to draw AK-47s." She gave Brian a mock glare, and he repaid her by shrugging his shoulders remorselessly.

Mona turned back to the child. "Are you ready to go see Daddy?"

The sheer amount of noise that came from the heart-happy child was almost startling. This little girl apparently had a very loving family if the noise of celebration coming from her lips was any indication. She and Jarren used to get excited like that when Dad would come home from work. The recollection was unexpected and painful and Laney shut it down. Giving those memories a voice was weakness. Nothing could be done about the people that were gone.

"This way," Mona said as she opened the door.

Mona and the child chatted happily with the ease of long-term companionship. Laney and her guard followed behind them as Mona led them to another hallway.

"What's your name?" Laney asked the thickly muscled guard who seemed to be trying his best to avoid her attention.

"Finn," he said in a deep voice.

Laney arched her eyebrow dubiously. The bruiser looked like a Finn about as much as she looked like a Tiffany. His face was stern and serious. Definitely not joking then.

"Okay. Well, it's nice to meet you, Finn."

The *I'll probably shake you within the hour* wasn't said. She didn't tend to keep guards for long, but Finn didn't need to know that.

The hallway opened up to an entryway. She stopped in surprise. This must have been the Denver leader's home. The walls were painted in shades of browns and greens, with lonesome landscape paintings hung in the hallways. The dark wood floors had taken a beating, but it only added to the masculinity of the home. A stairway lead to a second floor, and the furniture in the living area off the entryway was dark and functional. Mona motioned for Laney to sit in one of the chairs. The murmur of voices came from a set of French doors off the living space. The double doors were adorned with thin, ivory-colored curtains. His office.

Three more guards filed in and waited for their turn to talk to the colony leader.

"Wait here," Mona directed Laney and the child and walked to the office doors.

The little girl stood directly in front of Laney and studied her with a curious expression.

"Hello, there," she tried. "I'm Laney. What's your name?"

"Adrianna," Mona answered for the girl. Apology was already written on the woman's face. "Sean will be with you in a few minutes. Adrianna, you stay with Ms. Laney."

"Wait, you're leaving her here with me? But I don't know anything about kids!"

"Good luck," Mona said as she retreated back to the hallway they came from.

Face down a horde of zombies? That was just another Tuesday. The thought of entertaining a child, however, brought on the cold sweats.

Another group of guards came into the sitting area, and Adrianna fidgeted nervously as the room became crowded. When one of the men shifted his weight and bumped into the small girl, Laney reached out to steady Adrianna and unleashed a verbal lashing the guard wouldn't soon forget. The little girl's solemn brown eyes were filling with tears.

"Oh, geez," Laney muttered. She scanned the room in search of help, but the guards seemed to be trying to keep their distance after her little outburst. "It's okay. Everything is okay, Adrianna," she crooned. "Your daddy is just in the other room. You'll get to see him any minute now."

Adrianna's little lip quivered, and tears threatened to spill over to wet her rose-hued cheeks. The look on the child's face pulled at some deep, long hidden instinct.

"Come here. You want to sit with me? I won't let them knock into you again."

The child nodded slowly and crawled up into her lap. She tucked her head snugly against Laney's shoulder and sniffled softly. Laney rubbed Adrianna's back soothingly. Surely there wasn't a wrong way to give a hug, but it had been a long time.

The sitting room was quiet, and she could make out muffled conversation on the other side of the double doors. She sighed in profound relief, both that Adrianna seemed to settle into her arms and that the men in the office seemed to be wrapping up.

"One more thing, sir," came the muffled voice of a guard. "The outer fence on the east side has a large crack going up the entirety of it. It looks like Deads have been pummeling it, but no one has reported the incident before now. How do you want me to handle it?"

There was a short moment of silence before an authoritative voice answered him. "The repairs are to start immediately and any

Deads participating in the behavior are to be put down at once. We don't need them getting smart on us. Also, I want a list of guards who have had a post on the east side any time in the last three weeks. Someone has to have seen something, and I want to know why it wasn't reported."

The man's muffled voice was intriguing. There was no waver to his orders. No pause or hesitancy in his command, but it was clear he thought his orders out with careful consideration. Sean Daniels was a natural born leader, a man who knew his place in the world.

Laney tried to see him through the thin curtains but could only make out the shapes of three guards' backs. The man, Daniels, said something too low for her to hear, and the guards all chuckled and started for the door. She straightened back up in an attempt to appear as if she hadn't been eavesdropping.

"Mona?" the man asked.

That was her cue. "Come on. You ready to see your daddy?" she asked Adrianna.

The little girl jumped up and led Laney by the hand through the doors of the study.

"You!" Laney blurted out, instantly regretting her quicksilver tongue.

Daniels only had eyes for his daughter. Intense blue eyes that Laney hadn't been able to shake since he'd come to her rescue in the early hours of the morning.

He had Adrianna wrapped in a tight hug when those eyes came to rest on Laney.

"Yes, me. What are you doing here?" he asked gruffly.

"Well, let's see. I was up in this tree—"

"Not why are you in my colony. I mean what are you doing in my office? And where is Mona?"

"How should I know? I'm not your wife's keeper."

"My wife?" Sean asked, clearly taken aback. He adjusted his daughter up onto his hip. "You think Mona is my wife?"

"Well, yeah." Laney pointed to his wedding ring. "I thought Mona was Adrianna's mom, or stepmom. Why wouldn't I assume her mom would be the one taking care of her?"

Sean's face grew livid, so she backpedaled. "Look. I'm not trying to piss you off. I'm sorry. I just didn't know."

Daniels glared at her and then did an impressive job of ignoring her, choosing instead to focus on the reunion with his daughter. Laney took a seat in the furthest corner of the room. She felt every bit the intruder for witnessing such a tender moment between the stranger and his child, so she picked up a book from an end table and pretended to read.

"You like *The Art of War?*" Daniels asked as he set his daughter at his desk to spin her slowly in the chair. Adrianna giggled softly and held tightly to the armrests.

"If you can call war an art," she responded, confused by his question.

"No, I mean the book."

She flipped the book over to read the title and was legitimately happy to find that at least the book wasn't upside down. She cleared her throat. "Not much of a reader, I'm afraid. Not much time, what with the zombie killing and all."

"My wife is gone," he said, surprising her with the change in direction. From the look on his face, he had surprised himself as well.

"Sorry to hear that."

He nodded curtly. "Why did Mona bring you to meet with me?"

"Your guess is as good as mine. She just said she thought we should talk."

Sean looked at her blankly until anger flashed across his face. "If she thinks she is playing matchmaker, she couldn't be further off the mark on what would interest me."

That was a slap in the face. Why did he say the cruelest things he could think of? And how did he know her most painful insecurities? She was determined not to let him see he'd hurt her, but the careless venom of his words left a welt on her pride.

"I should go," she said quietly. She rose to leave and reached for the door handle.

Sean growled, a frustrated and angry sound. "I'm sorry." He didn't sound sorry at all.

She turned angrily at the door. "You know, I didn't know you were Sean Daniels. If I knew it was *you* leading this colony, I never would have come to your office. I like Mona, though, and she insisted I speak with you. It's not like it is on my bucket list to shack up with a man who clearly hates me. You jacked up my face with your helmet and you completely humiliated me in front of my own team and a group of total strangers." Her voice hitched embarrassingly, but she couldn't seem to stop herself. "You obviously had someone you cared for deeply." She waved her hand in Adrianna's direction. "Well, so did I. You aren't the only one suffering a loss, Mr. Daniels. I may not be your type, but I was someone's type and I don't deserve to be treated as cruelly as you have done today. And what is that smell?"

Sean opened his mouth to reply but frowned and shut it again. "What smell?" he asked. He was a wise man for choosing to only hit on the final part of her speech.

"It reeks of Deads in here. Not just in here but all over your colony. Do you bury their bodies inside the gates?"

"You can smell Deads at a distance?" He leaned over the desk on his knuckles, and the position made his triceps flex under his tight black cotton shirt. His appeal only made her angrier.

"Yeah, it's a gift," she said sarcastically.

"We bury the bodies a mile outside of the colony. There has never been a Dead inside. Not since we finished building the gates. Maybe you smell the ones outside of the gates. That I can't help you with. We don't have an unlimited supply of ammo."

"It wouldn't be this strong. Usually I get a break when we hole up in a colony. The smell is as strong as ever inside your gates, though."

"Maybe it's me," he said, looking completely unembarrassed. "It was a long supply run. It'll probably take a few showers to get all of the Dead reek off of me."

Every muscle in her body froze like a snake on a cold day as Sean walked deliberately toward her. He stopped directly in front of her and waited.

"What are you doing?" she asked through clenched teeth.

"Smell me."

She leaned slowly forward and took in his clean scent, finding momentary relief from the nausea. "Homemade shampoo," she murmured as she repressed a shudder.

"What?"

"You smell like soap and homemade shampoo." She looked down so he wouldn't see the heat rising in her cheeks.

Sean shrugged and moved back behind his desk. He pulled Adrianna into his lap and rocked the chair slightly as she snuggled against him. "I don't know what to tell you. We don't have Deads in the colony. Maybe your nose is wrong."

She sighed, tired and defeated. "It must be. It was nice to meet you. Adrianna," she clarified. She waved to the little girl who waved shyly back and then left the room without another word. Sean hadn't earned a "have a nice life" from her.

"What was your name again?" Sean called after her as she picked her way through the crowded sitting room.

"You can call me Landry," she said over her shoulder. She didn't bother turning around and stayed her course.

Sean's voice wafted across the muffled conversations around her. "Landry?" It was closer than before and held a note of interest in it.

Great.

"I heard a rumor about a girl named Landry."

She turned slowly. Everyone's attention had become directed at her. Sean was leaning against the open door frame, looking like a runway model with way too many articles of clothing still on. Damn, he was hot.

"Call me a girl again and I'll bust your lip," she said sweetly.

"Okay, all right. Retract the claws," Sean said over the whistles and murmurs of the waiting guards. "I heard a rumor of a *woman* named Landry."

She shrugged noncommittally. "Lots of Landrys out there."

"Hmmm," Sean said, his eyes narrowing to ocean blue slits. "Makes more sense for why Mona sent you in here. So, yes, I'll take you up on your offer."

"What offer?"

"You know, the one where you said you wanted to have dinner with me tonight."

The noise level from the guards enjoying the show was getting ridiculous. And there Sean stood, leaned against the door frame, scratching his forehead with the back of his thumb, the smirk on his face all but dripping with confidence. She wanted to kick him right in the sack.

"No thanks. You're not my type," she dished and turned back for the exit.

"See you around six, then. Don't be late!" he called after her through the laughter.

She flipped him off over her shoulder and disappeared into the hallway. She was shaking, her fists clenched at the anger that burned in her gut. She had spoken the truth. Sean wasn't her type. In fact, he was absolutely nothing like Adam. *Adam.* The thought cut through her like a knife. Why were her memories so bound and determined to haunt her lately?

She shook her head like it would put her demons back into their cages. She needed to find Jarren and the rest of her team.

Backtracking, she escaped from Sean's house. A quick, indirect glance at the sun said it was about one in the afternoon. She sighed in relief at being alone with her thoughts at last.

"You know you actually have to show up for dinner with him, right?" a deep voice drawled beside her.

She jumped and clutched her chest. She must have been exhausted to let a yeti like Finn sneak up on her like that. She had completely forgotten about her watchdog.

"I'll have to check my schedule, but I'm pretty sure I'll be sleeping." She hadn't the first clue where to look for her team, but there was no way in Hades she was swallowing her pride enough to ask the hulk behind her. West was as good a direction as any.

"Look, Mr. Daniels is head honcho around here. If he gives an order, it would be in your best interest to follow it."

"I suck at following orders," she said, taking a sharp right between two stone buildings.

"Yeah, that's pretty obvious."

"I miss when you used to be silent."

"Are you always this unpleasant?"

"Not generally, no." She stopped to regroup. She had come to the entrance of several massive gardens.

Finn sighed loudly. "All you had to do was ask for directions. This way."

She glared at his retreating back and, for lack of a better plan, followed. The stench of Deads grew stronger, if that was even possible, and she stifled a gag. Something wasn't right. Her focus was taken with the appearance of a very angry man in military dress, stomping dramatically their way.

"Fantastic," Finn muttered. "Try to behave."

"Who is he?" she whispered.

"Second in command."

The man was stout, with light hair shorn close to his head. His eyes were dark, and the color of his face would give a cherry tomato a run for its money. She became instantly enamored with a bulging vein at his temple. She could see his pulse! This was a man with little control over his temper.

"What is she doing here?" the man barked. "And why wasn't I notified of her presence in the colony?"

She held out her hand. "Laney Landry, pleased to meet you," she said with as much pestering cheer as she could muster.

The man's vein bulged even bigger. He looked at her hand as if it were full of pickled dog nuggets. She pursed her lips against a laugh.

Finn sounded genuinely confused. "I'm not sure why you weren't notified, sir. She has been here for hours. Daniels brought her in this morning, along with the rest of her team."

"Daniels is here too? Heads will roll for this, make no mistake. Keep her out of trouble, and for heaven's sake, keep her away from the gardens! We don't need her stealing colony food." The man did an about-face and stomped off the way he came. To roll some heads probably.

"I feel like I'll make fast friends with him," she said.

"I doubt it," Finn muttered as he watched the man disappear around the corner of a building. "That doesn't make any sense."

"What doesn't?"

"I have no guess where Erhard could have possibly been all day that he didn't know of your arrival. Or Daniels'."

"Hmm. Is he left out of the loop often?"

"No, never. It's his job to be in the loop. He runs this place when Daniels is gone."

She shrugged, unwilling to put too terribly much thought into affairs that didn't concern her. "Whatever. Let's go find my team. It stinks over here."

Finn shot her a puzzled glance. "I don't smell anything."

"Lucky you."

Finn led her back toward a group of buildings about a quarter of a mile away. "Are you really Laney Landry?"

"The one and only."

He let it rest. "We'll check the mill first and then the stables and barn. There is always plenty of work for outsiders. I bet your team is working at one of them."

They found Jarren hauling burlap sacks of flour at the mill. Mitchell and Guist were helping to clean up after the massive quantity of livestock the colony housed and bred. Jarren sent Laney to find Guist and told her he'd catch up after he finished his work. Guist had food for her, and she sat on a hay bale to eat as the men kept pace mucking out stalls and cleaning filthy pig pens. An utterly pointless task, if you asked her.

Her team didn't bat an eyelash at Laney's eating habits, but Finn couldn't seem to resist. "How can you eat in here?" he asked. "It smells like animal crap."

"Better animals than Deads," she said between bites. The barn was an unquestionably immeasurable relief from the stench outside.

"Your pack is almost resupplied," Guist said from a few stalls away.

He was hidden, but dirty hay flew into a wheelbarrow that sat outside of the stall he was working on.

"Already?" She shouldn't have been surprised. Guist was positively meticulous about having their packs together. "Thanks, Guist. You're the man." She unzipped her pack and rifled through it.

Finn glanced curiously at her pack, so she showed him a few necessities he might not have considered, being a guard and not a fighter. Flint and twine stored in a tic-tac case. A small plastic bag of pistachio shells that provided a fast-burning and oily tinder for fires. A small leather pocket of fishing line and colorful hand-made flies.

Laney came across her newly full clips. "Where did you find ammo so quickly?" she asked Guist. That had to be some sort of record for him. She'd worry about him except he'd been running on robot mode since the day she and Jarren met him.

"I got lucky and found a good gunsmith right off."

"Smith?" Finn asked him.

"Yeah. Does he do the guard's ammo?"

"Sure does. He's the best. Colony got lucky when he wandered in here."

"Wait, wait, wait. Smith?" Laney asked with a grin. "A gunsmith named Smith? Huh."

Finn chuckled as Guist started hauling the wheelbarrow toward them. "I'm supposed to meet back with Smith in a couple of hours about some tracer ammo."

Laney gulped a bite. "Don't you tease me, Guist."

He laughed as he hauled the soiled hay outside. With Jarren and Mitchell, he always tried to find their favorite available road snack. For her, he didn't try to track down chocolate, or magazines, or beauty products. Tracer ammo was her favorite treat.

She yawned so hard her jaw popped. The nap she had taken earlier hadn't been nearly long enough to make up for all she had put her body through. She was safe enough with her team so near, and the scent of living, furred flesh instead of the decaying stench of death had her comfortable enough to curl up on the hay bale that had served as her lunch table and fall promptly asleep.

Chapter Five

Jarren shook her gently awake. "Seems you've made an awesome first impression, as usual."

Laney sat up and rubbed her eyes sleepily. "What have I done now?" she asked testily as she removed pieces of straw from her hair.

"I was just notified by a very upset Drake Erhard that our team is supposed to leave immediately. Apparently he is second in command here and can do that."

She rolled her eyes. "Well, since I have a dinner date with the first in command at six o'clock, Erhard can suck it."

"Oh, so you are going to dinner now?" Finn asked from a few bales to her left.

"I suppose if it's the only way to keep us here until morning, I will make the sacrifice."

Finn shook his head and sighed. Mitchell and Guist were both eating on a wooden bench, and Jarren studied her with a worried furrow in his brow.

"We came here for a reason, remember?" her brother pointed out.

"Well, we better find some kind of scientist and quick because our time in this colony is limited," she said. "I met a doctor while I was quarantined. Maybe we can talk to him and he can steer us in the right direction. He seemed nice enough."

Jarren nodded at Finn. "Your doctor. He's good?"

"Yeah, he's great. Saved a lot of lives, but that doesn't sound like the type of service you need from him."

Jarren looked questioningly at her, but she only shrugged in answer. How should she know if Finn could be trusted?

"We need a type of science experiment performed."

"Well, I'd say Doc would be a good man to talk to about it. He worked as a doctor for the Centers for Disease Control before the outbreak."

The team looked at Finn, dumbfounded. How could they be so lucky? Jarren was making an effort to hide his excitement, but the corners of his mouth kept turning up when he spoke. "He'll do, then. Where is he?"

Finn frowned. "Uh, let me think. It's about dinner time. I don't think he'll be at the clinic. He's a self-diagnosed terrible cook, so I bet he's heading to mess hall."

"Great. Let's go," Mitchell said, wiping crumbs from his lap before standing. "Let's just hope we can avoid Laney's new boyfriend."

"Oh, I'm not supposed to meet him for at least another hour," she said absently.

"Not Daniels," Mitchell said, with the oddest expression on his face. "I was talking about Erhard."

"Oh," she said lamely. She grabbed her pack and avoided eye contact as best she could. She didn't want the boys to see how much this Daniels guy affected her.

Rays of rosy evening sunlight hit her face as soon as they opened the barn door. The gray, grassy field in front had grown tall during the springtime, and though it was dry in the colder months, it still waved an alluring greeting. It would have been a profound sight if it weren't for the stench of Deads that washed over her like a tidal wave. She keeled over and retched, her instincts like a fire alarm in her head. For a split moment she was in the woods again, and the sensation was dizzying.

"Whoa, Laney. You all right?" Jarren asked. He dropped his pack and patted her back.

Mitchell and Guist had crouched into position to cover them as they had done a hundred times before.

"Deads," she gasped. "It smells like Deads here." She put the back of her hand over the side of her mouth and tried to catch her breath.

"I don't understand," Mitchell said as he pulled a canteen of water from her pack. "It's not usually like that in a colony, right?"

"No, this is a first. Something doesn't feel right, but Daniels assured me there are no Deads in the colony gates." She thanked Mitchell and rinsed her mouth out with the offered canteen.

"You mean you've been smelling them this strongly all day?" Jarren stood and looked around. "That doesn't make any sense."

Finn spoke up. "Maybe your nose is becoming more sensitive. The rescue this morning was pretty intense. You've been through a lot."

"That's what I was afraid of," she admitted. "It's the reason I haven't told you guys before now. I think maybe I'm going crazy."

"Shut up," Mitchell said. "You aren't crazy. Look, let's follow your nose. If it leads us to the fence, we'll know it's just being sensitive."

"What about finding the doc?" she asked.

"He can wait," Jarren said. "If you think there's something wrong, we need to figure it out right away."

"I don't know about this," Finn said nervously. "Laney has dinner with the boss soon. And if Erhard catches you guys poking around, he'll shoot first and ask questions later."

"You can leave if you aren't comfortable," Guist offered. "We aren't trying to get you in trouble."

Finn rubbed his face vigorously. "Honestly, I'm curious about what's going on, too. The last few weeks have felt different here."

The group headed off with Laney the bloodhound in the lead. Her nose led her and the team back toward the gardens.

The relief was obvious in Finn's tone. "Looks like the smell is leading toward the fence. It's about half a mile straight ahead."

She plowed on. If it was the Deads on the other side of the fence, great. But she had to know for sure.

Daylight was fading as the navy dark of evening approached, and she quickened her pace. The men behind her also seemed to sense her growing urgency and walked faster to keep up. They passed through a group of storage buildings and headed for the fence. She started jogging and skidded to a stop after about two hundred yards. She doubled back and shook her head. She turned and looked toward the fence and frowned.

"The smell lessens when I go toward the fence, which makes no sense. Deads usually gather around the fences, right? Why wouldn't the smell be stronger there?" she asked Finn in a hushed whisper.

"There isn't much human activity on this side of the colony. The Deads tend to gather in areas they can smell us. They are rarely reported this far down the fence. We don't even schedule as many patrols down here because of a history of no action."

She readied her Mini as his words took hold. "They are inside," she whispered in horror. "What are those buildings?"

"Storage for the harvesting equipment," Finn answered, his voice thick with shock.

Click, click, click. The men readied their weapons. She checked the mag in her own gun to find Guist had been true to his meticulous nature and refilled hers completely.

"Let's go," Jarren said, lowering his stance and moving quickly and decisively toward the buildings.

She and the others followed closely. They walked the perimeters of all three buildings and found nothing. The doors of the first two buildings were open, and the receding light illuminated the lack of anyone in them, dead or living. The third building to the far right was slightly bigger than the other. The grayed wood paneling added to the aged look of the structure. The door had a thick padlock, and a faint shuffling sound could be heard from the inside.

"Give me a lift," she instructed Mitchell, and he boosted her up to a high window.

The window had a ledge on the interior that blocked her view, so she pulled herself inside to get a better look. The stench was the worst she had ever smelled. It was as if the odor had soaked into the wood with prolonged exposure.

She pulled a handheld flashlight from one of her cargo pockets and shimmied forward on her stomach, shining a spotlight on the opposite wall of the building. Four groaning figures snuffled slowly to the attraction.

One walked directly in front of her beam of light, and she stifled a gasp. The creature had some sort of muzzle over its mouth. She pointed the light at the other creature's faces to find the same treatment. Someone had even gone to the extreme length of tying their arms behind their backs.

"What the hell?" she breathed. She debated the distance it would take for her discharged weapons to fall unheard by the colony. They weren't far enough away to avoid attracting attention, and it did appear the Deads had been rendered mostly harmless. Blades it was, then.

"Guist," she hissed out the window. "Hand up your ax."

"How many?" Jarren asked as Guist loosed his newest weapon and handed it upward into her waiting hand.

"Four."

The anger in his voice sizzled like the crack of a whip. "No way are you offing four by yourself. Way too risky."

"Pipe down, Jarren. They're muzzled and tied."

The men erupted into a whispered frenzy at the news and were aiming questions that sounded suspiciously accusing at Finn, who sounded as genuinely shocked and angry as them.

She left them to it and set to her task. Shimmying to the edge of the ledge, she readied herself to lower down.

"Pssst," came a whisper from the window behind her. Mitchell. "I'm coming in, too. We'll get the job done faster with both of us."

Relief fluttered in her stomach for the help. That place was downright creepy.

The Deads smelled them, their human odor finally breaking through the stench of confined carcasses. The zombies groaned loudly and frantically searched for them. She and Mitchell dropped onto the unforgiving floor and rolled to cushion their impact. She came up swinging the ax at the nearest Dead and Mitchell drew the others away. He kicked in a female's brittle knee caps before he turned on the other two.

They were silent and efficiently deadly, and the deed was finished in moments. Mitchell hoisted Laney back up to the window ledge, and she climbed down to the waiting group. Mitchell followed directly.

She said nothing, only looked at Finn and waited for answers.

"I don't know anything about this. I had no idea there were Deads in our gates or I would have killed them myself long before now."

He was angry, and obviously felt betrayed. Truth rang from his voice. He had no part in it.

"Any guesses on who would bring them in here and why?" she asked.

"No," he answered miserably. "The guards have been acting off lately. It's like everyone has a secret and no one talks about it. I guess this is it. Muzzled Deads are the big secret." He shook his head. "How stupid could they be? Whoever did this, whoever brought them here, they could have killed off the entire colony! All of our family and friends could have died."

"We have to be careful who we tell," Jarren whispered to the group. "We have to make sure to flush out whoever did this or they will just rebuild their little project. They brought Deads in here for a reason. We need to figure out why. Laney, you should go straight to Daniels and alert him."

"What if he's the one who did it?"

"It's your job to find out. Go to dinner and make the decision either to tell him or out his plans. Finn, you go with her and act normal. Business as usual, okay? Don't talk to your buddies or family. You will cause a panic and send whoever did this into hiding. Mitchell and Guist, you two track down the doctor. We don't have much time here and we need to get things with Laney set into motion."

"What are you going to do?" Laney whispered to Jarren.

"I'm going to wait here. Someone will come and check on their little venture. I'm sure of it." He held up his rifle. "And when they do, I'll wing them."

She had never met a better gunman than Jarren. He really was the person for the job.

"Meet back at the barn if anything goes wrong. We'll sleep there tonight when everyone is finished," Jarren ordered. He lowered his voice to a whisper again. "Be careful, Laney." He squeezed her shoulder reassuringly and jogged off toward a grove of trees.

"You too," she said quietly to his retreating silhouette. "Come on, Finn. Don't want to be late for my hot date with Sean-Zombie-Puppeteer-Daniels."

"I think you're wrong about him. He gives everything for this colony. He wouldn't do this."

"We shall see," she gritted out as she turned her sights toward the populated center of the colony.

Chapter Six

"Is there another entrance?" Laney asked Finn from the shadows of the building they were hiding behind.

Erhard stood guarding the main door of Sean's house with a handful of other guards. The tension in his stance and the single-minded precision with which he scanned his surroundings while he gave hushed orders to his men said he must have caught wind of her scheduled dinner with the Denver colony leader. An unfortunate and irritating obstacle.

"There is a back entrance, but it will be just as heavily guarded. Follow me, but stay hidden. Stay close if you can."

If the other entrance was guarded too, what kind of plan was Finn hatching to get her in? She didn't trust anyone on the planet besides the team, so having any faith in Finn's ability was about as far a leap as possible. On the other hand, there weren't a ton of options. She slunk through the shadows as Finn walked casually around the house. He waved to other guards and talked cordially to a couple of them, and she smiled when she saw what he was doing. She liked it when people surprised her. To the other guards it would look as if Finn was thoroughly checking and re-checking if each bottom floor window was securely locked. One creaked promisingly, and Finn made a quick motion behind his back. He couldn't have known where she was in the dark, but he must have trusted her to be close enough to see the gesture. Maybe Sasquatch wasn't so bad after all. Finn strode over to a group of three guards who would catch her for sure if she ran for the window. He patted them on the back and joked easily with them while he positioned himself on the other side. When their backs were turned and they seemed engaged in conversation with a surprisingly animated Finn, she ran for the window and slid it open. Other than the creaking sound it made when Finn tested it, the window opened decidedly easily. In fact, if she were a betting woman, which she was on occasion, she would bet that window had been greased quite recently.

Hooking a leg over, she panicked when one of the guards started to turn in her direction, and she flopped through the window like a beached dolphin.

In a frozen pool of hope, she lay perfectly still on her stomach. Maybe she hadn't made too much noise falling through the window. She lifted her face just enough to come foot to eyeball with someone's boot. Busted.

"Shoot," she whispered.

Sean Daniels sat in his office chair with an amused smirk on his face.

He waved his hand toward the window. "Please don't shoot my dinner guest."

She turned her head just enough to find three assault rifles trained in the general vicinity of her ear.

The guard closest spoke first. "Sir, Erhard said—"

"I don't care what he said. At ease."

"Yes, sir."

The men lowered their weapons and withdrew from the opening. Sean stepped over her and closed the window before locking it securely in place. Laney cleared her throat and stood with as much dignity as she could muster. Which wasn't much. She sidled around him to stand on the other side of his desk.

"Seems like you've made a lot of friends while you've been here. Must be your accommodating demeanor."

She glared at him. "Your second in command is a thorn in my side."

"Yeah, what did you do to get him so riled up? He told me he kicked you out of the colony, so I just assumed you wouldn't be making it to dinner."

She shrugged. The real reasons she took the risk would have to wait for later. "I'm hungry. I figured the food here would be better than the crap I've been eating. He can kick me out tomorrow."

"Ah, a woman driven entirely by her stomach. You remind me of my three-year-old."

She opened her mouth to pop off but was cut short by the office door swinging open. A solemn-faced Finn stepped in and took a post in the furthest corner of the room.

"Glad to see you're still keeping our guest here out of trouble," Sean told him.

"She doesn't make it easy, sir."

Sean chuckled. "No, I don't expect she does."

"I have a question," she cut in with annoyance. "Why do you have an unlocked window, all greased up and ready for anyone who wants to mess with you or Mona or your daughter? Do you trust everyone in your colony so much?"

A flash of concern washed over Sean's face before his mask was firmly back in place. He looked to Finn and arched his eyebrow. "The lady poses an interesting question."

"You are right to be concerned, sir. We do regular window checks. I didn't think we had a shot at finding one unlocked, but it was the only way I could think to get Laney in here. I was pretty shocked when that one actually gave."

Sean drummed his fingers on the desk thoughtfully before he jerked his head toward the door. "Let's go eat."

She was surprised when he led her to an upstairs dining area instead of staying on the main floor. The upstairs was smaller but boasted a kitchen, dining room, and three bedrooms.

"This is the strangest house I've ever been in," she mumbled.

"That's probably because it wasn't originally a house," Sean said without offense.

"What was it?"

"It was a church when we found it. In fact, the original buildings and land used to belong to an extreme religious group, as far as we could tell. They were all gone before we got here."

"Extreme religious group? So a cult is what you are saying. Creepy."

"At first it was a little weird. We found an impressive cache of texts on the darker aspects of their beliefs, and if you lift up the carpet in any given room, there are strange markings in a red substance we can't seem to clean off. But if you ignore that stuff, the extremists gave us a huge advantage." He motioned for her to take a seat at an oak dining room table before he continued. "You see, the people who lived here had already started building the wall around the entire property. Not sure whether it was to keep outsiders out or members in, but it gave us a good foundation, not to mention a lot of the gathered materials to build the first wall. We worked constantly to get it built, but we still lost many in the first days of this colony. After we finished the first wall we were safe to build the interior gates in time. Without the gate having been started, we would have lost many more. Excuse me, I'm going to go check on Mona."

Sean disappeared into one of the bedrooms, and Mona and Adrianna both followed him back out.

Laney breathed out of her mouth, but she could almost taste the rotting smell of death. How would she ever be able to stomach dinner with such a strong, lingering aroma of Deads that seemed to be absorbed into everything in the colony?

Mona greeted her, and Adrianna waved shyly before she took a seat directly across the table.

"Dinner is on the plates and all ready to go. I'll be back later," Mona informed them, pulling on a jacket.

Laney's stomach flip flopped uncomfortably. "You aren't staying?"

"No, dear. I've been watching Adrianna for Sean while he was on a supply run, but tonight is my night to myself. Some of my friends have invited me to a ladies' dinner."

"Thanks for cooking again, Mona. We'll see you later tonight. Don't get too crazy on the moonshine though, huh?" Sean said with a wink.

"Scoundrel." Mona laughed as she waved goodbye and headed for the stairs.

"I'll grab the plates," Laney offered, only to be waved back down by Sean.

She watched him as he gathered their dinner in the adjoining kitchen. He wore the same black T-shirt he had on earlier but had changed into more comfortable-looking dark gray cargo pants. He had removed his weapons. Was it because he was in for the night or because he always removed them when he was around his little girl?

He was statuesque and fit, and the musculature of his back showed easily through the thin cotton shirt as he worked. She needed to get a grip, and fast. He could be harboring Deads in his own colony for all she knew.

Sean brought a plate and drink out and handed it to Finn. "You're welcome to join us. It's the least I can do for strapping you to this one all day."

"Aw, she's not so bad."

"Please, she has the demeanor of a deranged grizzly bear," Sean quipped.

"I can hear you, you know," she gritted.

"I wouldn't turn down a plate of Mona's lasagna, but do you mind if I eat at the kitchen table?" Finn asked, ignoring her.

"Whatever you want." Sean grinned and turned to her. "One day with you and he's already wanting to eat alone."

She rolled her eyes and padded into the kitchen to retrieve her own plate and water. One look at a fidgeting Adrianna had her setting the food in front of the child and heading back to the kitchen again. Sean didn't say anything when he came in with food for his daughter, who was already digging in. He just sat at the head of the table and went to work on the plate in his hands.

"Slow down, little bear," he said after a minute of watching his daughter eat with a concerned furrow between his brows. "Here, let me cut it up for you."

Mona had made lasagna with thick garlic bread and fresh green beans. The lasagna was made with goat cheese and had a much different taste than the kind Mom used to make, but it was easily the best food Laney had tasted in months. If she could completely ignore the stench of Deads, she might have been able to enjoy it more. As it was, she was only able to get a few bites in her before she felt queasy and started pushing food around her plate.

His eyebrows shot up. "What, the food isn't good enough for you?"

"No, it's not that." She really should've tried to eat more out of politeness. Her stomach did another flip flop.

"You one of those girls that doesn't eat? Is that why you're so scrawny?"

His observation pricked at insecurities she tried her damnedest to keep buried. That lash of hurt he caused, that obnoxious little affectation against her pride, was too much. "I wasn't meaning to be rude." She had to find a way to explain without giving too much. "I guess I just need certain conditions to eat."

"Like what? Filet mignon? You don't like the house? A different colored table? What?" Sean's serious blue eyes pierced hers. He wasn't going to let her get out of this conversation.

"She has a smelling problem, sir," Finn spoke up from the doorway.

"You're saying it smells in here?" Sean was only growing more offended if his tone was any indication.

"Daddy? All done. Can I play?" Adrianna asked sweetly.

Saved by the three-year-old with fresh tomato sauce all over her face.

"Yes, you can, but I want you to bring your toys in there." He pointed to a small sitting area at the entrance to the bedrooms, within easy view.

When Adrianna had disappeared to her bedroom, Sean looked back at Laney with exaggerated patience. He waited.

Stalling, she took a drink of water and wiped her mouth with a napkin. "I smell Deads. The smell of them is overwhelming for me sometimes and it makes it hard to eat when it is like that. I didn't mean to offend you. The food is delicious. I just don't feel very well."

"It's true, sir. She was eating just fine in the barn, but as soon as she came out of there she got pretty sick."

"Finn," Sean warned.

"Yes, sir." Finn disappeared into the kitchen.

"Seems you've bewitched him," Sean said.

"I'm much too scrawny and unwomanly to bewitch anyone." She took another bite and chewed it slowly, focusing on the pattern of her plate instead of the dizzying smell and the churning of her stomach.

Sean sighed and let his fork drop. The tinkle of the metal against ceramic sounded quite beautiful.

"I'm sorry," he said quietly. "For this morning. The way we handled the gate check in front of everyone. And for your face, too." He gestured in the direction of her newly stitched cut. "Losing Reynolds—" He cleared his throat. "Well, I didn't handle things like I should have."

She nodded her acceptance, impressed with Sean's ability to apologize but unable to trust her voice enough to respond.

"The tattoo on your back," he started. "Did you have it done before or after?"

His eyes never veered from her face as she answered quietly. "After. I had it done the first year of the outbreak."

A thoughtful look crossed his face as he chewed another bite. He seemed to find her answer interesting, though she couldn't fathom why.

"Laney Landry, is it? Do you mind if I take another look at that gunshot wound?"

She stood and lifted the hem of her shirt until Doc's new bandage was exposed.

"Do you mind?" Sean asked, gesturing to the gauze.

"Go ahead."

Sean unwrapped it slowly and gently before removing the pad of gauze from the wound. When the injury was uncovered, Sean leaned back in his chair and rubbed his jawline. "So you weren't shot. You were bitten." It wasn't a question.

"I have the same mark on my leg where I was bit for the first time two years ago," she admitted.

"And being able to smell them, that's been helping you and your team avoid the Deads when you are between colonies?"

"More or less. It isn't an exact science."

"Could you always smell them?"

"No. Right after I was bitten the first time, I noticed I could smell them from a distance."

"So you are the cure."

"No. Not the cure. I think the most they'll be able to get out of me is some type of vaccine. Something preventive if we're lucky."

"You think, but you don't know."

She sighed. How much should she admit to Sean? Could she even trust him? "I know enough. We've done experiments. My blood can bring the mind back but not the injured body. My flesh kills them."

Sean sat straight up in his chair. "Your blood brings back their mind. You mean they'll be human again?"

"Yeah, but just for a minute. Their bodies are decayed, Sean. My blood doesn't heal that and it hurts. It's actually really horrible. It's cruel to put a human mind back in a Dead's body. Lets them think about the things they've done. The people they've killed and eaten. We need to find someone who can analyze my blood and figure out why and how I am immune, and then we need to try to give that immunity to others."

Laney sat down and pulled the tail of her top back in place. The bandages lay in a pile on the floor. The wound would just have to get some air for a while.

She had left her pack and most of her weapons with Guist, but she still had a nine millimeter in a holster just above her knee. She pulled the handgun out smoothly and aimed it at Sean under the table. She needed to find out what he knew about the muzzled Deads.

"I killed your little pets."

Sean looked at her with the most peculiar expression. "I'm sorry? I think I heard you wrong."

"I found your project monsters by the gardens, and then I killed them," she enunciated slowly.

He shook his head slightly like he was waiting for the punch line. None came. "You took care of our rabbit problem?"

"I'm talking about the Deads you had hidden in the storage buildings behind the gardens, Sean."

The full minute of silence that followed was loaded as Sean's face went through a slew of emotions. It finally settled on anger.

"Is this your game then? You go from colony to colony and stir up trouble? Do you get some kind of kick out of it?"

"So you know nothing about four Deads, muzzled and tied and locked in your shed? It's why the whole damned colony stinks so bad, Sean." She was raising her voice but found it hard to rein it in. "You're in charge and you know nothing about this?"

A slow and chilling creaking sound came from one of the bedrooms, and her attention was drawn instantly to the eerie intonation. Adrianna still played with a small scatter of toys in the living area. Laney's unobstructed view of the girl as she played quietly made the next words from Sean's mouth sound terribly confusing.

"Adrianna," he warned. "I've told you not to ever go in Daddy's room. Back in here, right now, young lady."

The next few moments were the stuff of nightmares. The door that had slowly opened led to a darkened room, and a large Dead's face loomed out of it. Its face was completely focused on the unknowing child, and the sight ripped a gasp of horror from Laney's lips.

"Adrianna," she screamed. She jumped up so quickly the chair she was sitting in flung violently backward into the wall. The readied nine millimeter came up as if born of pure adrenaline-based instinct, and she popped one round into the Dead, and another to be sure.

The creature dropped like a sack of flour. The stiff, clawed fingers fell centimeters from Adrianna's turned back.

The child turned and screamed in terror, but Laney was already running for her. She pulled Adrianna away from the felled Dead and into her legs, which effectively shielded the screaming child's eyes.

Sean was right behind her and pulled his daughter protectively into his arms. "There's a Dead in my house. There is one inside the gates," he breathed.

"That's what I was trying to tell you. Shhhh," she hissed, holding up her hand.

Several people were screaming and a muffled peppering of gunfire sounded from outside. The lights upstairs suddenly flipped off, and when she tried the nearest light switch, she was rewarded with no reaction. Generators were down.

"Stay here," she said. "Finn, cover them."

Finn already hovered protectively near the child and his unarmed colony leader. She clicked her flashlight on and held it next to her handgun before she made sure the bedrooms were all clear.

"What's happening?" Sean asked when she returned.

"I'd say someone just made an impressive attempt at assassinating you." She held up a muzzle and a short length of rope she had found in his bedroom. "That Dead's been in there for a while from the smell of it." She kicked the body of the Dead with the toe of her boot. "I think he finally wised up and figured out how to open the door to let himself out."

The screams outside were becoming more frantic, and the gunfire more frequent.

"I have to help them," Sean said.

Laney nodded. "Weapons."

Sean flew into action. Any hints of shock or indecision vanished. He set Adrianna on his bed and strapped himself into a small arsenal of weapons he kept on a shelf in his closet. Laney provided the light from her flashlight and waited. The want for action pulled at her, too. Her team was out there.

Sean finished strapping in and rushed into Adrianna's room. He grabbed a small pink stuffed bunny in a floral dress and handed it to the little girl. Shoving handfuls of her clothes into a small pink backpack, he placed it snugly on her back.

A guard came flying up the stairs, talking so fast he couldn't be understood.

"Breathe!" Sean yelled. "Now tell me. What happened?"

"Sir, someone has opened the gates." He panted for air. "They let a bunch of Deads in and then closed the gates again."

"Which gates?"

"All of them, sir."

Sean cursed under his breath. Laney could almost see his mind racing, analyzing a hundred different ways to save his people.

"Sean," she said quietly. She picked up Adrianna, who was still wide-eyed and sniffling. "We have to get her out of here."

"Adrianna," Sean said in a rush. "You're going to go with Laney, okay? I'll meet up with you in just a little while."

"No, Sean. That's not good enough! You're all she has left, and you know as well as I do that if you go out there you won't come back. Not alive." She swallowed back all of the hurt and memories of her father not being around when she was scared. She couldn't allow that for Adrianna. Not if she could stop it.

"Sir," the guard said. "Colony is gone. Most are turned or turning. Any unbitten are gathering downstairs in the auditorium."

"You can't save them, Sean. But you can save her," Laney pleaded. "Come with me. My team and I can get you out."

"Follow me," Sean said, flying down the stairs. The man had an apparent penchant for ignoring sage advice.

She scooped up Adrianna, who was surprisingly light in her arms. Sean led them to a door opposite the bottom of the stairwell. The door opened to a small room with a wall of one-way glass. A dated diaper changing table with cartoon kangaroos was pressed against the furthest wall. The room must have been a baby room, built for moms with fussy infants to view the church services without interrupting. The lights were still on in the auditorium, making it easy to see everything. The acoustics were impressive. She could hear almost everything that was being said.

The majority of survivors were armed guards, not surprisingly. A thin stream of people were filing in through the double doors leading to the outside. A group of armed men were checking each survivor for bites, and Laney jumped and hugged Adrianna tighter when the men brutally shot a woman after finding a suspicious wound on her arm. There was no emotion involved and they went to the next survivor as if nothing had happened. Her stomach lurched, and she turned away from the horrifying scene. A figure stood in the pulpit. Erhard leaned across a podium as he gave orders and tried to rally the men.

"We have been a defensive colony for too long," he yelled. "We watch the Deads at our gates. We study their habits, and for what? A cure? They should never have lived to threaten us in the first place, but that was the will of our fallen leader. He made us weak. He kept our colony without proper defenses. He was a Dead sympathizer who gave specific orders not to shoot them, and now it is up to us to salvage what is left of our home. To avenge our fallen brothers, sisters, mothers, children, and friends who have all fallen because of Sean Daniels' weakness. Grab your weapons. It's time to learn to defend yourselves."

"I think you just found your attempted assassin, sir," Finn said solemnly.

The fury on Sean's face was indescribable. He was perfectly and utterly still as he watched the scene before him. Laney took an instinctive step backward until her back brushed the wall of the small room. She had been the victim of his furious wrath before and had the stitches to prove it.

"I have to talk to him," Sean said. "He's going to get all of these people killed. Finn and Greer, guard Adrianna with your lives. If something goes south, you get her out. Do you understand?"

"Yes, sir," they chimed in unison. Finn took Adrianna from her arms.

Sean left the small room and checked his weapons. "Landry, this isn't your fight. You are free to find your team and go."

She knew where the exit was. She could just go. Leave and live. Find her team and forget this horrible day like she had forgotten so many. She had to live with herself, though. She sighed and checked her ammo. "Look, I understand why you have to do this. You feel responsible for these people, so you have to try. Damned right it's not my fight, but you saved my hide this morning and I owe you one. So let's stop wasting time and get my debt paid, shall we?"

"Fair enough." Sean used his body weight to push up on the large bar over the doors that connected his living space to the auditorium. The bar groaned its discontent but conceded to the determination of the now former leader of the Denver colony.

"Erhard," Sean roared.

The room grew eerily quiet. The only sounds were the faint screaming and occasional gunfire coming from outside.

Erhard's eyes narrowed to dangerous-looking slits. He jumped down from the pulpit and headed directly for Sean. "Well, look who decided to seek our protection. The traitor himself."

"I'm no traitor. I've done nothing to earn that title." Sean turned to address the hundred or so gathered survivors. "Someone opened the gates and let the Deads in. Someone was hiding Deads inside the gates even before that, and someone hid a Dead in my bedroom, feet away from where my little girl was playing. Someone betrayed you all, but it wasn't me." Sean snapped his attention accusingly back at Erhard, who stood to the side with his arms crossed and a smirk on his face.

"No one here is interested in listening to your lies and excuses. Shoot him."

A few guards drew their weapons on Sean, but most just swung their heads from side to side in confusion, like milling cattle waiting for the first to stampede.

Laney drew her handgun on Erhard. The barrel of the gun fell decisively onto the pulsing vein at his temple. She hadn't the reserve Sean did. It was amazing how the barest touch of cold metal could wipe the cocky grin right off of Erhard's face. Several guns rotated to her direction in turn. Worth it.

"Can you not see," she gritted out, "that Sean is trying to save your lives. Like he has done for three years."

"Then why did he let the Deads in the gates?" Erhard asked calmly.

"He didn't. You did."

"Says the girl who got Reynolds killed. What a coincidence that the day you arrive, the Deads get in."

"Enough," Sean said. "We could stand around all night pointing fingers, but we're running out of time. Anyone who would like to get out and come with me to another colony, you are welcome. I'll do my best to protect you. We are leaving immediately."

"Everyone who wants to fight for your home and avenge our people, stay here," Erhard yelled. "There is no honor in running."

"You will get everyone killed. Is this what you have been after? You wanted the Denver colony? Surely there is a better way than this. I'll step down. We'll let everyone pick a new leader, but you can't turn them into an army. There are women and children here."

"Who need to learn how to fight these creatures. Now shoot them!"

"Shoot us," Laney growled, "and I'll die putting a bullet in your head, mister. Then all of your planning and treachery will have been for nothing."

Her bluff held. No one moved to kill them, and Erhard finally conceded with anger and defeat in his eyes. "You may go, but anyone who chooses to leave with you, be warned. You will be leaving the safety of the colony, guards, and weapons to head out on foot through Dead infested forests."

The crowd murmured amongst themselves, but none stepped forward. Sean gripped her shoulder from behind. As he guided her back toward the exit, she kept her gun trained on Erhard. She refused to lower her weapon until they were at the door. That man wouldn't lose any sleep over putting a bullet in someone's back.

"One more thing, Ms. Landry," Erhard called out tauntingly. "It was very clever of you to find our stash. And leaving your little watchdog in a tree? Also surprisingly astute."

Her heart jumped straight into her throat. Jarren.

"But you didn't honestly think your team was the only one with a sniper, did you?"

Sean pulled her bodily through the exit doors just before she did something that would get them both killed.

Chapter Seven

"Greer decided to stay and fight," Finn informed Sean as he shut the auditorium door firmly behind them.

Laney didn't give a fig who was going or staying. There was no time for any more delay, so she bolted. Jarren, Jarren, Jarren. He had to be safe. Her ears filled with the sound of her heartbeat and frantic breathing as she ran. She knew what she would find when she left through the doors of Sean's house, but her logic couldn't quite overpower her innate need to find her brother safe.

She came out firing, one shot for every Dead with unbridled focus and accuracy. The colony had been large, and from the numbers around the building, the majority of it had already turned. And who knew how many Deads were let in through the gates in the first place? Luckily, many were still feeding. Lucky for her, but not so much for the townspeople. Piles of Deads were feasting on the colony's poor dying souls. It made the numbers who noticed her exit of the building more manageable.

She bolted and left any Dead she didn't have time to take care of trotting clumsily behind her. Darkness blanketed the colony, but fires torched the buildings behind her in the chaos and cast an eerie glow across the landscape. The path was illuminated just enough for sure-footed progress. Her name being called was a faint buzzing in her ear, followed by gunfire behind her. It wasn't important. Nothing was important but finding Jarren.

The nine millimeter in her hand clicked, a truly frightening sound, as the firing pin found nothing to ignite. Out of ammo and a quick head count revealed twelve Deads closing in fast. She pulled a blade from her boot, but it wouldn't be enough. Not even close to enough.

"I'm sorry, Jarren," she whispered. She jumped on the first Dead with the knowledge that the others would be on her in moments. The night lit up with gunfire. It seemed to come from all around her, and the sheer volume of it disoriented her. The Dead under her put up a fight, thrashing and screaming and clawing. She had taken too much time to pin the Dead's arms under her knees, but the others seemed to be having trouble finding her. She found her opportunity and ended its struggle with a well-placed knife through the eye.

"Laney!" Mitchell's screaming finally got through to her, probably because he was shaking her hard enough to rattle her jaws. "What the hell are you doing? Are you trying to get yourself killed?"

Laney swung her head to look across the mass of slain bodies. The Deads in the immediate area were still and limp. Guist and Mitchell were staring at her like she was a maniac, and Sean and Finn had caught up just in time to ignore her completely and discuss strategy and escape.

Adrianna's small hand was encased in Sean's, but she wrenched it free when the child saw what Laney did. A woman walked unsteadily toward them, her long gray hair flowing with the breeze and illuminated by the burning building behind her.

"Mona!" the child cried as she ran for her nanny.

"No! Adrianna, stop!" Laney yelled as she saw the danger a split second before Sean did.

Mitchell and Guist had trained their weapons but were yelling about no clear shot. Adrianna was in the way.

Laney lunged, pushing her legs so fast her muscles screamed. She'd always been a terrible knife thrower, but for lack of other weapons she chunked her knife as hard as she could over Adrianna's head and directly at the face of Mona the Dead.

The monster's focus was directed only at the child, but as the knife hit her in the face, hilt first, that focus shifted decisively to

Laney. The creature bellowed an inhuman sound, and Adrianna skidded to a halt in front of Mona. Laney didn't slow, and with no other weapons at hand, she leapt through the air, over the child, and wrapped her legs around Mona. The collision caused the Dead to lose her already questionable balance, and both she and Laney reeled and landed hard on the unrelenting ground. Laney rolled on top of the Dead and punched her in the face over and over. Her blows damaged the creature very little as it didn't feel pain, but she had to keep the thing shocked until she could figure out how to kill it. Mother Nature gave no weapons. No branches strong enough to do the job were anywhere within reaching distance.

Mona's skin was still humanly warm, and the slap of the dying flesh against Laney's knuckles made her want to scramble off and retch. She had liked Mona.

A strong hand grabbed Laney's arm at the arc of her punch and placed a handgun smoothly into it. The split second hesitation gave Mona the Dead enough time to recover and stretch her neck as far as she could. The monster groaned and gnashed her teeth, desperate to hurt her. Laney put the gun to the Dead's forehead and pulled the trigger.

"Goodbye, Mona," came Sean's quiet voice from behind.

Laney stood to find him shielding the sight of Mona's limp body from Adrianna. She handed him his gun and retrieved her knife. Guist handed her pack and weapons over before he turned and popped a Dead that was getting too close for comfort.

"I have to find Jarren," she told them.

Their escape plans could wait. That or they could leave her to catch up later. Either way they needed to get moving. More Deads would be on them any second.

"Where is he?" Sean asked.

"This way," Mitchell answered. The lines in Mitchell's face grew grim. The fact that Jarren hadn't found them already wasn't an encouraging sign.

The group ran at a frantic pace. Sean carried Adrianna, and Finn covered them to make up for their disadvantage. The run took an eternity, with every step becoming more frantic than the last. When they approached the storage buildings, Laney turned directly toward the grove of trees Jarren had intended to station himself in. A wave of relief washed over her when she saw movement under the biggest tree.

"Jarren," Laney called as she rushed toward it. "Why didn't you come find us?"

The movement froze, and she raked the beam of her flashlight over the darkness. The light reflected off of a set of film-layered dead eyes staring back at them. The Dead was crouched defensively over something.

"No, no, no, no," she said, the chill of dread tingling to her very fingertips. She shot the Dead, inconsiderate of the noise, and pulled the carcass viciously off Jarren's body.

She kneeled beside her brother's limp form, chanting his name in a hoarse whisper. Mitchell kneeled on the other side of his body, and Guist cursed loudly behind her.

Jarren's body twitched, and then jerked in a string of spasms. Mitchell looked at her with the same resolve she had seen on Jarren's face when he had decided to kill Monroe.

"Laney, we can't leave him like this," he said at her hesitation.

She shook her head back and forth as Jarren's body struggled through its transition.

"I can't," she said. Tears fell down her cheeks, but she didn't care.

"You want me to do it?"

Jarren opened his eyes and a long, low rumble came from his chest.

Mitchell jumped up and sat on his chest to hold him down, but the Dead only rolled his head from side to side. Mitchell aimed his rifle at Jarren's forehead.

"Wait," she said, grasping Mitchell's arm to stop him.

"Laney, we've been through this before. You don't want that for him. You made him a promise."

"Pull that trigger, and I'll never forgive you, Derek."

She only used Mitchell's first name when she meant business, and it did the trick. He stopped. She pulled out her knife and cut a line into her arm, wincing at the sting of the cold blade. She placed her wound over Jarren's searching mouth and let some of her blood flow down his throat.

"I can't watch this," Guist spat angrily. "I'm going to find rope."

Her actions were wrong, but she had to talk to him one last time. She'd gone over it a thousand times in her head; she'd tried to convince herself she could obey Jarren's wishes if this situation ever came. In that moment, however, she was completely powerless to her emotions and attachment to the only family she had left.

Jarren the Dead panted and convulsed and his throat released pained sounds as his body seized. At last he stilled and his eyes closed. She wanted to take it back. What had she done? Torturing him before death wasn't what Jarren deserved, and now it was too late to undo her dark and selfish deed.

"Water," Jarren rasped through cooling and stiffening vocal cords.

Mitchell grabbed his canteen in a rush, but she slowed his hand. "Pour it in carefully. He can still infect you."

"Laney?" Jarren said after taking a small gulp. "What happened? Why can't I move?"

"Jarren," Laney cried softly. "Do you remember watching those storage buildings?"

His eyes searched hers in confusion. "Yeah, I remember."

She watched it come back to him and hated herself.

"Someone shot me. I fell out of the tree and that's all I can remember."

"Jarren, someone let Deads in the gates." Laney waited for him to comprehend what she was saying. He turned his head to the deceased Dead beside him. "I didn't get to you fast enough," she whispered as she cradled his head. "I tried, but I didn't know until it was too late. I'm so sorry." Her voice cracked and she bit her lip against a sob.

"Don't do that, Laney. You can't blame yourself for this. I don't." He swallowed and a far off look crossed his face. His chest rattled when he inhaled and it made him cough violently. "Why can't I feel my arms and legs?" he asked when he recovered. "The others you tried to save said it hurt really bad. I don't feel anything though. Does that mean I'm so new I can be saved?"

The hope in his voice shattered her already breaking heart. It was lucky that he couldn't feel anything. The Dead had done a number on his body and most of his chest and abdomen looked like hamburger. The injuries were more than any human could survive.

"I think you broke your back when you fell out of the tree," Mitchell said thickly. "That or the bullet broke it."

It was the first time she had ever seen Mitchell cry. A tear slid down his cheek and made a small splat against Jarren's arm.

"I can't be saved then, can I?" Jarren asked.

She shook her head and stroked his cheek. "I'm sorry." She was sorry for so many things. She was sorry she hadn't stayed in that tree instead. That she hadn't been there to protect him when the Dead found his body. And most of all, she was sorry she'd brought him back. So rarely did someone die as peaceful a death as Jarren had. He had gone virtually painlessly, and she'd brought him back to say goodbye, and then to die again.

Jarren coughed again and again, his body wracked with the effort to draw air into lungs that were filling with blood. "Let's do this quick then," he said bravely. "Laney, I love you, but you're wasting time, and I'm guessing he isn't the only Dead here. It's still important to get you to a lab, do you hear me?"

She nodded, unable to speak for fear of making it harder on him.

"I will die happy if I know you're safe. If I can keep the hope that you can end all of this suffering."

"I promise I'll try. I love you too, big brother."

"I'll tell Mom and Dad you say hi, okay? We'll look forward to seeing you soon. Not too soon, though. I'll have an ice cold beer waiting for you. Or maybe one of those horrible fruity drinks you used to like. The ones with the little umbrellas." He chuckled, but it turned into an uncontrollable coughing fit. "It's time, little sister," he wheezed.

"I can't."

Mitchell aimed his gun at Jarren again. "I'll miss you, man. You've been my best friend ever since I was a little kid. We've been through a lot together, me and you."

Jarren smiled weakly. "We have. Take care of her, Mitchell. I'm counting on you guys."

Mitchell nodded and stood, chambering a round in his rifle.

"Not you," Jarren instructed. "It has to be Laney."

She wiped her eyes with the back of her hand. "Please, Jarren. I really can't. I can't do it."

"But you will. We made each other a promise. It's how I want to go. You can't argue with a dead man, Landry." He tried to smile but failed. "Give me the Mini-14 special. Do it now."

Mitchell backed off to give her space.

"Do it, Laney. Do it. Don't hesitate. Don't make me wait anymore. Just do it," Jarren chanted.

She cried so hard she could barely see through her tears. "I'm sorry," she whispered over and over as she cradled his neck and brought her Mini to his temple. She had made this shot uncountable times, but this one would haunt and resonate with her for the rest of her natural born life. "Goodbye, Jarren," she whispered into his ear and pulled the trigger.

Chapter Eight

Pining screams were coming from Laney. The realization surprised her, but didn't help to ease her pain as she cradled Jarren's head in her arms. Later, she wouldn't remember much detail about what happened in the hour after that. She moved numbly, as if someone else controlled her body. The whispered escape plans caressed her skin like a summer breeze, but she didn't care so much about the words. They planned to climb the east wall where the Deads so rarely gathered. Guist and Mitchell dug a shallow grave for Jarren in the grove where he'd fallen. When it came time for her to say something beside the newly turned earth that nestled her brother's body, she found herself unable to speak. She wept for him instead.

Mitchell and Guist half-dragged her in turn as they ran for the twelve-foot wall that had them trapped inside the colony full of Deads. The men hoisted her up to the top of the first wall, and she lowered herself to the ground with a length of rope Guist had found in one of the sheds. The men held the end from the other side to give her leverage. Mitchell was up next, and Adrianna was passed up to him and then down to Laney. After that, she and Mitchell held the rope on their side while Finn, Guist, and Sean scaled the wall. They did the same for the other two walls that led them to the freedom of the woods beyond.

Free of the colony, the team didn't stop for rest. The distant sound of gunfire provided a constant reminder of what lay behind them. They headed into the woods with urgency until they were well away from the colony walls and all the carnage the gates held firmly inside.

The steady pace led her mind to wonder—a colossal mistake.

Finn and Sean were so loud when they ran. Sure, Finn wasn't trained for the woods and Sean was carrying a child, but just the same, Jarren would be shushing them constantly if he were there.

Jarren would have shaped them up and quick.

Jarren.

Jarren.

The grief rose to a level that caused her chest actual and poignant pain. After that, she wiped her eyes and pushed all thought, bar the next step and then the next, out of her tortured mind. She had a promise to keep, and dwelling on her sorrow would get her killed for sure. She would give in to her heartache in private. Somewhere she could feel safe, if there existed such a place.

She had taken Jarren's pack, and the extra weight had been a burden over such a distance. Sean had offered to carry it for her and she allowed it. She told him she wanted the pack back at the next colony, but until then, Sean and Adrianna were welcome to its contents. They were ill-prepared for their escape, and Jarren would have wanted his provisions used if it would help someone in need.

The team stopped running, and Finn pulled out a map. Sean squatted down beside him and pulled Adrianna close before pulling a flashlight from Jarren's pack. He and Finn quietly discussed their next move with Mitchell and Guist. Mitchell tried to include her, but she couldn't quite manage to take her gaze away from the pack that sat in lonely silence beside Sean's leg.

She pulled away. "I'll keep a look out," she offered, pressing her back into the trunk of a large pine tree. Like an animal who sought the solace of the forest in the final hours of its demise, her weeping soul also yearned for isolation.

"We trade with a colony about half a day's drive from here," Sean said.

"Drive?" Mitchell's tone was colored with frustration. "In case you haven't noticed, we're on foot here."

Finn and Sean glanced at each other, a significant look of decision passing through their eyes.

"We have a truck hidden on a back road not far from here," Sean said.

"Great," Guist whispered. "Then what are we waiting for?"

"Colony members only check on it every once in a while to make sure it still runs and hasn't been found by anyone else. Problem is, Finn and I haven't ever actually been on the patrol to check on it. We've never actually seen it."

"Fantastic." Mitchell's voice dripped with sarcasm. "Why are we even discussing this as an option then?"

"Because we know the landmarks to it, just not in the dark. We need to hole up somewhere close to here. I know where we are right now, but if we travel aimlessly I'm afraid we'll never figure out where the vehicle is."

"Fine. Up a tree we go," Guist said as he pulled his pack off.

Sean frowned. "Why would we go up a tree? We need to find shelter for the night."

"It's safer to sleep in trees," Mitchell said with exaggerated patience. "You don't wake up with a Dead gnawing on your leg bone."

"Yeah, but I thought she could smell if they're coming," Sean said, pointing toward Laney.

"I think she's earned a good night's rest, don't you?" Mitchell growled quietly.

"Okay. I get that, but I have a child. Even if I was comfortable sleeping up there, Adrianna can't climb a tree, much less sleep in one."

"Daddy, I'm scared," Adrianna chimed in.

"Shh. I know, baby. Everything's going to be all right," Sean crooned.

Laney spoke up. "He's right. We have to find some sort of shelter. Even if we rigged up harnesses for Sean and Finn, we don't have anything that would work for a child."

"What if we compromised?" Finn offered. He pointed to the map. "There's a gas station a couple of miles away if we are where I think we are. I know you like to get high up to avoid the night walkers. The gas station has a flat roof at a good height, and it's only a few miles on foot to the truck from there."

"Let's go," she snapped. She needed action if she was going to successfully continue to avoid her own head.

The gas station, as it turned out, was located in the middle of nowhere. Whoever had scouted out its location must not have been concerned with making profit. It had to have been a miracle that the small convenience store had been able to maintain enough traffic on the dirt road that snaked in front of it to stay open for any substantial length of time. But then again, maybe the old diner with the dilapidated Coca-Cola sign across the street had brought in some customers.

Laney glared suspiciously at the ladder that was attached to the side of the building and led to the roof. A ladder couldn't be trusted. Though Deads were terrible climbers at best and couldn't make it far up a tree, she had seen a handful of determined zombies figure out a few of the bottom rungs of a ladder.

She stifled her distrust and scaled up to the roof after Guist. He reached the top and raked his flashlight over the flat and slightly graveled floor of it. He cursed softly under his breath, and she looked around him to see what had stopped him in his advance.

Two bodies lay in each other's arms near the edge of the roof. They had died some time before. From the age of the sun leathered bodies, she would guess a couple of years at least. There wasn't even any noticeable smell to them anymore.

"They must have been treed by Deads," Guist observed. "Doesn't look like they had any provisions or weapons. Must have got stuck up here and the Deads waited them out."

Had they been as close in life as their loving embrace in death suggested? She sighed sadly. She should have been used to this. Death happened every day. She was drowning in it. So why, after years of being exposed to tragedy, did the sight of this sad couple etch another painful notch into her heart?

"Hey, Mitchell," Guist called down.

"Yeah?"

"Open that old Dumpster lid, will you?"

"You got it."

The thud of the large metal trash bin sounded below them, but she spoke against it. "We can't just throw them in the Dumpster."

The sigh that escaped Guist's lips sounded exhausted. "Laney, burying someone? That's for the living. These two are dead. They don't care."

"They deserve better, and you know it."

He searched her face for a long moment. "Can we at least bury them in the morning?"

"And store them in the Dumpster tonight?" She didn't mean to be a pain, but the thought of the couple breaking their loving hold on each other to be thrown carelessly in the garbage seemed really tragic.

"Laney!" Guist rubbed his face vigorously and whispered, "I lost him, too. I just want today to be over with. I don't want to dig another grave tonight. Please."

"Okay," Laney said, meeting his pleading eyes. "Can we just cover them up so the kid doesn't see them? Then we'll leave them as they are when we head out in the morning."

"Cover them with what?"

"I'll use my blanket."

"Laney, you are in a tank top and you are up a mountain in Colorado. You were supposed to trade for a jacket two colonies ago. Nights are too cold to go uncovered. I can see gooseflesh all over your arms from here. You can't gift those corpses your blanket or you'll be no better off than them by morning."

"You aren't throwing them in the Dumpster, Guist," she decided impatiently. "All clear. You guys can come on up," she called down to the others while she pulled the light blanket roll from the elastic strings in the front of her pack.

As she spread her bedroll over the two bodies, Guist growled in frustration from behind her. "Okay, but you should take my blanket so you don't freeze to death tonight."

"No, thanks." She stood and scoured the bodies to make sure no shrunken extremities were peeking out from the edges of her blanket.

Guist's logic often overrode any sensitivity he might have otherwise had, and it had been a long, horrible day. She knew she should cut him some slack, but she couldn't help how much he was irritating her.

"What's going on, guys?" Mitchell asked, no doubt interrupting the death glare Guist was probably giving her back.

"Laney's being stubborn," Guist gritted out.

Mitchell shrugged like *what else is new* in the dim beams of their flashlights. Ignoring them, she claimed the furthest corner from everyone. She couldn't explain it, but Guist giving her a hard time made her want to cry, a sure sign that her emotions were fried. Time by herself would be best.

She set her pack behind her and pulled her knees to her chest, curling in on herself to preserve any heat her malnourished body could manage to provide. The group settled onto the roof for the night quietly. Her frayed attention was pulled time after time to Sean as he settled in with Adrianna. He pulled his little girl into his lap and covered them with Jarren's bedroll.

Exhausted past the normal need to sleep, her arms and legs felt heavy and drained but she still couldn't manage to turn her thoughts away from the horror she had witnessed that day. The things she'd said and wished she had said to Jarren kept playing on a loop through her mind, her thoughts separated only by the resonating sound of the bullet she'd put through his head.

"Laney?" Sean asked from directly in front of her.

She had closed her eyes to try to find sleep and had utterly failed to hear his approach. Irritating. "What?" she asked, with little remorse for her short temper.

Sean squatted down to her eye level and rested an elbow on his knee. "Were you asleep?"

Thank the old world she hadn't fallen to pieces in her own little private corner of the roof. "It seems my mind won't let me."

"Yeah," Sean sympathized. "Listen, I'm really sorry about your brother."

"You didn't know him," Mitchell said testily from a short distance off. He got up and walked over to start a quiet conversation with Guist.

She glared back at Sean tiredly. She had stopped apologizing for Mitchell years ago.

"I also wanted to say thank you for saving Adrianna. Twice. She wouldn't be here if it weren't for you. I'll never forget what you did for us. I owe you. If you can think of anything, anything at all…" He waited, seemingly unable to think of what else to say.

Laney resisted a lip quiver and a *bring my brother back* reply. She had to hold it together. She tried instead to keep it light because he was suffering loss too. "That homemade shampoo your colony made was nice. It wouldn't suck if you found some of that."

Sean smiled in the dark. "I'll see what I can do."

"For what it's worth, I'm sorry, too. About you losing your people," she blurted.

Mitchell stood over her, interrupting. "You need to eat something."

"I'm not hungry," she said.

Sean got the hint and left to take his place by Adrianna.

"It doesn't smell like Deads around here, does it?"

She didn't respond. Arguing with Mitchell was a pointless endeavor.

"No? Then you need to eat. Here." Mitchell sat down beside her. "Guist got us some dried venison." He handed her a good-sized piece wrapped in brown crackling paper.

Laney's stomach growled at the sight. "If I eat, will you leave me alone?"

"Sure."

Mitchell pulled her pack from behind her back and rummaged through it until he came out with a tin of fresh grown carrots and a bag of biscuits. They shared the meal in silence. There was no point in talking about their heavy loss. Talking about sadness was too dangerous a pastime. If she let such potent agony in for even a second, it would consume her like the fires of hell.

She reached for a drink, but her hand fell on emptiness. "Shoot, I think I lost my canteen." She turned her pack around once more to find her thermos still missing. The saltiness of the dried meat made her thirst for a good swig of water.

"No, you didn't. Guist still had it from when he refilled them earlier. Here." He handed her the canteen, and she took a long pull from it. She offered it back to Mitchell, but he declined.

"It has a weird aftertaste," she noted, taking another drink and swishing it around her mouth. "Kind of metallic tasting."

"Yeah, Guist said it all tastes like that. It's from how they purify their water or something."

She leaned back into the cushion of her pack, and her body relaxed almost instantly. Her lips tingled, and her eyelids grew heavy. Mitchell solemnly poured the remaining contents of her canteen off the side of the building.

"Son of a —" she slurred before drifting off into a deep slumber.

Chapter Nine

Laney dreamed of a jumbled mash-up of events and people she had known and lost in her life. When she came to, however, all she could remember was Jarren, laughing uncontrollably at a game of Whovillopoly they had played one winter years ago with Adam, Mitchell, and Guist. The boys had always been so competitive, and Jarren always found great amusement in their insults and trash talk.

She smiled sleepily and refused to open her eyes. Instead she held on to the remnants of that dream for as long as she could. A rough hand shook her, and the layers of overwhelming drowsiness peeled away. The smell of Deads made its way slowly from her nose to her groggy brain. The inconsiderate hand shook her again.

"I'm not playing your games today, Jarren. Go bother Mitchell. He needs more practice than I do." She smiled again, finding amusement in her jab. She tried to roll away from the offending hand, but it stopped her.

"Laney. Wake up."

She froze mid-roll, muddled and confused. That definitely wasn't Jarren's voice, and the stench of Dead was growing stronger by the moment. She lurched forward, and her eyes flew open. The rough hand turned tender with a touch that steadied her. It was Mitchell's, and she began to kick frantically at the blanket she had become entangled in. The blanket, like the hand, was also Mitchell's.

"It's okay. We're all right," he murmured as he tried to help free her from the cloth cocoon.

She kicked free and lumbered to her feet, swaying dangerously. She held her head in her hands in an attempt to stop the world from spinning. The memory of the horrible day before came crashing onto her, weighing her down until she felt she couldn't stand. Jarren was gone, and that was the cruel reality of her life.

"We are definitely not all right." She rounded on Mitchell, desperately needing an outlet for her mental storm or she'd break. "You drugged me!"

He shrugged unapologetically. "You said you couldn't sleep."

"I smell Deads," she whispered angrily. "You could've got me killed. I'd be useless in a fight."

"You'd be useless trying to make it to the next colony half-dead, too. Why don't you just thank me and get it over with?"

She rejected the urge to claw his face, but could not help the angry screech that burst from her throat. She turned from him furiously and leaned on the wall of the roof. She scouted for the Deads she smelled, but with no visual sign of them she began to hope fervently that they were just passing through. She tried to relax until she saw her arms. They were crisscrossed with tiny scratches. She shook her head and blinked hard. She had to be imagining them with the help of whatever leftover drugs were still in her system.

Mitchell cleared his throat behind her. "I think you might have been hallucinating last night because you kept clawing at yourself and mumbling on and on about bugs under your skin."

"What did you give me?" She should have felt more embarrassed about how shrill her voice was becoming, but she was having trouble finding the energy to care.

"An Ambien."

"An entire dose?" she asked.

"And a few other surprise pills. Don't worry, though. Guist traded fairly for them and was assured they were all sleeping pills."

The amused smirk on his face made her want to slap it right off. She looked away from him and scanned the roof. Finn was playing some sort of game quietly with Adrianna, and Guist was sitting by himself with a sad, faraway look in his eyes. Sean stood on the opposite side of the roof with his back to them. He had one leg propped up on the low wall of the roof and was leaning forward. He was watching something with undiluted concentration, and the hairs on the back of her neck prickled.

Suspiciously, she asked, "What time is it?"

"It's just past ten."

"Why haven't we left before now? Why didn't you wake me earlier?"

"We have a bit of a situation."

"Deads?"

"Just one."

"So why didn't you just shoot it so we can leave?"

"That's what I wanted to do, but Captain America over there wouldn't let us. Said he'd shoot the person who killed her, and he seemed pretty sincere with his threat."

She eyed the gun in Sean's hand. Not much rattled Mitchell enough to keep him from accomplishing something he intended to do, so if he was being cautious, she would be wise to do the same.

"I'll talk to him," she said, snatching Mitchell's canteen away from him and sniffing its contents suspiciously.

"Wouldn't drug myself, love."

She glared at him and then emptied the canteen into her mouth, leaving nary a drop for him. She handed him the empty thermos, but just as he reached for it, she let it drop with a clatter to the ground. She smiled wickedly and slunk away.

She turned her head slightly to watch Mitchell pick up his canteen, but instead he was squatting down near it, rubbing his chin and watching her walk away. His liquid caramel eyes fell hungrily and unashamedly on her.

She snapped her head back around. Why did that look make her heartbeat pick up? She had caught Mitchell looking at her like that before but was just as confused about it now as she was then. He wasn't a safe man to give one's heart to. She had seen it time and time again with the women he left after their brief stays at the different colonies. Women that fell at his feet became expendable. And besides, she was not his type in any way. The women he preferred were mousy and sweet, two words that had never been said about Laney Landry. The revelation made his interest in her all the more confusing.

She swung her gaze back to the gun in Sean's hand. Nothing like a crazy man with a weapon to get her mind off of Mitchell's confounding attitude. "Hey, Sean. What's going on?" she asked as she approached the former Denver colony leader.

He gave her a glance out of the corner of his cat-like eye but remained silent as he turned his attention back to the woods below. Movement below signaled the source of the stench. The Dead was a woman, with flowing and mangled black hair. Her feet were bare and cut, but she walked without a limp. Her simple, once white dress was bloodstained and tattered, and she wandered aimlessly, turning this way and that. Sean's focus stayed riveted on the Dead like she was water and he hadn't had a drink in days.

"Who is she?" she asked him quietly.

"She," Sean admitted after a pause, "is my wife."

Laney dropped her head, unsure of what to say. The Dead turned to head in the direction it came from and then back again. Had the creature once been beautiful? She must have been to interest a man such as Sean Daniels.

Watching Sean pine for this woman reminded her of the years without Adam, and the pain of remembrance pricked achingly. "When did it happen?"

Sean sighed and rubbed his hands roughly through his hair. He looked exhausted. "Aria was pregnant when the outbreak happened. We were so happy. We had wanted a baby so badly, and when the outbreak came through I was desperate to protect my family. We found our way to Denver and had attracted a pretty large number of survivors. Safety in numbers and all." Sean chuckled softly without humor and his face grew dark. "We found the colony and it already had half of the fence built. We took it as a sign to stay. We worked night and day building the rest of the outer fence, but it took a long time and we lost so many in the early days. We were all sitting ducks, like a damned buffet for the monsters. For every survivor we attracted, we lost just as many, just as fast. Aria had Adrianna in the middle of that chaos, and I grew even more frantic to keep them safe. I didn't want them to leave the house we were living in. I didn't want people visiting them because we didn't know if there were other ways to spread the infection back then. Aria grew unhappy and lonely, but

I kept pushing for her to stop living her life in exchange for safety. I knew she wouldn't leave me. She loved me too much." Sean turned his attention back to his undead wife. "One day we got into this huge, stupid fight. I went out to work on the fence with the rest of our able people and left her in the house alone again. She was so upset she asked Mona to watch Adrianna and then met a girlfriend who was working to set up the gardens. They were attacked. I didn't even know what happened to her. She was just gone. And now, every morning at dawn she wanders over to the east side of the fence. The same time. Every morning. She goes to the part of the fence I was working on when she was attacked. I know because I watch her. Every morning."

"So she turned years ago? Why have you not put her out of her misery? She's dead, Sean. And she isn't starved, which means she's been eating people."

"Put her out of her misery?" Sean asked, disgust tingeing his words. "Is that what you did to your man?"

"I did it for my brother, didn't I? He isn't running around as a monster right now because I loved him enough." Her face burned with heat to match her rising fury. "With Adam, I didn't get the chance to. I never found him. If I had, you better believe I would've put him down. That—" Laney waved her hand in Aria the Dead's direction "—isn't what he would've wanted."

"And you just gave up hope that he's alive somewhere?"

"No, I didn't. I've sent word to every known colony in North America. I've spent three years searching for him. I didn't give up on him. I just know that if he were still alive, he would've found me or sent word of where he was. Don't belittle my loss because you assume I handled it wrong. You don't even know me."

"I couldn't kill her because there is still something there! Are you happy? Now you know my great shame. I know, *know*, she is a Dead. Her mind will never be right. But every time I point my rifle at her head, part of me argues that she comes to see me every day. That a part of her remembers."

"You can forget whatever romantic notion you have of her remembering you. She is tuned to your smell. I've seen it before too. Deads stalking their old haunts. Staying close to things and places and people they were comfortable with in life. But don't get it twisted, Sean. If you went down there and professed your love for her, she would eat your liver for breakfast."

Aria, apparently hearing the escalating argument, started searching frantically for the source of the commotion.

"She's not reconnecting with you," Laney said sadly. "She's *hunting* you."

Sean watched the Dead in silence as she made snuffling noises. Saliva ran down the sides of her mouth in anticipation of a meal.

"I guess a part of me was just waiting on a cure."

She watched the transformation in his face with a sense of dread. It was as if she could see the light bulb turn on in his mind.

"Laney," Sean started.

"Please don't," she whispered.

"I know I have no right to ask anything of you. You have already done so much."

"Then don't ask," she begged. She turned to leave, to flee from the words that were tumbling from his mouth.

Sean grabbed her wrist. "Please, Laney," he said. "You can put Aria and I both out of our misery."

"It's not a cure! I already told you how it works. You saw what happened with Jarren last night. It was awful. Save your wife from suffering and shoot her before she is aware of what she has done."

She pulled her handgun and aimed it straight for Aria. Sean put the barrel of his own against her temple in a movement so fast she didn't have time to register it before she started talking again.

"She will feel everything. Her body is dead. Has been for years. She will feel the pain of that decay. It is *cruel*. I was cruel and selfish for putting Jarren through it."

"Laney, listen to me. Do you know how often I've wished someone had just disobeyed my orders not to kill her? Just so I could find closure. So I could move on."

"I'll do it for you," she whispered hoarsely, her eyes burning with unspilled tears.

"No, Laney. I have to be the one to do it. Just like you were brave enough to end Jarren's suffering. And now I have a chance to say goodbye to her. I'm begging you. Please." He set his gun down and put his hands up in surrender. "Please."

She glared at the Dead, so tempted to pull the trigger and provide the means to move on for everyone. All she had to do was pull the trigger. Seconds ticked by before she holstered her weapon and waved Mitchell off. He had been waiting impatiently behind with an assault rifle aimed at the back of Sean's head. Sean probably hadn't even been aware of the danger. More likely, he didn't care.

"Adrianna, you stay with Mr. Finn for a minute. Daddy will be right back, okay?"

The child looked frightened but nodded slowly. Laney stopped Sean's descent down the ladder behind her.

"I'll subdue her. You stay high and safe until I say so," she directed him. "Mitchell and Guist, keep an eye out. Pick off any Deads attracted to the sound."

They both nodded and picked their positions on opposite sides of the roof.

"Why should you take that risk?" Sean argued as he started down the ladder behind her. "It's my decision to do this."

She was so done arguing. "I'm immune from a bite. You are not. You've got a kid and I've got nothing left. We are doing this my way or we aren't doing it at all. I get it. You are used to being boss man." She stopped her descent and looked him squarely in the eye. "Not today."

She started back down toward the pine-needle-riddled ground below, and Sean stayed put. Aria the Dead caught the movement and lumbered toward the gas station. Laney hopped off of the last rung and sprinted for the Dead. She needed momentum. At the last moment, she dropped down and swung her leg around as she slid through the dirt toward Aria. She didn't land gracefully, but the move did as it was intended, and Aria flew forward, landing face first and hard on the ground. Laney recovered quickly and pounced on the Dead's back. She flipped Aria over and pinned her arms and flailing legs under her body weight.

"Sean!" she yelled as the undead creature beneath her bucked and screamed with fury.

Sean came running up behind Laney and dropped to his knees in the dirt. "What do you need?"

"Cut me."

Sean froze.

"There's a knife in my boot," she rushed. "I need both hands to hold her."

Sean hesitated only a moment before he pulled the knife. "Where?"

"Neck. I swear I'll haunt you if you nick an artery, though. She won't need much."

Sean placed the edge of the blade against the side of her throat but pulled back slightly, second guessing himself.

Aria made the decision for them when she chose that moment to buck wildly. She arched her body and pushed Laney's neck into the point of the knife, puncturing it deeply.

Sean cursed loudly, but she had no time to dwell on the pain. She leaned over Aria's mouth and bled into it until the Dead went slack and then rigid with the first of many seizures. Laney fell onto her backside and scrambled awkwardly backward as she held the gash at her neck. Flashback after pain-soaked flashback about the night before pummeled her, as she remembered when it had been her turn to pull the trigger on someone she loved.

Sean hovered over Aria and stroked the matted hair out of her face while crooning nonsensical things to her. Aria moaned, but this time it was with pain, not with hunger.

Laney couldn't bear to watch or hear any more. She stood. "She can still infect you. Steer clear of her mouth," she advised him. She turned to leave, unperturbed by the hitch in her voice.

"Laney, please stay." Sean looked at her with fear-filled pleading.

She imagined those piercing eyes got Sean a lot of the things he wanted in life. He had, however, asked much too much of her.

"Screw you, Daniels." She turned and ran for the gas station and didn't look back. Instead of crawling back up the ladder, she went in through the front door. She looked around the small convenience store and spied a door that led into a small office. Bingo. She was running out of time. Her walls were peeling away, and fast. When she was inside, she slammed the door only to find that warped hinges made it fly back at her. Oh, come on! Could she not catch a break? Was a door that actually shut and locked too much to ask after everything she had been through? She slammed the door over and over, venting her emotions before letting out a scream and sinking to the floor. She buried her face in her arms and cried for her brother.

The patter of her own blood hitting the stained tiles beneath her brought her a step back from the cliff's edge. She pressed her hand over the gash and brought blood-soaked fingers back. Great. If Jarren were there he would already be stitching her up. How would she survive without him?

A shot rang out, making her jump. Her sniffles quieted as the weight of what had happened fell over her like a tarp, heavy and suffocating. She knew how Sean felt in that moment. She had been called on to pull the trigger too. It was something that would be with them for the rest of their lives. Footsteps came for her some time later, and she fought the urge to push her feet against the door for a few more moments of uninterrupted time alone.

She would have to face them sooner or later.

The door to the small gas station office opened, and Sean stuck his head in. He didn't ask if she minded him being there, just closed the door behind him as best he could.

"Brought your knife back," he said. He handed over her weapon and sat directly in front of her. He glanced at the puddle of blood on the floor and slowly reached for her hand. He pulled it off of her neck. "You need first aid."

She nodded. She knew she did, but having some time to herself had been essential, too.

"I'm sorry," he said softly.

"You didn't mean to."

"Not just about cutting you too deep." He ran a feather-soft finger over the healing gash on her head. "For everything I've done and asked of you."

She put her hand back to her neck and dropped her eyes. The last thing she needed was for Sean Daniels to see her cry over an apology. She needed to rein it in, and fast.

Sean surprised her and pulled her into an embrace. He pulled her to her knees and held her. He didn't cry, or talk, and when she didn't respond, he pulled her arms around his neck. His hands were strong on her back, and the stubble of his unshaven face prickled her neck. She relaxed into him and tightened her grip around his neck ever so slightly. It had been so long since anyone had just held her, and something in her shifted and opened up. Something that had died and caved in on itself long before.

"I'm sorry," he said again into her ear. His voice was brimming with raw emotion.

Whether Sean was saying it to her or to Aria, she couldn't quite tell.

"I'm bleeding all over your shirt," she said. Pulling away, she wiped her eyes.

"It's okay," Sean said. "I'm going to go get our packs and we'll get you stitched up."

Sean started to stand but the door flew open, and Mitchell burst into the small room. He punched Sean across the jaw without warning.

"Mitchell!" Laney yelled in shock.

He ignored her and placed all of his furious attention on Sean. "The next time you point a weapon at anyone on my team, it'll be the last thing you ever do."

Sean spat blood out onto the dingy floor and sat up, wiping his mouth with the back of his hand.

Mitchell turned eyes that had darkened to charcoal black on her. "Well, crap, Landry. If I knew Sean slit your freaking throat, I would have been here to stitch you up a long time ago." He pointed to the door and gave Sean a warning look. "Get out."

Sean left without a backward glance and Mitchell knelt in front of her to get a better look at the gash. "I was trying to give you some space. I didn't know he'd cut you so bad."

"He didn't mean to."

Mitchell grunted, seemingly unconvinced. He rummaged through the first aid and started to clean the wound without so much as a "this-might-sting-a-little." She knew the drill. It certainly wasn't the worst injury she'd ever had, so there was that.

A sheen of sweat broke out on her forehead, and she held her breath as Mitchell worked. The tender skin on her neck hurt worse than the rougher bits of her did. She searched desperately for a distraction, both from the pain and the recollection of Sean's embrace, which kept making a stubborn and persistent appearance into her frayed mind. The man just lost his wife. Again. She couldn't name a more unavailable man.

"Do you think you'll ever settle down?" she asked a silent Mitchell. The words fell out of her mouth, and as soon as they did, she wished she could swallow them back down again. They were out though, hanging in the air between her and Mitchell, breaking an unspoken rule that forbade them from talking about a future they likely didn't have a chance at.

Mitchell chucked. "What? You want to go steady with me, Landry?"

"No, not like that." She searched for a way out. "I mean, do you ever think of picking a colony? I don't know. Jarren was always the fighter. I wouldn't have left him for anything, so I became one too. But now he's gone." She swallowed hard. "He's gone and I don't know where I fit anymore."

He kept working silently. His face was thoughtful, but his lack of immediate response had said he likely wouldn't give one. She closed her eyes against the pain and waited for Mitchell to bandage her wound.

"If it were the right colony, I think I could eventually settle down. I don't think I could work in the gardens or anything. I'd need more action. After the way we've lived, I don't think we could be satisfied with a boring existence. Maybe I could be a guard or something. I know the wise decision would be to cash our chips in now, you know? We're pretty lucky to have survived all of the impossible situations we have. Guist talks about picking a colony, so it's been on my mind lately too."

That was news to her. She had never once heard Guist talk about slowing down. She assumed he would be a fighter until he died. How sad that she was just then learning of her team's wants for their futures. She didn't know how to respond to such a candid conversation with Mitchell. "Guess all of our wants don't matter anyway." She grinned, trying to lighten the seriousness of their talk. "We'll probably die tomorrow."

He chuckled and put the medical supplies into his pack. He reached out his hand to help her up. "Better live today then," he said in a velvet soft voice. He gazed down at her, his light brown eyes full of indecision and hesitation. It was impossible to ignore his dark haired perfection when he was so close. He leaned forward and opened his mouth as if to say something but shook his head slightly and did an about face instead. He left the room and left her flustered, her lips throbbing for something she couldn't quite understand.

He was notorious for ribbing her constantly, and the semi-mature conversation they'd just delved into was definitely a first. She waited for him to turn back around and call her a sentimental idiot, but instead he left without another word.

Men were complicated and confounding creatures. She would need to smother her questioning heart quickly if she was to avoid being irreparably damaged by the consequences of such pursuits.

Chapter Ten

The hike to the hidden truck was blissfully uneventful. The path was rural, and Deads tended not to hang around for long if there wasn't food. Laney's new team encountered exactly two walking corpses, both of which were put down with a single shot, from the time the group solemnly buried Aria Daniels until they found the concealed pickup.

It was late in the afternoon, and the shadows from the evergreen forest stretched across her hiking boots. Down in a large crevice, a truck was backed into a ledge and half hidden by Mother Nature. How on earth someone was able to get that vehicle down there in the first place, she couldn't guess. When the boys removed the brush that had served as camouflage, a midsized four-wheel-drive Chevy was exposed, fully jacked up in every sense of the word. Maybe it hadn't been so hard getting that lifted, red, roaring beast in the hole after all. She smiled sadly. Jarren would have loved it.

Sean tried to start it a few times with no luck. Laney, Finn, and Guist patrolled nervously at the noise. They definitely didn't need to attract Dead attention with their getaway car stalled in a ditch.

Mitchell popped the hood, and the annoying half of him disappeared to tinker inside. The bearable half of him was on display as he balanced on one foot in his gray cargo pants and boots. Damn, that man could wear a pair of pants. He had found a pair that was tighter on his assets and looser in the legs, effectively lengthening his already impressive height and accenting his athleticism.

She jerked her gaze away from Mitchell and mentally strangled herself. What was wrong with her? It was Mitchell. She got over her crush on him in high school. She couldn't even name a more dangerous man to give her heart to. Her gaze fell on Sean, who was turning the engine over again. Well, maybe she could name one.

Mitchell leaned against the open hood and stared at the truck's innards with a slight frown. "I think it's just the gas. It's been sitting too long in the tank and it's settled." He shut the hood of the truck and pulled the tail of his shirt up to wipe his hands.

Sean jumped out of the truck and pulled a canvas off the bed, exposing a row of red sloshing gas cans. They added more gas to the tank before Sean said a little prayer and tried to start it again. It took a couple of tries, but the engine finally roared to life, to the relief of everyone watching and crossing fingers for something, anything, to go as planned.

Mitchell jumped in the bed of the truck, and they made their way slowly but steadily up the ravine to where the rest of the group waited.

"Come on, Adrianna," Laney said as she picked up the little girl who had taken to clinging to her leg while Sean was busy. "You can sit in the back seat with me."

The truck was a four-door, and roomy enough, but Finn was roughly the size of a Clydesdale, and they had six people to fit into a five-seater.

"I'm staying back here," Mitchell announced when they pulled up.

"Why?" she asked.

"Because there is no room to spread out inside, and I need sleep. I was up all night watching you twitch and moan."

She rolled her eyes heavenward. "Fine. More room for us." She grinned at the little girl firmly holding onto her hand.

Sean drove, and Guist took the front seat, leaving the back seat to Finn, Laney, and Adrianna.

"I'm hungry," Adrianna said after they had picked their way a couple of miles through the dense woods.

Laney had opened the window that separated the bed of the truck from the cab so she could hear Mitchell if he saw Deads. It also wouldn't hurt to keep her nose in the wind. She thought Mitchell was already asleep, but at the child's complaint he started rifling through his pack. He handed Laney a bruised but still edible apple through the window.

"Can she have an apple?" Laney asked Sean.

"Yeah, but she can't chew the skin very well yet."

She pulled a pocket knife out of her pack and peeled the apple with an unbroken cut. She handed the long coil of skin back to Mitchell, who arched his eyebrows with impressed approval. She sliced the apple into manageable slivers for Adrianna, and as the child munched hungrily on the fruit, Laney searched her own pack for something to add to the meal. All she could find was more dried fruit, two leftover biscuits, and half a package of colony-made wheat crackers. Guist had obviously planned for them to hunt on the way to their next mission when he had packed for them.

She divvied up the stash between herself, Adrianna, and the men, but after having consumed her small portion, she concluded it wasn't nearly enough. Finn pulled out a plastic bag that contained thick squares of homemade granola bar in it. The sight and faint smell of the peanuts alone were enough to elicit a rumbling growl from her unsatisfied stomach.

Finn pulled out a square and handed it to her without saying a word. She nodded her appreciation and knocked it lightly against Finn's own granola bar in silent cheers. She offered some to Adrianna, but the little girl was satisfied and nodding off with her head resting in Laney's lap.

She looked up to see Sean watching her in the rearview mirror. His radiant eyes looked curious and tender.

She leaned her head on the window and finished her meal, and before she knew it, she had fallen into an unexpectedly peaceful sleep to the gentle pulling of the truck as she stroked Adrianna's hair.

Laney's head snapped forward as the truck jerked to a stop. "How long have I been asleep?" she asked Finn as she looked out the window to unfamiliar surroundings.

"Half the day."

She must have heard him wrong. "As in all of the waking hours of a day?"

"Yeah, we stopped like six times for munchkin here to take a potty break." Finn nodded his head toward a fidgeting Adrianna. "You didn't move a muscle."

At the mention of it, she felt the strain against her own bladder to the point of discomfort. "Why didn't anyone wake me?"

"For what? We were just driving. Besides, your mind and body are trying to heal from a whole lot of hurt. You needed the sleep."

She had to admit that, besides a seriously stiff neck and constant dull ache where all of her injuries were, she hadn't felt so well-rested in a long time. "Did we run into any Deads?"

"A few groups but we outran them all. This truck has some get-up-and-go. There just aren't as many of them this far up in the mountains. There wasn't a huge population to turn Dead in the first place and fewer humans for food up here. This colony is kind of in the middle of nowhere."

Sean had pulled the map over the steering wheel and was discussing the route in a hushed voice with Guist. Apparently traveling the woods for such a distance had thrown them out on an unfamiliar road.

"I think we're almost there," Finn said, sounding relieved.

"Need a moment," she called up to the front seat. She hopped out of the truck to relieve her bladder. She could feel Mitchell's eyes on her from the bed of the truck, but she did her best to ignore him. She focused on scouting out the perfect forest toilet instead. She smelled the faint, sickly sweet musk of Deads, but they were too far off for immediate concern.

When she was back in the truck again, Sean turned to her.

"We're going to be there in a few minutes, but I wanted to touch base with you guys first."

Mitchell stuck his head in the window.

"There were closer colonies, but this one houses one of Doc's old buddies. Name is Dr. Mackey and they met back in their days of working at the CDC together. I figured this would be a better option to start work with Laney."

"You mean *on* Laney," she grumbled.

"We trade with this colony and their leader is a good lady," he continued. "But she is strict. If you guys want to stay here and give Mackey some time, you will have to mind colony rules to the letter."

Mitchell made a snoring sound and retreated from the window.

Sean frowned slightly and folded up the map. He put the truck in drive and took a hard right. Within minutes the truck pulled up to a makeshift gate that flanked a fence of strewn barbed wire.

Guist leaned forward in the front seat and squinted at the fence. "I don't think that would stop a Dead. They don't feel anything. The best you could hope is that they get tangled up in the wire to buy some time."

"True," Sean said as he pulled the truck to a stop. "Which is why they also electrified it and attached bells every few feet. Not even a rabbit gets in without the guards being alerted. It's still not as safe as the colony needs, though, which is why they're building that." Sean pointed out his window. Through the foggy mist that had descended upon them Laney could make out an imposing wooden fence in progress. "The wire fence is only temporary. The colony is fairly new and it takes time to create safety." Sean waved two fingers to a guard who had spied their truck and was approaching. There were ghosts in his voice. "And even then, no matter how safe you think you are, things can still go horribly wrong."

The guard talked quietly to Sean through his open window and then spoke into his walkie talkie. He requested backup and was rewarded with four more guards that appeared out of the fog. They ordered everyone to exit the truck, and the other guards gave respectful greetings to Sean. They apologized for subjecting him to the required bite check.

"I completely understand. I do have one request though."

"Certainly, sir."

"The woman in my crew, Laney, has been shot on her side," he told them. "We put her through the ringer a couple of days ago because we thought it looked suspicious." He smiled. "I assure you she isn't turning and the wound is already healing. I just wondered if you would conduct both her and my daughter's search with respect and as much privacy as can be managed."

The four guards looked to the first who had approached the truck. He consented.

"Behind the truck," a short, stocky guard commanded.

Laney took Adrianna's hand and pulled the little girl behind her. She stopped when they were out of direct view of all but two armed guards and began lifting the child's shirt and pant legs as instructed until she was cleared.

"Okay, baby. Go back over to your daddy while we finish up here," she told her in a low voice. If this was the time she was going to be shot for her Dead bites, it was best if Adrianna was out of the line of fire.

"Clothes off," the shorter guard instructed.

She started to protest the complete removal of her garments, but he cut her off.

"We have orders. If you don't comply to the bite search, you don't enter the colony."

She bit her lip and scurried farther out of direct sight from her team before she peeled off her clothes for the second time in a week for a group of complete strangers. Light rain spattered across her bare skin and raised gooseflesh in waves across her arms. The men were professional, obviously doing their best to ignore her feminine assets other than to do a quick check that her skin was unblemished by teeth marks. They ignored her tattoo, choosing instead to focus on the atrocious injury on her side. She didn't look down at it. She stared straight ahead and waited for the verdict. She knew what it looked like. It looked exactly like what it was.

"Sir?" the shorter guard called to Sean.

He appeared around the side of the truck.

"Seriously?" she exclaimed angrily. "Can I at least put my pants back on?"

"Yes," Sean told her, as he glared down the guard. "What is the problem?"

"Sorry, sir. It's just *that*—" he pointed to her side as she tried to scramble into her pants "—doesn't look like any gunshot wound I've ever seen. Surely you can see why I'm going to have to call it in to Mel."

"Get her on the radio. I'll talk to her personally. Did you even bother to notice it is an old injury?" he asked angrily.

The anger must have been for show since he'd recently made the same assumption that she was in danger of turning into a brain-eating zombie at any moment, too.

"Landry," Sean barked. "Put your clothes back on!"

She was already hurriedly zipping her pants up with her back to the argument. If he was waiting for a "yes, sir" from her, he was clearly deranged. She turned her head to tell him so, but she stopped when she noticed his eyes raking down her bare back. She resisted a shiver and a smart remark. Instead she reached for the black shirt still draped over the side of the truck bed, and slid directly back into her semi-modest comfort zone. She grabbed her vest and weapons and slunk around the truck to stand by the others. Maybe the color in her cheeks would go down before the boys got a real look at her face.

"I'm either never leaving this colony or we are living in the woods forever. I can't handle any more gate checks," she complained as she straightened her shirt.

"Aw, don't be a spoil sport, Landry," Mitchell said through a rakish grin. "The rest of us like gate checks just fine." He slapped her backside firmly and went back to fastening his belt.

She glared at him and scooted out of physical harassment range, rubbing her bottom gingerly. "Mitchell, you are a bunion."

"Oh, come on, Laney. If I didn't annoy you, you would be completely bored with your life. You would! So you're welcome," he said with a devilish wink.

He went back to work redressing. He was standing unashamedly beside her in all of his shirtless glory. No matter how much the man made her blood boil, she couldn't deny that he was a beautifully made, masculine creature. He was tall and lean, and his defined chest delved directly down to an elongated and muscular abdomen. His pants hung low on his waist, but not annoyingly so. They showed just enough musculature retreating to regions below, and try as she might to feel differently, she couldn't help but find the fashion obnoxiously intriguing on his physique.

She squinted at the tiny script tattoo across his ribcage. It was located under his arm and done in such a fashion that it was almost indecipherable. She always tried to make out what it said, but thus far had been disappointingly unsuccessful. He had his done the same night she had gone in for her peacock tattoo. He had never let her look closely at it though and so far had absolutely refused to tell her what it said or meant. Probably to annoy her. He would say, "You aren't ready to know yet," with an obnoxious grin.

He noticed her interest in his tattoo and pulled the shirt over his head. "Nice try."

She didn't know why he looked so amused with himself. "It probably says bunion," she muttered.

Sean and the guards rejoined the group. "We're cleared for gate check, but we have to report directly to Melony Benton. She is the leader here. By we, I mean Laney and I."

"Where Laney goes, we go," Guist said in a tone that invited no argument.

"That's what I figured. Let's load up." Sean hopped in the driver's seat and started the truck.

She hoisted Adrianna into the back seat, and the shorter guard jumped into the bed of the truck with Mitchell.

"Where are we, anyway?" she asked as Sean pulled the truck through the opening gate.

"Blue River, population six hundred eighty-five," Finn offered. "Or so the sign said. I'm assuming the last few years has maimed that number a bit."

She wiped condensation off of the window with her forearm as they climbed a steep mountain road. Buildings made of logs peeked from between thick groves of pine trees. Every colony was different, but this one was the most unique and picturesque she had seen. Most colonies felled the trees near living quarters so the people who dwelled there could spot danger at a distance and feel a little safer. In contrast, this high altitude colony used trees to camouflage its very existence. Each building was one of a kind with snaking, thin walking trails that connected them all. All of the cabins were small, but some were of newer, cruder construction while others seemed dilapidated, though sturdy. Her ears popped as the truck climbed a zigzagging switchback. To the left of the truck was a leveled area that housed three rows of RVs someone had taken the time and substantial effort to track down and haul in. They were placed in close proximity to each other but as far as housing went, it was highly efficient. Farther up the mountain, long wooden cabins made of fallen pines jutted out of the forest. Each had ten doors, evenly spaced, which indicated the cabins were made of separated bedrooms for different families.

The space between the wooden logs that comprised the construction was packed tightly with what looked to be concrete of some sort. She counted six of the long cabins before Sean pulled the truck into a parking area filled with other four-wheel-drive vehicles and one giant eighteen-wheeler. How they managed to get that huge supply truck up the mountain road Sean had just maneuvered was beyond her.

"Let's go," Sean said as he parked the truck.

He led the group up a trail through the dense woods. They crossed three small bridges where one of many rivers snaked its way down through the Rocky Mountains. The bubbling and gentle rushing of the water relaxed the tension in her shoulders almost immediately. How could a place so beautiful still exist in this world? She paused on a small wooden bridge and looked over the edge into the flowing water beneath.

"Do you think it has trout in it?" she asked Finn. She wasn't quite able to keep the excitement out of her voice. The thought of a fish dinner had her stomach aching for sustenance.

"I know it does. I see one right there." Finn pointed.

"Colony tour later. Business first," Sean called from up ahead of them.

The end of the trail brought them to the front steps of a cabin much larger than the others they'd seen. She was panting like a freight train and feeling light-headed by the time they arrived.

"Geez, Laney. Forget the Deads. It's a little hike uphill you have to worry about," Mitchell teased.

"It's the altitude," Finn defended her. "The air is thinner and it will take some conditioning to get used to it."

The front door opened, and a tall woman in her mid-thirties stepped out to greet them. Her medium brown hair was pulled back into a ponytail and her smile was easy, natural and unforced. Her jogging outfit was a light blue color, and it made her bright green eyes seem animated and bright.

"I'm Melony Benton. You can call me Mel, though. Everyone around here does," she said. "Welcome to Dead Run River."

Well that was surprising. "Dead Run River? I thought this was the Blue River colony."

"Ah," Mel said with a smile. "The town was originally called Blue River before the outbreak. The new name came later when we started setting up a colony. When we started building this place, Deads were attracted to the water for some reason we still haven't figured out. It seemed every Dead from any town around here gathered at the same place, all along the river's edge. Like they were waiting for something. It was quite the job to thin them out. The Deads ran this place in the early days. People started calling it Dead Run River and wondered if we would ever be able to set up here. Humans persevered, but the name stuck." She studied everyone as she spoke, and when she finished her eyes fell on Sean. "Good to see you again," she said with sincerity. "Though I thought it would be a while until your next visit. You were just here a week ago."

Something on Sean's face made the woman's green eyes fill with worry. "Come in, please." She led them into the great room of the large home and turned to Laney. "First things first. Let me see it."

Sean nodded to her in encouragement, and she lifted the hem of her shirt until her unbandaged bite was exposed.

"Mel," Sean said in a low voice. "She's Laney Landry."

The woman's green eyes snapped up to Laney's face. "Is this what it looks like, then?" The woman gestured to her side.

She nodded. "The Dead that bit me died almost instantly."

"That's not all, Mel," Sean offered earnestly. "Her blood, it brings back their minds. She can't do anything for their bodies, but for a few minutes, they are themselves again." His face took on a grim and haunted look. "I've seen it."

"Well, it's actually a cruel thing to do to them," Laney said, trying to stifle the excited look on Mel's face. "But if you have a doctor or anyone really who can try to start figuring me out, I'm at a point where I'd be willing to be a lab rat for a while."

"Why now?" Mel asked curiously.

"I made a promise to someone."

Mel knelt back down to examine her healing bite.

Laney cleared her throat in search of anything that would clear her head of her persistent thoughts of Jarren. Mel's home wasn't the place to cry.

Hello, leader of Dead Run River. It seems you have heard a lot about me. I'd like to squash that by blubbering uncontrollably on your shoulder. Nope.

"Beautiful house you have," she said instead as Mel gestured for everyone to take a seat on the comfortable looking couch and chairs around a great stone fireplace.

"Thank you. I decorated it myself. Believe it or not, this is the house I lived in before the outbreak. I used to be a ski instructor in the winters and I would pick up a couple of jobs in the summers down in Breckenridge. For me, this place was paradise. Still is in some ways." She took a seat in a large dark leather chair across from them. "I think being a native and a survivor and knowing the area so well is what established me as leader of the Dead Run River colony."

"Don't sell yourself short," Sean interjected. "You are the leader here because you are capable. People flock to your colony, and even choose to settle right outside of it because you are a natural at providing structure and safety for them."

"Flatterer," she laughed.

Sean shrugged unapologetically.

"I must say," Mel said, turning her attention back to her. "You look so much like your picture. Whoever drew your likeness must have had real talent."

What in Hades was that woman talking about? Laney looked to her team, who seemed to be exactly as confused as she was. "I'm sorry," she said. "Are you saying you have a picture of me?"

Mel smiled attractively. "Follow me. I have something to show you."

Chapter Eleven

Mel led them to an office space, which was exactly as one would expect such a room to look like, except for one thing. The largest wall of the rectangular room was completely covered with lists, pictures, letters, and pleas. Organized chaos at its best. Most colonies had a bulletin board to try to reunite friends and family members that had gone missing or been separated. Most went sadly unanswered, but everyone living had heard a tale or two about the success stories. The boards gave people hope.

Mel walked directly over to the left hand side of the wall and plucked a small, gray piece of paper from the pin that held it securely in place. She handed it to Laney. On it was a simple picture of her and Adam. It had brief descriptions of them both and a short plea that gave directions on how Adam Leary could get in contact with Laney Landry, who was searching for him.

She crumpled the paper against her chest as her heart shattered into a million shrapnel fragments. The picture of the man she thought she'd marry was so unexpected that for a split second, all she had been through promised to become too much.

Mitchell had drawn the flyers up in the beginning, and they had sent them with everyone they knew to be traveling in different directions. All had gone unanswered.

If she talked quietly, maybe the shake in her voice wouldn't be so noticeable. "May I please throw this away?"

"But why? I mean—" The woman opened her mouth to say more but seemingly changed her mind and switched directions. "This drawing made it to the Breckenridge colony. When Breck fell, we recovered the board and it was the beginning of our own."

She nodded and swallowed hard as she handed the picture to Mitchell. History or not, she didn't want it. "You can do whatever you want with it, Mitchell. May I use your restroom?" she asked.

"Sure," Mel said. "There's an outhouse in the back."

"Thanks."

She ignored Mel's directions and veered toward the river. Darkness had fallen, but the moon was full and enough light filtered through the thick trees for her to see. She washed her hands and face in the frigid snow-melt waters. She wiped her face dry on the bottom hem of her shirt and pulled clean, pine-scented air into her lungs once. Twice. She clasped her shaking hands together to steady them. The gooseflesh on her arms told her that though it may still be early autumn, the nights in the mountains would be bone chillingly cold.

A deep and familiar voice interrupted her thoughts. "Guist and I are going to work for a jacket for you first thing. You'll get sick in weather like this."

She tried to smile her thanks to Mitchell, not bothering to stand. His tiny, perfect nipples were puckered tightly against the thin shirt that covered them. "You need one too."

"True, but you are more important. You know, being the cure and all."

She snorted. "I'm nobody's cure."

"You okay?" he asked her after a few moments of contented silence.

Genuine concern from Mitchell was new and uncharted territory. She must have looked even more pathetic than she felt. "It was just unexpected, you know? I haven't seen Adam's face in so long."

"I know," he said simply. "Come on."

He pulled her hand and held it as he led her through the back door of Mel's house. His hand was strong and warm, and somewhat disturbingly comforting. When they were back in Mel's great room, Mitchell motioned for her to take his seat closest to the fire and he took her seat on the couch next to Finn and Guist.

Guist filled them in. "Sean is speaking with Mel in private to talk about what happened to his colony. Mel said her second in command is coming in to give us housing assignments and take job assignment applications. She's going to set up a meeting with the colony doctor first thing in the morning and she'll hand out our official job assignments tomorrow."

Finn leaned forward. "Guist asked Mel where they should trade for a jacket for you and she said to grab one out of the front coat closet before you leave. She doesn't want you catching cold."

"Lucky," murmured Mitchell. He stood and walked briskly to the coat closet near the front door. He rifled through an impressive selection of winter jackets before he held up two for her to choose from.

She tried them on and settled for a simple, fitted, navy blue one that hugged her curves. It was surprisingly warm for feeling so lightweight. She peeked in the closet to find a plethora of pink and leopard skin printed coats. She gave Mitchell a nod of approval before she sat back down, cuddled snugly into her new jacket. He was a jack-wagon ninety percent of the time, but that man knew her tastes and didn't tease her for it. Usually.

The second in command, Nick Creedy, made his appearance a few minutes later. He was a grizzled man with a long, full, graying beard and deep wrinkles covering skin leathered from time spent in the sun. After they all put in their applications for guard duty, Nick pulled out a large clipboard with a list of available housing. He assigned Sean and Adrianna to a detached cabin and Finn a trailer that was located a short distance away from it. Mitchell and Guist would be roommates in one of the larger attached cabins, and Nick assigned her to a single room in one of the long cabins a little farther down the mountain. Her room was located closest to the doctor's cabin.

She would have a room all by herself. She couldn't even name the last time she had privacy or a space of her own.

Nick provided them with a packet of information and maps to everything in the colony including a mess hall, gardens, doctor's office, outhouses, and showers. There were short papers on the history of the Dead Run River colony and surrounding areas and a schedule that listed their times to do kitchen duty. Nick also handed them little welcome bags containing a bar of handmade soap, a small tube of lip balm, a disposable razor, and a plastic baggy containing three chocolate chip cookies.

"Sorry," Nick said with a sheepish grin. "The welcome bags kind of just have whatever we can get our hands on."

"Don't apologize," Laney said. "This is the nicest reception we've ever had at a colony."

Nick highlighted their housing assignments on the maps. Before he sent them off he told them, "At your job assignments, you will be paid every Friday in credit to the general store and market located here." He highlighted it on Laney's map. "They'll have everything you need, and if they don't you can put in a request to get it. We always see what we can do on supply runs."

Sean came out of Mel's office as the rest of them were finishing up with Nick. He took his offered packet from the second in command and shook his hand in greeting. Sean looked pale and drained, but he talked to Nick cordially for a couple of minutes before he met up with the rest of the group. "I'm familiar with the housing in this colony if you want me to show you where you'll be staying."

Mitchell looked like he'd rather lick a toilet seat than accept Sean's help, so Guist was the one to speak up. "Sounds good, man. We could use the help, especially in the dark."

As they started down the main trail that led back down the mountain to the housing areas, Finn swerved off toward his own trailer. It was located right beside Sean's cabin, which was about two hundred yards away from Mel's house. He said his goodnights and left the group for the first time since he had been assigned as her guard in the Denver colony.

The trail looked different at night, as all things did. Small solar lights had been stuck low to the ground every few yards, and the dim blue light reflected off vegetation that edged the dirt path. The noise of breeze and river and bugs singing into the night air made the place feel like magic. If only Jarren had lived to see this place. He had been so close. The group walked quietly as if they were also affected by the weight of such a perfect night. Or it could have been that they were all in different stages of despair and exhaustion. The latter was more likely.

Adrianna asked to be held, and Sean picked her up. Laney followed behind him, and the little girl smiled sleepily over his shoulder.

Mitchell and Guist, accustomed to forest footing, followed behind her as quietly as a whisper. If she weren't so attuned to their movements, she wouldn't have even guessed they were there.

Lantern light swung lazily back and forth up ahead. Sean didn't miss a step, so they must have been common when the colony's inhabitants chose to walk the trails at night. The dim light coming from the gently rocking lantern was quite mesmerizing, so other than a quick body count when the small group of five passed by them, she didn't catch faces or genders. They were talking easily as they passed and one of the women greeted Mitchell, but she barely registered their conversation.

"Adam," Mitchell said quietly.

The context was confusing. She most definitely didn't want to relive their earlier conversation. In fact she wanted to stop thinking about her past altogether.

"Mitchell, I don't really want to talk about him anymore."

Mitchell had stopped and was looking back toward the group that had just walked by. "Adam," he said a little louder.

His exclamation brought a man in the middle of the passing group to a halt. He froze so quickly, the two women behind him ran into his back. The man swung his head around, and his gaze landed squarely on Mitchell. Laney's heart stopped.

The man was at first unfamiliar, though she could never forget his face. His blue eyes had aged a hundred years since she had seen them last and weren't quite as bright as she remembered them. His blond hair was thinner, and he wasn't as tall as she remembered, but she still thought him a handsome man, made more attractive by the wit and humor that hid just beneath the surface of those pooling cerulean eyes. The light from the lantern in his hand danced across his face, and his nostrils flared ever so slightly as recognition lit his features.

"Derek? Is that you?" he asked in shock.

Her hand rested on Mitchell's still back, but she couldn't recall how it got there. His muscles were tensed, and she brushed his back lightly, searching for softness where only brute power resided. She was sure that if she took it off, the beast in Mitchell would escape. Her hand was the only thing that kept him frozen in place, of that she was certain.

At his failure to respond, Adam approached slowly, as if his mind had convinced him he was dreaming. Every step he moved closer to

Mitchell moved him closer to her. She stood, shocked into complete silence, behind the hard planes of Mitchell's back.

Adam was alive.

When he was close enough to see Mitchell and Guist clearly, he let out an excited yell. He grabbed Guist in a rough hug. "Oh, man! I thought I'd never see you guys again. I thought surely I'd never see anyone I knew again," he said with exuberance.

Guist patted Adam on the back stiffly and pulled away without saying anything. He walked past Mitchell, and stood loyally by her. He looked as if he had no idea how to react to the situation, and the questioning glances her teammate threw her out of the corner of his eye snapped her out of the trance she was in. When Adam approached Mitchell with his arms out to embrace his old friend, Mitchell side-stepped to reveal her presence.

Adam froze in his advance. He let his outstretched arms fall limply to his sides.

"Adam," she whispered. Tears were welling up in her eyes, but she didn't care. Adam was alive. Her Adam.

She threw her arms around his neck and felt his hands gently slide up her back. "I thought you were dead, Adam," she said quietly. "I tried to find you. I've searched dozens of colonies for you, but nobody had ever seen or heard of you. I thought you were dead. I thought you were dead."

"Who the hell is *she?*" a woman spoke up from behind Adam.

Adam pushed Laney away, and she wiped her eyes in confusion.

"She's — " Adam started. Unable to explain her away, he gave up with a shrug and looked to her for help.

"I'm Laney Landry. Who are you?" she asked the woman, who had stepped into the lantern light to reveal she was very pregnant and very pissed.

"I'm Adam's *wife*," she growled.

Wife. He was married and very nearly a father and Laney couldn't seem to remember how to shut her gaping mouth. That was supposed to be her. Silence stretched on as she fumbled for any words to relieve the maddening embarrassment that consumed her under the woman's murderous glare. "Oh, of course," was all she could think to whisper. She wiped her eyes and gave a trembling smile. The lantern light flickered across the harsh planes of the woman's face, which only served to make her look angrier. Was she pretty by daylight?

"For three years I've watched Laney pine for you," Mitchell ground out.

"Mitchell, please. It's okay. Let's just go." She tugged at his arm, but he wouldn't be moved. She had one too many helpings of embarrassment, and to make matters worse, Sean was staring in bewilderment at their humiliating reunion.

"No, Laney. He should hear what he did. Why should a man not be held accountable for doing this to a woman?" Mitchell rounded on Adam again, who was trying unsuccessfully to pacify his seething wife. "Do you know how hard we searched for you? And you couldn't even send word? I want to know why!" He pulled the crumpled piece of gray paper from his pocket and flung it at Adam's chest.

Adam looked at the wrinkled, hand-drawn picture on the ground without surprise.

"That's what I thought," Mitchell said with a cruel and humorless smile. "You've probably seen this a hundred times. What, you couldn't be bothered to send a notice out? Too much effort for you? You moved on, so the girl you left behind doesn't matter anymore?"

Adam looked from her to Mitchell and back again. "I'm sorry," he said, looking wholly uncomfortable. "I met Sabrina when the outbreak first happened. We came here together, and I knew she was it for me. I'm really sorry."

"We were still together, Adam," she said through her acute disappointment in a man she thought she knew. "If you'd found another woman, fine, but you could have sent word and let me know what was happening. You kept me from moving on."

Adam slumped his shoulders and looked miserable. He looked from one face to the other and tried to look through them to Sean. "Jarren, you have to help me out here, buddy. I know you understand why I had to cut myself off from her completely."

Who did he think he was talking to? She looked around in confusion, and Mitchell spoke up with an unmitigated fury. "That's not Jarren, ya dick. Jarren died. Yesterday."

Adam's wide eyes darted from face to dimly lit face, and his eyebrows furrowed in pointless apology. "Man, I'm sorry, Derek. It was an honest mistake. It's dark out here."

"Don't do that," Mitchell said, shaking his head.

"Don't do what?"

"Don't call me Derek. *You* can call me Mitchell. You don't know me anymore. You don't know any of us anymore. Your choice," he said jabbing a finger in Adam's direction.

"Look, Laney seems like she's doing all right without me, so it all worked out. Right?"

She stopped mid-scurry, effectively putting a halt to her retreat to the shadows where the men hopefully wouldn't be able to see how badly she was affected by it all. Mitchell's eyes looked black with anger in the dim lantern light, but they softened when they fell on her.

"Yep, I'm awesome," she called out overly cheerfully. "Congrats on the baby. And the wife. She seems super nice." She was probably hysterical.

"Shhhh," Sean said quietly, interrupting her awkward tirade. He put his arm around her and pulled her back to continue on the trail. "He doesn't deserve you."

"Do you think Mel knows?"

Sean sighed and squeezed Laney's shoulder before he released her to adjust a sleeping Adrianna in his arms. "Mel knows everyone in her colony."

The betrayal stung. Why hadn't the woman told her? Given her some kind of warning that a horrible encounter in the woods with *the* ghost of her past was a possibility. Without a heads up, she'd been shamed in front of two men she was completely confused and torn over. Damn that woman.

The hike back to the cabins felt like it took a hundred and thirty-seven years. Realistically it was only a fifteen minute trek at the slow pace they adopted because of the darkness, but it was tinged with a shade of desperation to escape the witnesses to that ghastly ex-boyfriend scene. Did no one want her? Adam was married, with a child on the way, so she had wasted three good years looking for a man who was happy with another. How silly she had been for having imagined that man to be more than he was.

At the first row of cabins, Sean pointed out the room Mitchell and Guist had been assigned to. Guist gave her a squeeze on the shoulder, but Mitchell kept his distance when they parted ways. Both men from her team gave parting, comforting words in the form of colorful curses at Adam, and it made her laugh, despite the wretched clenching in her gut. Mitchell leaned up against his doorway until she and Sean had disappeared down a smaller trail that connected the newly built rows of cabins.

Her cabin was only a few minutes' walk from Mitchell and Guist's room, and she and Sean went the rest of the way there in silence. Not even the crickets felt brave enough to interrupt their private, awkward moment. When they got to the door and checked the number to make sure she wouldn't be walking in on some poor, unsuspecting family who had long been asleep, she hurried in to try to avoid conversation with him altogether.

"Laney, wait," he said, catching the door before it closed.

She stifled a groan and opened the door back up, waiting.

Sean hesitated. "There should be a lantern in there for you and some matches to give you some light. The sheets will be on the bed, and there is a row of outhouses through there." He pointed to a small trail that led off through the trees. "The showers are back up by Mitchell and Guist's cabin though."

"Oh, okay. Thanks." She could sleep for a week, and the bed was calling to her like a siren's song.

He spun to leave, only to turn back to her again. "I'm sorry about that, back there with Adam. It was pretty brutal and I wish it hadn't happened like that."

She tried to smile at him through the dim light. "It seems we have both been holding on to people we shouldn't have."

The corners of his mouth turned up sadly. "So it seems. Good night, Laney."

"Good night."

Good night. Right.

Chapter Twelve

A thunderous knock on Laney's door made her lurch ungracefully from the bed she had been blissfully sleeping on exactly one second before. She landed with a thud on her hands and knees, the wooden floor proving itself a completely unforgiving companion. Another knock blasted in her ears.

"What!" she yelled testily. It was barely even light out.

"It's Guist," came the reply.

She threw open the thick wooden door so she could better glare at him.

"Eeek," Guist said, taking a step back.

Why in Sam Hill was he so surprised? She had never been a morning person.

"What do you want?"

"Nick came by and said he'd meet up with us at breakfast to give us our job assignments this morning. Said mess hall stops serving breakfast at eight, and work starts at eight thirty." He turned to head back up the trail to his cabin. "Get ready," he called over his shoulder.

A quick look in the mirror brought the cause of Guist's startled reaction to light. Nightmares had kept her tossing and turning through the short night, and her hair was sticking up in all directions. The thin pillow had left creases across her face, and in light of no pajamas to be found in her cluttered backpack, she had greeted him in her black tank top and a pair of red cotton underwear. Attractive.

She took in the small room that was to be her home for the duration of her stay at Dead Run River. A mixture of exhaustion and laziness had kept her from lighting the lantern the night before so her view of her new home had been drastically narrowed. The little cabin Nick had assigned her was actually quite homey and warm.

There was a table with a washbasin that came up to the height of her hips on the wall opposite the door. An old bucket just showing its rust had been placed beside it and the bowl where she had rinsed her face the night before was under the mirror. A simple pine bed took up most of the wall to her left, and the mattress had been accompanied by a stack of clean linens and a thick blue comforter. A small, old fashioned wood burning stove sat in the corner with a stack of firewood just below it. A silver pipe that vented smoke from the stove to the exterior of the cabin snaked up the wall. Opposite the bed was a small dresser with three drawers, and a chair and modest table beside it with a pen and a small stack of linen paper for writing. The dark metal lantern was on the wooden table waiting to be lit by the box of matches that sat beside it. The wooden floor was simple and bare except for a small, blue fuzzy bath mat that someone had thoughtfully placed just below the washbasin and mirror.

It was perfect.

She pulled her pants on and emptied the small amount of clothing she had in her pack into the top drawer of the dresser. She made the bed and stood back to admire the tidied room. When she was satisfied, she rifled noisily through her pack and pulled out the few toiletries she owned. She placed them in a large plastic baggie and headed for the door. On second thought, she turned and grabbed the disposable razor and bar of soap out of her welcome bag and tossed it in with her other shower supplies. When her new jacket was snugly in place over her shoulders, she left the room and dropped the wooden latch into place to secure the door. There was no lock. Apparently Dead Run River ran on the honor system.

A wooden porch ran in front of the row of rooms, and she stopped to admire the scenery that surrounded her. She leaned against the crude wooden railings that encased the porch and felt the hairs on the back of her neck prickle. Someone watched her. A girl in her early twenties stood to her left, giving her the foulest glare. What had she done to cause that look? Laney tried to put a finger on where she had seen the faintly familiar girl before. She waved and placed the face. The girl had been a witness at her little reunion with Adam the night before. She had been the one standing next to him and his wife. Laney shoved her hand in her jacket pocket to halt the awkward wave.

The girl spun around and disappeared into a room two doors down from hers, slamming the door loudly behind her. She hated to make an enemy so quickly in a colony. Maybe if she apologized for…what? Existing while her boyfriend cheated? Whatever that girl's problem was, she could keep it. Laney resisted the urge to flip off the door and set out for the trail that led to the showers. First impressions had never been her thing.

The biggest and probably best surprise of her recent life was that the showers had hot water. She tried not to act too shocked, as it seemed very normal to the other women who were bathing themselves in the wooden stalls on the girls' side of the shower room. "Room" was a loose term. There was a row of ten showers housed in wooden stalls out in the open. In between the fifth and sixth shower stalls, a thick wall divided them, and a hand-painted sign enlightened her that ladies were on the left and gentlemen were on the right. Laney tried her best to ignore the hairy legs under the doors of the gentlemen's side and instead tried to focus on the beautiful steam that was rising out of the stalls as hot, moist air battled the morning chill.

Her turn came up quickly when a stall became vacant. A line was forming behind her so she tried her best to hurry through her own shower, though it was tempting to stand under the blissfully warm water for much longer. It wasn't until she was finished washing that she remembered she didn't have a towel to dry herself off with. She poked her head out of her stall and looked around in desperation.

"Here," a girl said with a smile. She kindly held a towel out for Laney. "You must be new around here. The towels are in a bin over there." She pointed to a green plastic storage container. "When you are done, just throw the dirty one in the black bin."

"Thank you so much," Laney started. She didn't get to talk to girls very often. Was she supposed to shake her hand?

"I'm Eloise," the girl offered.

"Laney," she said, taking the towel. "Nice to meet you."

"Same," the girl said as she disappeared into the empty stall next to her.

Laney dried off hurriedly. The cold air was slowly seeping into her bones, and she didn't want to be wet and naked in it any more than she had to be. She redressed, wishing silently that she had something else to wear, and dropped her towel into the black bin before she headed back to her room to stuff her shower supplies into the bottom drawer of her dresser. She asked directions to the mess hall and was rewarded with another kind response. The hike took her about ten minutes and was all uphill, but with the smell of eggs and bacon came new motivation to move. She gave her sore muscles a light workout and eagerly jogged to the door.

She waited in line and picked up a tray of food before scanning the large building. Rows of long picnic tables held happy groups of acquaintances and friends talking softly as they ate their early morning meal. A hand shot up from a bench in the farthest corner, and she snaked her way between tables. It was Sean who had hailed her. Finn sat on one side beside Sean and Adrianna, and Guist and Mitchell were on the other. The back of a girl's head bobbed excitedly by Mitchell as she talked to him over her meal.

Laney frowned. Figured.

She took a seat by Guist and dove into her breakfast. Sean watched her from across the table, but she didn't feel like talking. She was agitated, testy even, but she couldn't explain the exact reason why. So much had gone wrong in the past few days. She didn't even know where to begin deciphering what she was upset about that morning.

When Nick arrived with their job assignments, the girl hanging on to Mitchell got the hint and took her leave. When she stood, Laney got a look at her face. It was the same girl who had been there with Adam and his wife, the same one who'd slammed the door on her that morning. She waved as she sauntered by, but the look on her face made it clear they weren't friends. The girl was thin and petite, with a swing to her gait that said she liked the way it felt when a man watched her leave. She had blond hair and crystalline blue eyes. She looked like Barbie—if Barbie was five foot two and pissed.

"She's really nice," Laney said through a bite of scrambled eggs.

Mitchell watched the girl leave with a thoughtful look on his face. "Yeah, I think so, too."

Maybe he had missed her sarcasm.

"I've got your job assignments," Nick said. "Sean, for now we will have you at the sawmill. Mel might have you helping her some days, though. Finn, you will be a guard but when Sean needs you, you will have leave to help him. Mitchell and Guist, you are both guards also. You'll report to Steve Mercer at the front gate right after you are done with breakfast." He swung around to her and wrote something on his clipboard. "Laney Landry. You are assigned to the gardens, but this morning you will meet with the doctor before you report out there."

"Whoa, what?" she sputtered. "But I applied for guard duty. I can't be in the gardens. I'll go insane!"

"That's where Mel wants you. Sorry."

"Can you check it again?" Mitchell asked him. "There has to be some mistake. Laney is a fighter. She's more qualified for guard duty than any guard you have posted."

Sympathy lined the creases of Nick's somber eyes. "Look, I get it. It's not what you wanted, but it's where Mel wants you right now. And what she says goes. My advice? Try it for a while, and if you really don't like it, take it up with her. Maybe she could put you somewhere else."

Deflated, she took the offered work outline from his hands. There wasn't a job in existence she would have wanted less than gardens.

"I got everyone Fridays off, but the other day off I couldn't swing with you all together. Sean, Finn, and Mitchell, you'll have Mondays off, and Laney and Guist, you'll have Wednesdays off. Since you are coming in during the middle of a work week, your credit will still hit the store on Friday, but it won't be as much. It should still be enough for you to get some warmer clothes, though. Okay, good luck with your assignments and I'll see you later. Laney, I'll show you where the doctor's office is."

He headed for an exit without delay, and she followed him without looking back at the table. She couldn't handle their pitying looks.

Though she had full intentions of ignoring Nick as punishment for bearing bad news, the mountain man had different ideas. He gave her exactly two minutes of silence on their hike back down the hill to the doctor's office.

"Did you like the warm water in the showers?" he asked.

His excitement was infectious, and she was unable to be rude. "Yes, it was lovely. How is that possible? Seems like a waste of the generators."

"We don't use the generators on them. I rigged up a way to use water power to heat the showers. It runs a bunch of our larger equipment too. Like our antique sawmill. It is up and running because of the work we did with miles of piping farther up the mountain. We use the river's naturally strong current to power machines that conduct that energy to the areas we need it. Took me a year to get the kinks out, and even now the pipes get clogged and we have to do repairs often, but all worth it for a hot shower, I think."

"Agreed," she admitted. "It was a really happy surprise. I don't even remember the last time I had a hot shower."

She followed Nick down a narrow path that led away from a group of cabins.

"What do you use the sawmill for?" she asked curiously.

"Ahh, we use it to cut the boards for the cabins for one. We use the boards to build our fences as well and then we trade large loads of it with other colonies farther down the mountain that don't have the resources of the mill. Here we are," he said, hopping up onto a small wooden porch that bordered a medical building. "Knock, knock." He opened the door a crack and looked inside.

"Come on in," an older gentleman called. He was wearing a baseball cap over thinning hair, and glasses perched firmly on his nose. He was short, barely as tall as Laney, and his dark and observant eyes seemed to miss nothing.

"Hi, I'm Dr. Mackey. You must be Laney." He reached his hand out and shook hers vigorously.

Nick excused himself and waved to her before he left. Dr. Mackey motioned for her to have a seat on the sterile-looking table in the middle of his office, and she did so. She shifted her feet in an attempt to get comfortable, but it was likely she'd never feel completely relaxed there. Whatever was coming was going to hurt.

"All right, Mel has told me a little about what is going on with you, but let's start from the beginning. How long have you known of your immunity to Dead bites?"

"Don't you want to see the bites first?" she asked him.

"I'll get to that. Mel is a pretty straight shooter and I believe what she has told me. How long?" he repeated.

"Two years."

"And what were your side effects?"

"Heightened sense of smell."

He pulled a small pen light out of his medical coat pocket and flicked them to her eyes. "Any vision loss or change in eye color?"

"None that I could tell."

"Any dietary changes, or wants?"

"None. I was always a meat eater, but I still prefer it cooked, and animal in nature."

On and on it went. Dr. Mackey seemed as if he would never run out of questions for her, and he jotted every answer down on a brown clipboard. When he was finished grilling her, he finally asked to see the bite scar on her leg and then the newer one on her side. Her wounds were all in different stages of healing, and Dr. Mackey cleaned them and bandaged the ones that needed it. Her new bite and the gash on her hand were the worst, so she sported sanitary looking white bandages on both.

"Come with me," the doctor told her, and he led her to a room in the back of the building.

Inside, Dr. Mackey had set up an impressive lab equipped with microscopes, stacks of charts, and medical machines with functions she couldn't even guess at.

"I think the source of your immunity comes from both your blood and your living tissue. I will need samples of both."

Well, that sounded painful. She squared her shoulders and tried to wipe any emotion from her face.

"We'll try to take only small samples of tissue but you will have to give blood regularly until I can get us closer to figuring you out. I have a small team who will be assisting us. You will meet them later. They have a day off today unless we have an emergency. We'll take some tissue samples and draw your blood before you leave here if you're feeling up to it."

He said the last sentence as if he were asking her a question, so she nodded. Not even a little part of her wanted to do any of that, but she had promised Jarren she'd try. And she'd be damned if she was going to invite him back to haunt her for not following through with her promises.

"Let's get this done, Doc. I have a riveting day ahead of me at the gardens."

He chuckled and prepared a short row of medical instruments and a roll of gauze. "I take it you don't appreciate your new job assignment."

"Let's put it this way. If I had a choice between picking weeds or petting a porcupine, I'd pick the latter."

"Well, you are in luck then, because as per doctor's orders, on the days you have to give blood I insist you lie down in my office for observation for at least an hour before you go to work there."

"Whoa, doc. You sure know how to charm a lady."

"I'm afraid my wife would thoroughly disagree," he said with a laugh. "All right, Laney. Where would you like your scars?" He held a terrifying instrument that was shaped like a metal tube with a rectangular blade on the end.

She looked away. Best if she didn't watch. "Let's keep the party centralized." She lifted her shirt and pointed to the area directly beside the bite. It would look mangled even after it had healed so what would a few more scars hurt? It wasn't like boys were lining up to ogle her bare body anyway.

"Okay. You're going to feel a pinch, but it will be over before you know it."

"Pinch, my ass." Laney lifted her shirt enough to glare at four small red slivers that had been covered with butterfly bandages on her hip bone. Those little suckers had burned like a hot iron when Doc not-so-gently took them. They were large enough that they would scar, but small enough that over time they would be unassuming. The first of many. Dr. Mackey had been true to his word and insisted that she rest for an hour after he drew her blood, but the time had come to head to the gardens to start work. Goody.

She scuffled along slowly. She didn't mean to meander, but the scenery was breathtaking. It was baffling how small groups of happily chatting residents who passed her on the trail could ignore such a view. Would she ever get used to it as they obviously had? Hopefully not.

The doctor had given her spotty directions to the entrance of the gardens, and after half an hour of bumbling around the wrong trails, she finally stumbled upon a hand painted sign that read *This way to Gardens* with an arrow. Another pointed to a trail that would lead to the antique sawmill Nick had told her about. Sean was working there. She shook her head like the obnoxious thoughts would leave by way of ear and headed toward the gardens.

Two armed men guarded an exit to the colony. She pulled up short and looked back in the direction of the sign she had followed. She could have sworn it pointed to the path she was on.

"You looking for the gardens?" one of the guards asked.

"Yeah, did I get turned around?"

"Nope," he answered. "You're in the right spot." He pulled out a clipboard and scanned a list of names. "Laney?" he guessed.

"That's me."

"Come on through." He and the other guard opened a tall wooden gate and let her pass. "You're pretty late for your first day on the job."

She smiled. "I like to make a good first impression."

"I can tell. Good luck with that."

She waved and found herself on a narrow path edged in thick barbed wire fence.

"I wouldn't touch the fences," the guard called out. "They'll lay you out."

"Eeeeuh," she muttered, pulling her arms in closer to her sides.

The path led her about a quarter of a mile outside of the colony gates. She scented the air often and scanned the trees for any signs of Deads. The Dead Run River gates had provided a safety she hadn't felt in a long time. It was amazing the difference when she was all alone, exposed between the electrified barbs. Pausing, she tilted her head back and looked skyward to the top of the wooden fence looming in front of her. Unlike the partial pine fence that was in progress around the colony, this one had been completed. The fence line followed a jagged path, connecting still living trees with rows of felled pines between them. She pushed gently on the gate, but it didn't give. She pushed again, throwing her weight behind it, and still nothing happened. She stepped back and looked up again. The sun shone over the top of the mountainous gate, a blinding orb that threw rays of light onto the pine needle carpet below.

"Knocky, knocky," she called out.

A latch clicked and the wooden door swung open slowly to reveal two more armed guards. One of them pulled a walkie talkie to his lips. "Yeah, she's here."

"Copy that," came the static laced voice on the other end.

"You're late," the guard said.

"Got a doctor's note."

The guard snorted and shook his head in amusement. "You're supposed to report to Vanessa." He waited and stared at her as if she should recognize that name and then shake in her boots.

"Awesome, thanks," she said, skirting around the guard and into the garden gates.

She squinted at movement in the distance and headed up a main walking path that cut right through the center of the farming area. When she reached a woman working feverishly with a hoe over rows of small plants, she asked directions to the apparently very scary Vanessa. The woman stood straight up and wiped her sweating forehead with the back of her long sleeved shirt. She took in Laney's appearance with an expression completely unreadable, and finally jerked her head in the direction of a small cluster of storage buildings.

"Thanks," she murmured before she strode down a thin walking path that led to the buildings.

A woman was bent over three burlap sacks overflowing with some sort of leafy greens. Laney cleared her throat, but the woman ignored her and hoisted a sack up onto a small trailer pulled by a four-wheeler instead.

"Excuse me," she said in a tone that dared to be ignored.

The woman turned around and glared at her.

"Shit," Laney muttered as she looked into the ferocious glare of Vanessa. The girl who witnessed the most embarrassing moment of her life to date. The girl who had slammed the door on her friendly wave that morning. The girl who had attached herself to Mitchell's side like a barnacle almost immediately after their arrival.

"Vanessa, I presume. Lovely to meet you," she said cheerily. Or as cheerily as one can manage through gritted teeth.

"You're late."

"Why does everyone keep saying that? Look, I might as well let you know it won't be the last time."

"And why is that?"

"Ahh, you'll have to take that up with Dr. Mackey."

"Oh. Got an STD?"

Laney glared. "Or Mel. You could take it up with Mel."

"I saved a special job for you," Vanessa said. "There is a great big pile of fertilizer over by that building. Make yourself useful and shovel it into the wheelbarrow next to it. Then distribute it evenly over that section over there." Vanessa jabbed a finger at a plot of land to their left. "The big one."

Unamused, Laney asked, "You want me to shovel poop?"

"I do, and since I'm running the gardens, you get to answer to me. If I feel you aren't doing your job adequately, and make no mistake, Ms. Landry, I'm not an easy girl to please, then I will, as you recommended, take it up with Mel." Vanessa smiled as if she were thoroughly enjoying herself. "If you hurry you could be done by Friday."

Chapter Thirteen

Laney gently flexed her blistered hands. The shovel wasn't a kind tool to those who had never used one before. The only area spared on her hands was the heavily bandaged part that protected her cut.

The day hadn't been her best one, but it definitely didn't go down in the history books as one of her worst ones either. Her side was uncomfortable and itchy as she sweated freely from physical exertion into the tiny wounds Dr. Mackey had made. Her other injuries were screaming with the hard labor she had forced onto her body. Lunch had been called only for her to find out that she was supposed to pick up a sack lunch from the kitchen before her work day. She also was made aware that she was supposed to bring her canteen to work with her own water. Thankfully, a teenaged boy named Nelson had offered her a drink out of his canteen just as she thought she would die of thirst. He was young, awkward, and a little wonky-eyed, but he was nice enough, so she didn't mind that he spent a substantial amount of his time looking at her chest. He had shared his water and he certainly wasn't the first pervy glancer she had met. She could throw him a bone, so to speak.

Shoveling manure had been monotonous and laborious work, but she had done it without complaint. Even the fact that she smelled like a cow tail couldn't keep away the little shiver of excitement at the thought of seeing Sean at dinner. The downside would be that Vanessa would no doubt be attached at the femur to Mitchell and sitting at her table, but she had learned to take the good with the bad.

She couldn't even put a finger on why the girl bothered her so much. Mitchell was a grown man, free to bone whatever ditzy skank he wanted to. Far be it from her to judge his bad taste. She had spent three years searching for Adam Not-Worth-The-Effort Leary. Stones and glass houses.

"Hey, wait up!" a girl's voice sounded from behind her.

She turned on the small path that connected the colony to the gardens. It was the young woman who had given her a towel at the showers. "Hey," Laney said, smiling and genuinely happy to see Eloise again. After Vanessa's maiming glares all day, a friendly face was as unexpected as it was comforting.

Eloise was attractive, with sandy brown hair and a light smattering of freckles across her nose, making her look much younger than she probably really was. "How was your first day?"

"It was glorious. I have a newfound respect for fertilizer."

Eloise laughed. "You're funny."

"Hmm," she said thoughtfully, squinting suspiciously at the girl. "What do you want?"

Eloise's face lit up with a crooked grin. "I wanted to know about one of the men you came in with."

"Aw, really? You too? What *is* it about him? It's the dark hair, right? His jokes aren't really that funny, you know. He thinks he's wittier than he really is."

Eloise looked at her with such a profound look of confusion that she stopped talking.

"Not the dark haired one. The other one," the girl clarified.

"Sean Daniels?"

"No, not him, though he is a handsome man too. No, the other one. The quiet one."

"Guist?"

"His name is Guist?"

"Well, everybody calls him by his last name. His name is Aaron Guist."

"Aaron," Eloise whispered, like she was tasting the sound his name made on her tongue.

"I have to tell you, this is a first."

"What is?"

"Guist, he just doesn't really shack up with a lot of ladies when we go to colonies."

"Good. Wait, does that means he doesn't like girls?"

"No, no." She shook her head vigorously. "No. He likes the ladies. He's just shy when it comes to them."

"Oh," Eloise said through a slow smile. She looked embarrassed, and her cheeks turned pink enough to make her freckles stand out even more.

All right, so she would throw out two bones that day. "Look, if you come by our table at dinner I'll introduce you."

"But what would I say?"

"I don't know. Just say some stuff about the importance of pruning or something."

"No, not to you. I mean what do I say to Aaron?"

Laney glanced at her out of the corner of her eye to judge her seriousness, but the girl seemed genuinely lost in thought. She shrugged and waved to the guard at the colony gate as they passed through. "That I can't help you with. I have zero game. If you want advice on how to swoop into the friend zone, or how to unattract men, or even how to become like a little sister to the object of your affection, I'm your girl."

Eloise giggled. "I highly doubt any of that is true. You came into this colony with a harem of the hottest men in the universe, and they circle you like planets. I suspect you have more game than you think."

She snorted and held in a retort about said men only wanting to be around her for her zombie-sniffing abilities. Let the girl think what she wanted.

Dinner wasn't as eventful as Laney had anticipated. She was the first one there, so she filled a plate and picked a table near the area they sat in at breakfast that morning.

"Where is everybody else?" she asked Guist as he approached the table with a full tray of his own.

"Mitchell volunteered to do a night shift tonight. We have to do two a week. He's back in the room catching some sleep before he has to report for duty again." He sat down and held up a cloth sack that sagged at the bottom with the weight of its contents. "I'm bringing him dinner after I finish up here."

She waited for more information, but he dug into his food instead.

"What about Sean?" she asked innocently. Too innocently because Guist looked up at her and squinted thoughtfully.

"I don't know where Sean is. I haven't seen him all day." His gaze lingered on her as she took a drink of her water. "Laney, I'd be careful with that one."

"What are you talking about?"

"You know what I'm talking about. Mitchell wouldn't like it," he said in a low voice.

She narrowly avoided sputtering her drink all down the front of his shirt. "And why would I give a fig what Mitchell would and wouldn't like?"

He opened his mouth to answer, but apparently thought better of it and went back to spearing broccoli florets with his fork. The bewildering man had closed up. She would get nothing more from him until he was good and ready. Which could be the day after never.

A movement caught her eye. Eloise nervously approached their table and waved timidly from behind Guist's silent figure.

Laney smiled and waved her over like she had just seen the girl in passing. "Hey, Eloise. You want to come sit by us?"

Guist glanced behind him.

"Uh, would that be okay with you?" Eloise asked him.

Laney had no guess as to what passed between her new friend and her teammate. They stared at each other for a loaded moment before he nodded his head slowly.

"S'okay with me," he told her.

Eloise walked around the table and set her tray down beside Laney before taking a seat.

"Guist, this is Eloise," she introduced them, pointing at them each in turn with a forkful of mashed potatoes. "She works at the gardens with me. Eloise, this is Guist."

"Nice to meet you," Eloise said shyly.

Guist smiled, a rare sight, and cleared his throat. "Likewise."

Laney pursed her lips happily and looked from Guist to Eloise and back to Guist. "Well, I'm stuffed." She lifted her tray and headed to a trashcan nearby.

"Where are you going?" Eloise squeaked, mortification evident in the tremor in her voice.

"Lots of stuff to do," she lied. She cleared her tray and set it on a table beside the trash. Eloise looked partly frozen, and mostly like she wanted to flee. "Enjoy your dinner. See you tomorrow morning." She waved at Guist who was looking at her like she had lost her mind. "Later, Guist."

"Later," he said suspiciously.

When she reached the cool crispness of the night, she rubbed the gooseflesh on her arms. What should she do first? Her jacket was in her room, but Mel's house was only a ten minute trek up the mountain from the dining hall. If she went back for her coat it would take much longer. She had decided she wasn't above begging for a better job from Mel. One that preferably involved deadly weaponry.

She could live without a jacket for half an hour, so she marched determinedly up the path that led to the leader's cabin. The lights were on. Nick must have hooked a generator directly to the cabin, because while everyone else in this colony lived by lanterns and candlelight, Mel was afforded more luxury. Laney knocked. Jubilant voices could be heard from the other side of the door, and Mel was laughing as she opened it to find her on the other side.

"Laney," she said in surprise. "What's happened? Are you all right?"

Sean and Adrianna were putting their coats on in the entryway. So that's where they'd been at dinnertime. She dragged her eyes back to Mel. "Yes, I'm fine. I just wondered if I could talk to you about something."

"Of course," Mel answered, sounding concerned. "Sean and Adrianna were just leaving. We can talk in my office."

Laney pursed her lips and nodded. "Fine. Yes, that sounds good."

"Hey, Laney. What are you doing here?" Sean asked as he noticed her coming through the door.

She opened her mouth to respond, but Adrianna shrieked and ran to hug her legs, eliciting a surprised laugh from her instead.

Sean chuckled and turned to the woman holding the door. "Mel, dinner was delicious."

"You are welcome anytime, Sean."

Gag. Laney zipped up Adrianna's jacket and stepped out of their way.

Sean cocked his head to the side and looked at her curiously. He squeezed her bare arm as he passed. "Why aren't you wearing a jacket? You're going to get sick, Laney. It's really important that you take care of yourself."

She warmed despite the dropping temperature. He cared. "Come on. If I can survive Dead bites, I'm pretty sure a little breeze isn't going to do me in."

They said their goodbyes, and Mel led Laney into her office. "How do you like your cabin?" Mel asked.

"It's fine. Perfect, really."

"And the mess hall? Were you able to find it all right?"

"Yes, yes. Mel, why didn't you tell me?"

Mel sat behind a huge mahogany desk and motioned to a plush looking chair on the other side. Laney sat and waited.

"You'll have to be more specific," the woman said.

"Adam?"

"Ahhh. Well, I wanted to, but I didn't know how."

"Why didn't anyone send word that he was here? He still looks just like the drawing and his name was on it."

Mel sighed. "Look, Laney. Adam just came to this colony a few weeks ago. His home base is in Fairplay. He and his wife came up to have Dr. Mackey deliver their baby. He is the best doctor around and a lot of pregnant women want him to deliver them. They'll be leaving again after the baby is born to go back to their colony."

"You still could have sent word that he was alive."

"He requested I didn't, and my colony members' privacy is their right. He asked me not to say anything the first time he saw the board.

I didn't have a problem with it because, honestly, I didn't assume you were even still alive. The Laney Landry I'd heard about was a fighter. You guys tend to have short expiration dates."

Laney bit her lip calculatingly. "You could make it up to me, you know."

"I can't give you guard duty."

"Why not? I've been fighting for three years and my nose could be a huge asset to your colony. I can smell Deads from a distance. I could be the colony's own personal Dead warning system. There is no reason for me to be working in the gardens."

"There is, actually."

Laney waited, eyebrows arched.

"Look, I promised a friend I wouldn't put you on guard duty."

"Sean?"

Mel nodded. "And part of me agrees with him. You're important, Laney. We could potentially get a vaccine from you in time and it is too big a risk to put you in life or death situations."

She was baffled. Did Sean care for her, or for what she could provide? The difference mattered. "Look, Mel. I will wither if I have to stay on garden duty. It isn't about not wanting to work hard at my job. It's about not finding any joy or fulfillment in it. I've been a successful fighter for three years and now I'm shoveling fertilizer all day. Can you please just think about another job placement for me?"

Mel tapped a pen on the table in quick rhythm. "Give gardens until the end of the week. If you still feel as strongly, I'll try to come up with a new placement. It won't be what you want though, Laney. It'll still be a safe job with no action."

She clenched her teeth against more begging. What was the point in pouting? Mel had made up her mind, and she wouldn't be moved.

Laney left for her own cabin with a quiet goodbye and a heavy heart. Things were not turning out the way she had dared to hope.

Laney remembered to bring her canteen and sack lunch to the gardens the next day. After a gloriously warm shower, she ate breakfast with Finn and Guist and, surprisingly, Eloise, who had been invited by Guist himself. Mitchell was still nowhere to be found. Probably working the last of his night shift or crashed out asleep in his room. Or with Vanessa. She was putting a substantial effort into blocking that possibility from her mind, though. The most surprising thing was that she never even looked for Adam or his wife when they gathered for meals. Surely it was a good sign that she was over him, or at least well on her way.

She and Eloise said goodbye to the boys and headed off to the gardens in companionable conversation. When they approached the exit gates to the colony, she assumed the guards would be the same as the day before. She was stunned to find a much more familiar face instead. Mitchell looked exhausted, and his rifle hung limply at his side as he leaned against the gate. He talked in a low, deep voice to the other guard on duty.

"Hey, stranger," she said as they approached. His absence had done her good. Even exhausted, Mitchell was a fine specimen of a man. She could almost forget how much he drove her nuts.

He looked up at her voice, and his face brightened considerably. He whistled a catcall, and she rolled her eyes.

"Any action?" she asked as she came to a stop in front of him.

"Not a bit," he said as he ruffled her hair annoyingly. He laughed when his move had the desired effect of sticking it out in all directions.

She punched him in the arm and tried to smooth her unruly tresses back into place. "At least you have a shot at some. Working the gardens is going to put me in a coma just to escape the boredom."

"Glad to hear you love your job so much," a feminine voice sounded behind her.

Vannessa and Nelson approached the gate.

"Hey again, Mitchell," the girl said flirtily. "Don't tell me you requested this gate just so you could see me again."

"Uhh," he stammered as Vanessa elbowed her out of the way to put her arm possessively through his.

The move angered Laney into silence. She couldn't even explain why she cared. Or why she watched Mitchell's face as he looked down at the attractive girl clinging to him.

"Permission to pass," she gritted out.

The other guard checked their names off of a clipboard and opened the gate.

"Later, Mitchell," she grumbled before pulling Eloise through. She sniffed the air. A cautious look around showed the coast was clear.

Vanessa chattered happily away at his side, but his eyes stayed trained on her as she left. Why was that so important to her? Two other guards approached the gate to relieve the night shift.

She turned back around and growled in frustration.

"That guy is hot. Not as hot as Aaron, but he's still an Adonis," Eloise said.

Laney took another quick glance behind her. Mitchell was taking his leave. He hadn't even waited to see if she got to the gardens safely. He was so different from Sean and his overbearingly protective requests. She sighed in an attempt to relieve the annoying ache in her chest and picked up her pace to catch up with Eloise. She couldn't sift through her feelings or emotions. They swung so wide, there was no point in trying to understand them.

"Yeah, he is good looking," she admitted.

"I don't know how you don't just jump on his leg when you're around him. That man is sexy."

Laney shrugged and knocked on the garden gates. "We're just friends."

"Put that down," Laney commanded as she heard the click of her Mini behind her.

Nelson put it back down on the bale of hay that it and the rest of her weapons were lying on.

"Can you teach me how to use it?" he asked enthusiastically.

"No."

"Why not?"

She straightened her spine and leaned on her shovel. She huffed air out of her mouth and blew a sweaty strand of hair out of her face. "Because I am obviously busy, Nelson."

"I can get Vanessa to give you a break so you can teach me."

"If you could wrangle a break out of Vanessa, I would have a newfound respect for you, kid."

"I can, I know I can. Vanessa is my sister. She'd do it if I begged."

"Your sister? I'm sorry."

Nelson snorted. "She's not so bad to me. She just doesn't play well with others. I'm on her good side. I'm family."

"Speak of the devil and she shall appear," she said loudly enough for an approaching Vanessa to hear.

"Nelson, I need to speak with you," Vanessa said quietly with nary a smarmy retort for her.

Laney went back to fertilizing.

"You," Vanessa said, rounding on her.

"What did I do now?"

"You came in with Sean Daniels, right? Right?" she asked frantically.

"Yeah, why?"

"Is it true?"

Laney sighed. "Could you be a little more specific?"

"Everyone is talking but no one knows any details. Did the Denver colony fall?" Bad Attitude Barbie was bordering on panic.

Laney looked from her to Nelson, who had gone white as a sheet. "I don't think I should be the one to talk about it with you guys," she said, searching for an escape. A storm was coming, and every instinct pushed for her to take cover.

"Yes or no?" Vanessa screamed.

"Yes," she whispered.

"Did anyone escape?"

"I don't know. There were survivors. We tried to bring them with us, but Sean's second in command had them convinced they should stay and fight. We couldn't get a single civilian to leave with us."

Vanessa grabbed her arm, sinking her nails in, and dragged her to the nearest building. She jerked her arm out of Vanessa's grasp and rubbed the torn skin gently. The cat had claws.

"Describe the survivors," she demanded. "Do it!"

"Uh, I don't know. They were mostly armed guards. There were some women and children in the auditorium too." Laney wracked her brain for faces but came up short. Her mind had already started to block the memories from that night to protect itself. "Look, your best bet is to ask Sean. Maybe he would have recognized faces, names—"

"Sean wouldn't talk to me. He doesn't even know me." Vanessa gave her a predatory glare. "But he would talk to you. Where is he right now?"

"What? I don't know."

"Where is he?" Vanessa screeched, barely in control of herself.

Best to give the crazy lady what she wanted.

"He was assigned to the sawmill. He's probably working there today."

"Good. I need you to take a four-wheeler and a trailer and go pick up a shipment of wooden stakes for the garden. Nelson will tell you how to work it."

After a brief lesson on the ins and outs of a manual transmission ATV, Vanessa slapped a piece of paper with a list of names into the palm of Laney's hand. There was no please or thank you, and she was off without further ado.

Eloise lifted her hands in question as Laney headed out, but she just shrugged. She'd tell her about it later. The guards at the garden gates let her out without question, and she guided the four-wheeler down the narrow path between barbed wire fences. It barely fit, and by the time she pulled it to a stop outside of the colony gates, she was sweating with the stress.

The guard Laney recognized from the day before opened up the gate. "Where you headed?" he asked.

"Vanessa wants me to pick up a load of stakes from the sawmill."

The guard wrote on the clipboard, and then opened the gate wide enough for her to pull through.

"There is a trail through there for the ATV. It'll take you straight to the mill." He pointed to a double row of small wheel tracks headed off through the pine trees.

"Okay, thanks."

The actual blades of the antique sawmill were in an open area, covered by a roof with no walls. A large building stood close by, and the place was surprisingly busy with men and woman loading, unloading, running logs through rows of blades, hauling wood, and stacking finished lumber. A few of them looked up at her arrival but kept to their work. Sean was nowhere to be seen.

She turned off the four-wheeler and headed for the building beside the mill. The smell of sawdust was overwhelming and comforting at the same time. It was the smell of newness. Inside the building there was just as much hustle and bustle as there was outside. It seemed to serve as storage for much of the lumber they cut until it was ready to be shipped off or used for construction or fences. The lumber was stacked so high in places that it was impossible to see around it. On tiptoes, she scoured the rows, looking for Sean. She was on the farthest wall, still not having located him, when she spotted a man and woman arguing beside a stack of two-by-fours. The woman blocked the man, and Laney could only make out the woman's back, so she advanced and did her best to ignore them. She searched the rooms one by one with no success. The last one to check was the closest room to the argument. No help for it.

The woman moved a little to the side to reveal Adam. Laney drew up short and panicked. She in no way wanted to interrupt Adam and his wife arguing, so she ran into the last room and pressed her back against the wall. With her breath held frozen and her eyes squeezed tightly shut, she waited for them to bust her. Had they caught her movement?

"Hey, Laney. What are you doing here?" Sean's deep voice asked from a desk in the corner.

She squeaked and held her chest. "Shh!"

The arch in his eyebrows said he thought she was insane, but the room was quiet enough to hear the argument between Adam and his wife.

"I just don't understand why you didn't destroy that damned picture of you two in the first place," Adam's wife said shrilly. "Was it so you could go look at her picture and remember her face?"

"No, Sabrina. It's not that and you know it. You are all I need. It just didn't feel right to rip something off of the board is all. She's nothing. I barely remember her, it was so long ago."

Sean had tiptoed to where she was frozen to better listen. Sympathy pooled in the deep blue of his eyes. If only she could plug her ears against the world. Just drown out everything so she could have one uninterrupted moment of peace.

"You said she was ugly," the woman accused with a hitch in her voice. "She isn't ugly at all, Adam!"

"Baby, yes she is. You barely got to see her in the dark. She isn't beautiful like you. I'm not attracted to her in any way. You have to believe me."

Sean clenched his jaw. He reached across Laney and tried to shut the door against the horrible things being said, but the door creaked loudly and they both froze. The argument stopped.

"Wait here," Adam told his wife.

The rhythmic thud of slow, booted steps sounded against the rough wooden floorboards, and she looked around frantically for a hiding spot. The room was small, and besides the cubby hole under the desk that was easily visible, there was nowhere to disappear to.

"Well, that's unfortunate," Sean growled.

He pulled her to the desk and lifted her hips until she sat on top of it. Shock stifled her protests. His strong hands opened her legs and pulled her until they were wrapped on either side of him. Sean threw one last glance at the door and then slid one hand around her waist and the other behind her head. His piercing eyes held hers for just a moment before he leaned closer.

And then he kissed her.

Chapter Fourteen

Laney had been leaning back on her hands, but at the gentle caress of Sean's lips, she pulled forward, closing the space between them. The kiss was slow, an undulating fire on her mouth that made her stomach clench and warm.

The door creaked as it opened, but she didn't care about anything other than the physical connection that tethered her to Sean.

He pulled away and glared at Adam. "Hey, man, do you mind?"

"Oh. Laney? I am *so* sorry. I thought—"

"I couldn't care less about your thoughts," Sean said furiously. "Shut the door!"

Adam backed out and shut the door firmly behind him.

"You sure know how to pick them," he said after Adam left.

"Yeah, well you know. I tend to like boys that borderline hate me."

"Nasty habit, that one."

"You'd think I'd learn my lesson," she said through a smirk.

Sean held her gaze questioningly for a moment more and then helped her off the desk. "Why are you here?"

The smile faded from her face as she remembered the reason for her unannounced visit. It was hard to fall back to earth after that kiss. "I was looking for you." She handed him the list Vanessa had given her. "Rumors are swirling about the fall of your colony. My boss wanted me to ask you if any of these names were still alive when we left."

"I didn't get a good look at everyone, but I will see if I can remember any of these from the auditorium. It may take me a while. Do you mind if I give these to you at dinner?"

"Sure. Does that mean you are actually going to eat dinner with the peons tonight?"

"No, I mean at dinner. With me." Sean smiled and looked at the ceiling as if he searched for inspiration. "What I mean to say is will you come over for dinner tonight? I think we need to talk."

She tried to control the slow smile that made its way across her face and nodded. "That sounds nice."

"All right, well I've got more work to do here." His voice was dismissive.

If the man was anything, he was definitely confusing.

"Okay, can you tell me where to get a load of wooden stakes for the gardens before I go?"

"Of course. This way."

After the stakes were loaded into the trailer, Sean waved his goodbye and jogged back to the warehouse, disappearing into the large building. How was she supposed to feel about their encounter? He had kissed her and invited her to dinner, but then he acted as if he couldn't get away from her fast enough. Maybe he was just really swamped at the mill. She pointed the four-wheeler to the well-worn ATV path and headed back to the gardens.

"You'll have to wait until tonight," she told Vanessa and Nelson when she arrived back at the storage buildings. "Sean said it will take him a while to remember. I can bring you answers after dinner if you want."

Vanessa looked angry and impatient, and when she didn't answer, Laney turned and started unloading the stakes herself. When she turned back around, Vanessa was gone.

"It's just…we know a lot of people at the Denver colony. *Knew* a lot of people," Nelson corrected himself.

She heaved another bundle of stakes out of the small trailer. "I figured it was something like that or I wouldn't have helped your crazy sister."

Nelson mumbled his thanks and left her to her work and to her thoughts.

The nerves crept in as Laney checked her hair in the mirror for the third time. Without an option on clothes, all of her anxiety had gone straight into fussing over her hair, which hung long and straight across her shoulders and back. The nine millimeter was a comforting weight in the holster on her leg, and she checked the knife at her ankle out of habit. The drawer of the small dresser made a hollow *thunk* as she placed her Mini into it and slid it closed. Without her trusty rifle, she was as good as naked.

After bundling up in her jacket and shutting the door firmly behind her, she made her way to the main trail that led up the mountain. She didn't know exactly where Sean lived, but she remembered Nick saying his cabin was near Mel's. If she got lost, she would simply ask for directions.

The light was fading, and she was struck by how beautiful the foliage looked right before dark. It was her favorite time of day. The green of the ferns seemed to deepen, and a calm peace hung in the air. How could a place like this exist on the brutalized earth? If magic still endured in the world, surely it would be found in that forest.

Sean's cabin was easy to find. Finn's trailer sat close by and identified the log home as the right place. She knocked on the door and waited. A minute with no answer had her knocking again. She leaned back and checked around the corner of the house. A lonely ax stuck stubbornly out of a large tree stump surrounded by splintered wood shavings. No one was outside.

The door flew open, and Sean stood there pulling his jacket on quickly.

"Laney?" His eyes widened. "I forgot about our dinner. I'm so sorry. I just got word that a large group of Deads are at the gates. Mel wants me down there right away to identify if any of them are from the Denver colony. Since you're here, can you do me a huge favor?" His words were clumped together and hard for her to keep up with.

"Uh, okay. What do you need?" she asked, making the effort to conceal her disappointment.

"Can you watch Adrianna until I get back? I shouldn't be long. If you missed dinner there is food inside. Ade can show you where. I'll be back soon. Thanks, Laney." He squeezed her shoulder before he jogged off toward the main trail. "Oh! Almost forgot." He ran back and slapped Vanessa's list of names into her hand. "I didn't see any of these people in the auditorium before we left. Sorry." Sean left without a backward glance.

"Ms. Laney?" Adrianna said from the doorway.

She tore her frown away from the direction Sean had disappeared to. "Yeah, sweetie?"

"Where did Daddy go?"

"He just had to go check on something real quick." She shifted her weight and glanced inside Sean's cabin. She couldn't just make herself at home without him in there. "Hey, do you want to go on an adventure?"

Adrianna nodded slowly. "Mm-hmm."

"You want to go fishing?"

"Yeah!" Adrianna squealed as she jumped up and down excitedly.

Laney laughed. "Okay, let's go check and see if Mr. Finn is home. See if he wants to go too. And then we'll go get my pack with my fishing line in it."

The girl was already tugging her hand down the steps. Laney slowed her down enough to retrieve her jacket from a hook in the front hallway and shut Sean's door behind them. When Adrianna was all bundled up, they knocked on the door to Finn's trailer.

He was home and opened it with a surprised but happy grin. "Hello, ladies. To what do I owe the honor?"

"Mr. Finn! We're going fishing," Adrianna exclaimed breathlessly. "You come too?"

"Heck yeah, I'm coming. A fishing trip with two pretty ladies? I'm in."

"Heck yeah!" Adrianna repeated.

Laney burst out laughing. "That one's on you. I'm not getting in trouble for it."

"Did you girls eat already?" he asked them.

At a shake of their heads he invited them in to wait at the small table inside while he made three cheese sandwiches. With their picnic in tow they headed to Laney's cabin and she explained Sean's absence to Finn.

"Do you think those Deads could have traveled here from the Denver colony that fast?" Finn asked as Adrianna scrambled ahead to look at a huge exotic-looking plant that was growing on the edge of the trail.

"I don't know. I guess it's enough time. Do you want to go check to see if you know any of them?"

Finn shook his head vigorously. "I don't even want to know. I wouldn't want to see them like that. I just want to remember them like they were when they were human."

After she had grabbed her pack and lantern, given a swift tour of her room, and latched the Mini securely to the strap across her chest, she followed Finn and Adrianna to the widest part of the stream. It had a small gravel beach, and they ate their picnic just as the setting sun kissed the horizon.

She didn't know anything about night fishing for trout, but even if they didn't catch a thing, Adrianna would still have fun.

Finn found a long, sturdy stick while Laney showed Adrianna how to unroll the line and tie a fly on the end. Adrianna picked a tiny yellow feathered fly, and Laney complimented her fly-picking abilities. It was her favorite too.

They tied a substantial length of the line to the end of the stick, and she showed Adrianna how to flick it back and forth so the fly landed on top of the water for a few seconds at a time. The little girl needed constant help and supervision, but she stayed focused enough and was rewarded with a small cutthroat trout. They didn't have a reel, so when the fish was on the line, she helped Adrianna back up the bank until Finn was able to pull the remaining line out of the water. Adrianna was elated, and Finn couldn't seem to stop grinning. The little girl giggled and screamed happily as she held and dropped the flopping fish in the grass.

"We're going to cook this up back at my place," Finn told Adrianna. "Have you ever tasted fish before?"

Adrianna shook her head, her little black ringlets bobbing and her grin infectious.

"Come on," Laney said as she wrapped up the line and put it in her pack. "Let's go see if Daddy is home and then we can show him your fish."

The threesome headed back to Adrianna's home with their catch, but as they approached the cabin, an eerie calm came over Laney. Something was off.

Sean barreled toward them off of the porch he had been uneasily pacing. He scooped Adrianna up in his arms.

"Where were you? I was worried to death! I asked you to take care of her, Laney. Not kidnap her."

A cloud of anger seemed to waft from his very skin, and she was shocked into silence.

"Whoa, whoa, whoa," Finn said with his hands out in front of him. "We took Adrianna fishing, not across state borders."

"Daddy, I caught a fish," Adrianna said quietly. The child seemed confused over the fuss.

"Surely you can understand," he spat. "There were Deads at the gates. Twenty of them! I thought Adrianna was safe inside my cabin, but she wasn't."

"I trusted you guys to handle the Deads," Laney said. "Deads outside of the gates are a constant thing, Sean." Her own anger was a slow boil in her gut. "Do you honestly think I would let anything happen to her?"

"How would I know that, Laney?"

"Because I brought Finn and a small arsenal with us. And because I have already thrown my body at a Dead to keep Adrianna safe. Twice!" She turned and stalked off. She didn't have to listen to his ridiculous accusations.

Sean sighed loudly. "Laney, wait."

She quickened her pace to escape him. Unnecessary as he didn't come after her.

Why on earth she let that man get to her was beyond her comprehension. Sean's reactions always left her disappointed, yet she always hoped the next time would be different. Was she insane? Einstein had once said that the definition of insanity is doing the same thing over and over again and expecting different results. Maybe her habitually bad taste in men did in fact confirm she was crazy.

She knocked at Vanessa's door. If she was lucky, she wouldn't be home. Her luck hadn't changed. Vanessa opened the door almost immediately.

She handed her the list of names and shook her head. "He doesn't remember seeing any of these people in the auditorium."

Vanessa's face fell.

The girl's sadness reminded Laney of her own. She knew all about loss at the Denver colony. "That doesn't mean they didn't survive somehow, though," she said sympathetically. "We were only in the room with the survivors for a minute and some were still coming in."

"They're dead, Laney. Spare me your pity." Vanessa slammed the door.

The force of it pushed cold air into her face and rocked her weight back on the heels of her feet.

"Cow," she grumbled before retiring to her room for the night.

Gunfire woke her from a deep sleep, and she lay there in the dark listening to the pepper of ammo as it made contact with the herd of Deads scratching to get into Dead Run River gates. She lay awake for a long time. What had taken the guards so long from the initial realization that there were Deads outside of an unfinished gate to taking care of the problem? Colony defense strategies were always drastically different from her own views. It was simple to her. See Dead. Shoot Dead. Colonies, however, always seemed to want to study them, their behaviors and patterns, as if it would give them the upper hand to know their enemy. Maybe this time was different though. From the way Mel spoke, it seemed like they were taking descriptions of the Deads at their gates. What they looked like and the clothes they wore. Maybe Mel was trying to give closure to people who might have known them.

Morning came quickly, and as she sat down with her tray of food, she was quickly joined by Guist, Eloise, Finn, Mitchell, and Vanessa—the latter of whom was giving her the beginnings of an impressive eye twitch with her snide remarks. She did her best to ignore the girl. There was no point in engaging with a personality like that one. She was one part wolverine and two parts rabid badger.

Finn didn't mention the night before, and she was grateful. She in no way wanted to rehash the Sean debacle in mixed company.

"Laney," Sean said in a quiet voice behind her. "Can I talk to you for a minute?"

She froze in mid-stab of a piece of sausage link.

"I have to get to work," she said without turning around.

"Can I walk you to the gardens, then?" he asked.

"Look," Mitchell said through a cold glare, "it doesn't sound like she wants to talk to you, so piss off."

"It's okay, Mitchell," she said in efforts to avoid an argument. Or another well-placed punch to Sean's face by Mitchell's unapologetic fist. "That's fine," she told Sean as she stood to put her tray away.

She left without waiting to see if he followed. He could come or he couldn't. Either way, she was astonishingly unaffected.

"I'm sorry about last night," he said as he caught up with her quick pace. "I was wrong to get so angry. I didn't tell you the rules before I left, and I had no right to take my fears out on you."

Why were half of their conversations arguments and the other half apologies?

"It shouldn't be this hard, Sean."

"What shouldn't?"

"Getting along with another person."

"Look," he said, pulling her to a stop beside him. His impossibly blue eyes searched her face. "This is a really crazy time for me. And not the good kind of crazy, just the crazy kind of crazy. I don't know how to handle all of this. Losing the colony, Aria, my life in a new place. I'm just treading water here, Laney. And then you come along in the middle of it and part of the time I just want to strangle you, and then the rest of the time I can't stop thinking about that damned peacock tattoo on your back." Sean's sigh tapered off into a growl and he ran his hands through his hair. "I guess I just want to spend some time getting to know you better, but I don't want it to mean anything. Not right now. Does that make any sense?"

"No! It doesn't! And you're so confusing that I just want to give you a swift punch to the spleen!" Or at least that's what she wanted to say, but didn't. Though from the way Sean took an involuntary step backward, she suspected that much was written on her face anyway.

Maturity was best. "So, you think of me naked but you just want to be friends?"

Sean looked miserable and, after a loaded moment, he nodded. "Can we call a re-do on dinner?"

"I don't know, Sean," she said, picking up her pace again to get to the gardens. She had to get to work, preferably before Vanessa verbally assaulted her for being late.

"When is your day off?" he asked, unperturbed.

"Friday. Tomorrow. I'm off tomorrow."

"Perfect. Dinner tomorrow then. I won't forget this time," he said with a boorish grin.

"Ha," she said without humor. "Maybe I'll show up and maybe I won't."

"Maybe be there around six."

"Bye, Sean." She threw a little wave behind her. He didn't follow. At least the man could take a hint.

"What did he want?" Eloise asked in breathless excitement as she caught up to her at the colony gates.

"To apologize."

"For what?"

Laney waved to the guards at the gate, both of whom she didn't recognize, and filled Eloise in on the disastrous almost-dinner with him as they walked the quarter mile to the garden gates.

"Ooo-wee, the drama. The intrigue!" Eloise exclaimed.

Laney snorted. "The drama at least."

"Hey, I heard something about the Denver colony falling. Is it true you were there?"

"Yeah, it's true. Did you know anyone in the Denver colony?" she asked cautiously.

"No, I didn't personally. Lots of other people at Dead Run River did, though. It's so sad. And scary!" Eloise snapped her fingers. "Just like that everyone could be gone."

A vision of Jarren's last moments flitted across her mind. "Yep," she agreed somberly. "We have to live our lives as best we can while we have them."

"Landry!" Vanessa screeched.

Laney hunched her shoulders against the grating sound. "What?" she asked at a more reasonable volume.

"No more fertilizing for this week. I need that area tilled and prepared for next spring. Cold weather is coming and we need to get the gardens ready for snow. Eloise you help her, but keep your traps shut. I want you actually working today."

"I'll show you what to do," Eloise told her.

Thank goodness for Eloise's know-how. Laney could identify any handheld weapon with a glance, but "tiller" was new to her vocabulary.

The girls dragged handheld tillers out to the area Vanessa had pointed to and worked diligently for the rest of the day, only stopping for water breaks and lunch. When they were done, they removed clumps of plant material from an old crop and tossed them in a big pile. At the end of the work day, Vanessa had her load the huge pile of old plant clumps into the trailer on the back of an ATV with instructions to take them outside of the garden gates and throw them over the electric fence.

"Hey," she said, stomping down the shiver of excitement that came with seeing Mitchell open the colony gates as she pulled the four-wheeler up. She had full intentions of swindling some help tossing the plants from one of the guards. She didn't even have to ask. He saw what she was doing and jogged over to help.

"What about your post? Will you get in trouble?" she asked him.

"Nah, we just changed shifts. I'm off duty."

They worked in companionable silence until the trailer was almost empty. Mitchell stopped and looked toward the garden gates. She followed his glance and saw Eloise, Nelson, and Vanessa heading their way.

"I'm going to go hit the showers before dinner. You got the rest of this?" Mitchell asked with a frown in the unwary group's direction.

"Sure," she said, baffled by his quick exit.

He left, and a few armloads of plant bundles later the trailer was empty. Laney rubbed her itching nose. The smell of plants was overpowering. When she pulled her arm away from her face another smell struck her. Deads.

She looked around and caught movement through the trees. He was a big monster, with the bones of his skull showing through strips of hanging flesh. All of his teeth were exposed as his lips had rotted away and his mouth was open in anticipation of a meal. He was running full out with startling speed. When she swung her head in the direction of his target, her horrified gaze rested on the slow moving and completely unaware threesome meandering between gates.

"Dead at nine o'clock," she yelled the guards at the gate behind her.

A guard talked rapidly into a radio, but the Dead was getting close to his targets. It wasn't going to be enough.

"Eloise!" she screamed.

Chapter Fifteen

"Eloise!" Laney shouted again as she pulled her nine millimeter from the holster on her thigh.

Eloise and the others snapped their heads up in confusion over the panic in her voice. The barbed wire fence would hold the beast, but only for a few seconds. He had caught their scent and wouldn't be put off by the damage the fence did to his body. Eloise looked on in terror as the monster came crashing through the trees directly for them.

Laney aimed her gun and fired. Miss.

She let out an expletive and ran forward a few steps, then inhaled slowly, training her sights on the Dead. Her arms swung in a graceful arc as the gun followed its target. He was getting too close. She couldn't miss again. She held her breath and pulled the trigger lightly, as a finger brushes forbidden frosting off a birthday cake.

The Dead's legs buckled under him and he flew forward. He landed on the fence and went rigid as the electricity filled his body. Bells jangled as the fence rocked under the new weight, and the monster's gaping mouth was frozen only a few feet away from Eloise, who was screaming in terror.

The electricity stopped working as the force of its energy drained the limited power source. The Dead hung limply across the labored fence, the hole in his head confirming her last bullet had found its mark.

Vanessa was bodily dragging Nelson to the safety of the colony gates, but Eloise remained frozen in place. Laney scanned the woods for more Deads and sprinted for her. The girl sank to her knees as Laney approached and slid to a stop beside her.

"It's okay. You're okay," she crooned, propping the crying girl up beside her.

"Laney!" Mitchell yelled. The fear in his voice made the fine hairs on her neck stand on end. It had been too close and they both knew it.

He ran through the colony gates, unwavering dark eyes trained on her.

"Mitchell, I need help," she said, struggling under her friend's weight. She was pretty sure Eloise had fainted on her.

Mitchell didn't say a word. He scooped up Eloise's slight frame easily, and Laney covered him as they ran for the safety of the gates.

After the guards closed the heavy gates behind them, Mitchell laid Eloise down gently onto the grass beside the path. In one fluid motion, he stood and crushed Laney to his chest. She could hear his heart as it threatened to hammer right out of him. Strong, and so loud against her ear it almost seemed tangible. *Thump-thump-thump-thump.*

"Mitchell, I'm okay," she said, finding it hard to breathe in his crushing embrace.

He pulled her back and put his hands on either side of her face. His dark eyes oozed concern, which melted to fury as he pointed his gaze toward the two guards.

He released her and exploded. "Why the hell didn't you help her? Even I could hear she missed that Dead on the first shot. There's no way there should have been only one gun trained on him! Where was her backup?"

"We have protocol we have to follow. No Deads are killed without Mel's permission."

"Hang your protocol! You have unarmed civilians out there and you didn't lift a finger. This would have been the time to bend the rules!" Mitchell shook his head in anger. "Laney deserves that guard uniform more than any of you guys and they've got her working in the freaking gardens."

"We didn't make the rules," one of the guards said defensively. "We do have to obey them if we want to live here, though. If you don't like the way things are run, you can complain to Mel."

Mitchell glared at him through angry, slitted eyes that had darkened to the color of volcanic rock. "That's a fantastic idea." He turned and stomped back up the trail.

Crap. She looked between Eloise's limp figure and Mitchell's quickly receding back. Where was she needed most?

"I'll take care of her," said the guard who slumped as if he felt miserable and inadequate. "We have reinforcements on their way as well as Dr. Mackey. They'll be here any second."

Eloise lay peacefully in the grass, pale, but otherwise uninjured. Laney's instincts warred over which friend to protect. "You let anything happen to her, and you'll regret it. That's a promise." She gave him what she hoped was a Vanessa-worthy death glare and sprinted after Mitchell.

"You can't go talk to Mel like this, Mitchell. She'll kick you out of here," she pleaded. He hadn't slowed his pace in any way. "You have to at least wait until you calm down."

Silence.

"Mitchell! I don't want you to leave," she admitted as she skidded to a stop.

Mitchell slowed and then stopped. He sighed as if it would expel all of the anger and emotional turmoil from his body.

A small group of guards and Dr. Mackey ran up a nearby trail toward the colony gates where Eloise and the guards were. Mitchell glared at them and then blazed his own trail through the woods. She followed.

He eventually found a place that seemed far enough from civilization to afford him the peace he sought. He sat against a tree, back to the rough bark and a seat of pine needles to cushion him. She chose a tree directly across from him and waited. Mitchell wasn't an easy man to talk to when he was angry. If she just waited him out, he would eventually talk or just get over whatever was ailing him.

With the birdsong and chilly breeze and distant river waters as a calming music, she relaxed into the tree trunk. The rays of late daylight filtered through the thick branches of the mountain trees, and she searched in vain for the bird that was making the soundtrack to their rare moment of peace. Her body complained as her adrenaline wore off and her side burned with a heat that hadn't been there earlier. She must have pulled at her injuries in the scuffle.

She pulled her shirt up to check on her half-healed Dead bite and noticed the four cuts Dr. Mackey had made. The butterfly bandages had pulled apart, and all but one were open and bleeding. Dr. Mackey had said he needed to take deep samples so he could test all layers of her tissue, and they were taking longer to close up than she had expected.

"What are those?" Mitchell said, finally breaking his silence.

His voice startled her. "Oh, they are just the skin samples doc took off me a couple of days ago. I guess I pulled them open."

He scooted closer and examined them. "Here, let me," he said, swatting her hand away from the bandages. "These look really deep."

"All in the name of science."

He reattached the bandages as best he could and sat back on his heels. "I knew you would be undergoing some tests, but I guess I just thought they would be taking some of your blood. I didn't know it would be like this."

She shrugged. It was just an unfortunate and inconvenient part of her life now.

"When do you go back?"

"Dr. Mackey wants me to come in for some more samples tomorrow morning. He says fresh samples are the best."

"I'll meet you there. You shouldn't be going through that alone."

She was touched. And speechless. In rare moments, Mitchell surprised her with his thoughtfulness. "Okay. I'm going at eight."

He stood and held out his hand. "Let's go eat. Rampaging makes me hungry."

She stifled a laugh. "Yeah, I was sure you were going to kill someone."

He smirked. "I'm not going to lie. The thought crossed my mind."

Mitchell ate and left dinner early to catch a few hours of sleep for another night shift. He was likely trying for a bigger credit at the general store with all the extra shifts. Guist was also working that night, so he disappeared with Mitchell, and Eloise was still recovering in Dr. Mackey's office. Finn, Sean, and Adrianna were probably eating filet mignon at Mel's place, so she ate quickly and left for her room.

Someone had been there. The latch to her door hung loosely, swaying gently in the breeze. She made it a habit to shut it firmly into place every time she left, so that was her first clue. She threw the door open with a handgun at the ready. Her room was empty and untouched, other than a small package on her bed.

She closed the door behind her and tore the brown paper and string off gently. Inside were three small bottles of homemade shampoo that smelled exactly like the kind she'd used at the Denver colony. Underneath was a book.

"The Art of War," she read aloud. Sean had placed a handwritten letter inside the front flap of the book.

I do believe I owed you some of Mona's handmade shampoo.
See you at dinner tomorrow.
Sean

She held the letter for a moment longer as she stared vacantly at the wall over her bed. What a confounding man. Her emotions churned as she struggled for a way to feel about the gift.

She put the shampoo with the rest of her shower things and took the book and a blanket out to the porch. Two wooden rocking chairs graced the end, and she cuddled into one, propping her feet up on the railing and draping the blanket across her legs. She used the rest of the daylight to read. She so appreciated tiny, rare moments like these. Life in such an unforgiving world could be unkind if ill-managed, but despite all odds, she still lived and breathed to enjoy a moment of peace and undiluted tranquility.

The fact that Laney wasn't a morning person would never change. The doctor making an appointment so early in the morning on her day off just seemed unfair. She knew he didn't mean to, or even think about it, but she grumbled soft curses for him anyway. After she dragged herself out of bed and up the hill to shower, she stumbled onto the doctor's front porch about an hour late. If Mitchell minded her tardiness he would have kicked her door down much sooner. As it was, he was fast asleep in a sturdy wooden chair on the doctor's front porch. He looked exhausted, but the planes of his face seemed relaxed in his slumber. Laney studied him until the hidden, tender places in her heart began to bother her. It was Mitchell. She had to get a grip.

She gently shook his arm until his eyes opened and fell on her. He smiled sleepily and stretched. He didn't even grace her with a single grievance about her belated arrival. She squinted at him suspiciously, waiting for the other shoe to drop. Maybe he was so tired he didn't know what time it was.

"You ready?" he asked in a voice deep with fatigue.

"As I'll ever be," she said. She led the way into Dr. Mackey's office.

Mitchell sat in a chair beside her as Dr. Mackey pulled the samples from her flesh. She didn't watch, but Mitchell observed the procedure with frank curiosity. He asked a constant string of questions, and the sound of his voice was comforting. It gave her mind something more than pain to focus on. After the doctor was finished drawing blood from the crease at her elbow, Mitchell helped her to a row of cots in the corner of the recovery room. She felt faint, as she always did after having her blood drawn.

Dr. Mackey showed Mitchell one of the samples he had just taken under a microscope, and the sound of their quiet conversation lulled her back to sleep.

She woke with a start from a dream she couldn't quite remember. Mitchell was nowhere to be seen, but Dr. Mackey and two other men were mulling over what looked like clumps of odd shaped cells thrown up on a wall by a slide projector.

"Your friend already left," Dr. Mackey told her as she sat up and pulled her hair into a ponytail. "He said he had to get some stuff done."

"Oh." Was that a twinge of disappointment? "All right. Well, I'm going to head out. See you next time, Doc." She waved her goodbye and left the office to find the day sunny and bordering on warm. Her stomach rumbled loudly, and she looked around self-consciously to make sure no one had heard. She had skipped breakfast in her haste to get to Dr. Mackey's, and it was already time for lunch.

She hopped off the stairs and headed up a trail that would lead her to the mess hall.

"Baaaah!" Mitchell yelled as he jumped from behind a huge tree trunk.

"What the hell, Mitchell?" she exclaimed as she fought the urge to viciously kick him in the kneecap and/or punch him in the esophagus.

"Where are you headed?" he asked when he had stopped laughing enough to talk.

"I'm starving," she said shortly.

"I've got that covered. Come on." He grabbed her hand and led her onto another trail.

"Wait. Where are we going?"

He turned and looked at her with eyes fever-bright with excitement. "Hunting."

She tried to keep the smile out of her voice. "Hunting? Like what kind of hunting? Bunny hunting or Dead hunting?"

"Maybe a little of both if we're lucky. I grabbed our lunch from the mess hall already. Where is your Mini?"

"Back in my room."

"Go grab your arsenal and your pack and meet me at the front gates, the ones where we came in."

She looked at him dubiously. It sounded too good to be true. "Are you sure they're just going to let us walk out of here for the day?"

"I already got it cleared. Mel specified that I could take one other person with me. She just didn't specify who."

"So she meant Guist but you are getting around her wording."

"Yep," he said proudly. "We're going to have to do a bite check again when we get back, though. Are you sure you still want to go?"

She mulled it over for a few seconds. She had worked hard that week, and after the emotional roller coaster she had been on lately, going hunting with Mitchell sounded downright exciting. "Worth it," she said, grinning. "See you in a few." She scurried off to her cabin to grab her things.

She tried not to look too suspicious as she half-walked, half-ran to her room, but the thought of an adventure was too enthralling after days of the steady and stable schedule kept by the colony. She wasn't used to it yet, actually finding it a nice change most of the time, but the restless corners of her heart hungered for deviation. And maybe for a little trouble too.

Mitchell talked to the gate guards easily as she approached them. It seemed he had made fast friends with many of the armed members of Dead Run River. Not surprising. He was a notoriously happy person, a prankster, a charmer, and though he had a temper, it usually came out for good reason and on people who more or less deserved it. People always flocked to Mitchell at the colonies they visited, and she was in awe of his easy way with them. She, on the other hand, tended to offend everyone she came into contact with, no matter how much she tried to secretly learn by watching him.

Mitchell grinned when he spotted her and made introductions to the three men at the gate. She had never met them before and they stayed to chat for a few minutes before he pulled her over to an ATV that was parked beside the gate.

"We're going in style, Landry," he said as he hopped on and turned the key.

The little engine roared to life, and she pushed her Mini to her back so she could better hang on to him. The guards waved and opened the gate just enough for them to squeeze through, and she threw her arms around Mitchell's chest in time to hold on for dear life. On a spectrum of safe to reckless drivers, Mitchell bordered on terrifying. He wasn't much safer with her on the back, but probably because he trusted her to hang on. If he was anything, he wasn't one to invite another to change him, so complaining about his speed was a fruitless endeavor.

They were laughing breathlessly by the time the gates had disappeared behind them. If she hadn't been worried about falling right off the back, she would have raised her arms above her head and let them catch the wind. The freedom was jubilating. Out in the forest, there were no rules but survival.

They stopped for lunch soon after they left the colony and ate it up in a tree for old time's sake. Mitchell had insisted she keep her tree climbing muscles limber, so they picked a pine and hoisted themselves up the crowded branches before eating the sizeable spread Mitchell had grabbed from the mess hall. They watched as dark clouds drifted slowly over the mountains, and she buttoned up her jacket to protect her from the chill that crept in.

"Looks like bad weather," she observed.

"Smells like it, too," Mitchell agreed from the branch he straddled.

He had always been more sensitive to the smells of earth and changing weather. Her nose had been more accustomed to death.

He gestured with his sandwich to the covered openings in her skin. "How does your side feel?"

"Fine. Honestly, I don't really notice them unless the bandages pull." She lifted up the edge of her shirt to check the four old samples and three fresh ones just above them. "Maybe I'm just getting used to pain."

"Probably. Come on. Let's get some hunting done before these clouds open up on us."

The day was spent joyriding. They weren't successful in their rabbit hunt, which was not surprising, as they put very little effort into it. They did, however, get into it with some Deads. They found two groups, one with three Deads and a larger band with seven. Both aggregations were headed straight in the direction of Dead Run River. The smaller group stumbled upon them while they were at the edge of a stream discussing whether or not to fish. She smelled them early, and she and Mitchell were both prepared and waiting. One shot for each was not much of a risk for seasoned fighters. The larger group was a different story.

When the distant stench of Deads hit her, Mitchell pointed the ATV they were riding in the direction she told him. When they saw how large the band of Deads was, she was prepared to pull off of their trail and escape. Mitchell had something else in mind.

He pulled around them, let them get a good whiff of human, and took off laughing.

She looked behind her at the group that was sprinting clumsily to keep up with the meal on wheels. "Thanks a lot, Mitchell. You know they are going to eat me first, right?"

He chuckled. "Better get to shooting then."

And shoot she did, though not well. She was turned the wrong way and bouncing this way and that as he maneuvered the ATV out of the groaning Deads' reach. In a situation that shouldn't have been funny in any way, she and Mitchell found themselves in a fit of laughter every time she missed.

"Come on, Landry. A few days in a colony and you forget how to shoot?"

"I swear," she muttered as she pulled the trigger and missed again. "You have the worst man plans."

When the last Dead had fallen and no more followed, he pointed the four-wheeler toward Dead Run River just as a few flurries of early season snowflakes floated down around them.

They had been right in their assumption that bad weather was coming, but they weren't in any way prepared for the storm that hit them when they reentered Dead Run River gates.

Chapter Sixteen

Sean barreled down on them like an avenging angel. "Are you out of your minds? No! Don't even answer that. I know you're out of your minds."

"Sean, stop yelling. What're you talking about?" Laney asked, trying desperately to pacify his barely checked anger.

Mitchell stared at Sean with his head cocked to the side as if he thought the man had taken a swan dive off the deep end of sanity.

"You," Sean accused, jabbing his finger at Mitchell. "Do you have any idea what could've happened out there? What would even possess you to drag Laney beyond the gates, unprotected?"

Mitchell leaned against the four-wheeler and shrugged. "She wasn't unprotected. She has her weapons, and if she got in a jam, we'd get out of it together. Like we've done a hundred times."

"Uh, Sean," she said patiently, "Mitchell didn't drag me out of here. I wanted to go. We had permission."

"You don't have permission, Laney!" Sean yelled in exasperation.

"So…what?" she asked. "I'm a prisoner here, then?"

"No, Laney. But you're the one who wanted to stay here. You have to mind the rules. You and your entire team don't get that. Obey the rules, stay in the colony. Break the rules, and this colony can't offer you protection anymore." Sean stepped forward menacingly and lowered his voice. "And whether you like it or not, you need protecting. And this guy doesn't cut it."

"Hey, whoa, whoa," Mitchell said, sliding his arm between her and Sean. He pulled her back from Sean's angry countenance. "I can protect her just fine. I've saved her life too many times to count, and she's done the same for me." Mitchell stepped into the space he had created between them and glared at Sean accusingly. "Why do you care so much what Laney does and doesn't do anyway?"

Sean shook his head and didn't answer.

"Why?" Mitchell barked out.

"Because she's the cure!" Sean blasted. "She's the cure, I know she is. She could change the tide for our survival, and if you get her killed we're all doomed. Don't you get that?"

At his admission, her heart sank to the soles of her boots. She put her hand gently over her mouth to hide the tremor in her lips. Stepping around Mitchell, she walked away from them. Let them have their pissing contest. She'd rather die than let Sean see how much his insensitive statement hurt her. Why had he kissed her? Just to make her seem more desirable to Adam? How could he toy with her in such a way and feel nothing? Nothing more for her than a mad scientist caring for his lab rat.

She ran for her room, and once inside the safety of her own space, she let herself go as a part of her heart pulled painfully further from Sean. It was weak. She shouldn't cry for a man who didn't deserve her tears, but she'd been ready, for the first time in years, to have a relationship, and the vulnerability of that revelation was overwhelming. She didn't know whether it was the loss of Jarren, or of finally finding Adam only to realize he was settled with another woman. She didn't know if it was either, or both, or none at all. Maybe it had just been too long since she'd cared for a man in such a way and her body and soul needed it to find some sort of balance, to fill some gaping hole she didn't know existed.

A soft knock at the door pulled her out of her abstraction. A quick wipe to her puffy eyes and a regrettable glance in the mirror and she opened her door a crack. Guist stood there.

"Hey, Laney. Somebody wanted to know where you lived so they could thank you." He stepped aside to reveal Eloise, looking decidedly better than the last time she'd seen her.

"Come on in," Laney offered.

Guist took the chair by her desk and immediately started doodling on the blank paper before him. The bed creaked as Eloise and Laney sat on it, facing each other.

"I wanted to thank you for saving me yesterday," Eloise said quietly. If the tone of her voice was anything to go by, she was still rattled by the close encounter.

Laney tried to reassure her. "Anytime. I'm sorry I bolted before you woke up. I had to stop Mitchell from giving Mel what for. What happened when you came to?"

"It was all a blur. Dr. Mackey was there and one of the guards carried me back to his office." Eloise smiled mischievously. "He said you'd shoot him if I had even a scratch on me. I wouldn't have believed him but I saw your face yesterday. That Dead didn't even faze you. You're kind of tough, Laney Landry."

"Oh, it fazed me all right. He got way too close to you guys for comfort."

Eloise slid a glance to Guist. The scratching of his pen was the only sound in the room. "Are you okay? It looks like you've been crying," she observed quietly.

Guist spun around and studied her face. "What's happened?" he asked gruffly.

"Simmer down. It's just a little bit of everything got to me. It's been a rough week." Nope. There was no way she was telling Guist she was having boy problems.

He frowned. "I thought you had a good day. Mitchell said you guys went hunting. Did he piss you off?"

Laney snorted. "When does he not piss me off?" She bit her lip. "Actually today is the first time I can remember that he didn't annoy me. The hunt was kind of exactly what I needed."

"Huh." Guist went back to scribbling.

"Was it Sean?" Eloise mouthed.

She nodded.

"Are you ladies about ready to head up to dinner?" Guist asked over his shoulder.

"I was supposed to go to dinner at Sean's," Laney admitted. "I think I'd much rather eat with you guys though. I'm pretty sure he rescinded my invite when he was screeching at me for leaving the colony anyway," she said with a grin.

So she had a knack for ticking people off. It had never seemed like a trait Guist minded. She washed her face and tucked her backpack and Mini away. She zipped her jacket up as they left her room, and the trio walked together up the trail to the mess hall.

"Laney!" Finn hailed as she reached out to open the cafeteria doors.

"I'll catch up," she told the others. "What's up?" she asked the imposing man.

"What're you doing here? I thought you had dinner with Sean tonight."

"I did, but—"

"But nothing, woman. The man has been cooking away up at his cabin. You don't stand a man up when he's put that much effort into a meal."

She internally groaned. She was still angry, and Sean was literally the last person she wanted to see or talk to. Not even a little piece of her wanted to deal with him, but she couldn't just not show up if he expected her. She was brash and stubborn and sometimes a little irresponsible, but her mother had instilled manners in her and she'd feel guilty for a long time if she left him hanging.

Growling in frustration, she headed for the trail that led up the mountain, offering no response to Finn's confused goodbye. She didn't feel like shooting the messenger, but she sure felt like ignoring him.

The smell of the food Sean was cooking wafted down the trail in front of the cabin. Her mouth watered. At least something good would come of this.

She knocked on the door and waited. Laughter emanated from the cabin, and her stomach dropped. Sean finally opened the door with a wide grin on his face, as if he were enjoying some inside joke, and she shifted her weight to look around him.

Mel sat in the dining room, happily eating and joking with Adrianna. Sean's grin dropped the instant he realized who stood on his doorstep.

After a quick glance inside, Sean stepped out and closed the door quietly behind him.

She threw her head back, and the cold air caressed her exposed neck. She laughed without humor. "Are you serious right now?"

"Laney, I didn't think you were going to come after earlier."

"So you had another dinner date on standby? You know what? Forget it. Why would I have expected anything different from you, Sean?" She spun and left the porch. "I didn't want to come anyway."

"Laney, I'm sorry."

"Apology not accepted," she called over her shoulder.

The tragedy of the entire situation was that she really wasn't surprised. He hadn't done anything out of character. Sean was a great leader, a great father, a great protector, but he wouldn't be a caring partner. No matter what her loyal heart said to the contrary, her logic couldn't argue with experience. Despite this knowledge, the rejection stung like the crack of a whip.

He'd made it clear she was unattractive to him, other than her tattoo of course. With this repudiation coming on the tail of her discovery of Adam's years of refusing to contact her in the shadow of another woman, she was low. Lower than low. Rock bottom low even. She'd had her insecurities throughout the years, as all women did, but on the whole she was a confident woman. She had to be to keep up with the men on her team. If she showed frailty, they'd eat her alive.

She walked the trails she'd become familiar with. Meandering to the river, she picked a place to sit near the water's edge. The river was shallow there, and the rocks on the bottom made small and melodious rapids. She leaned her chin on her knees and watched small trout making their way upstream. The tiny snow flurries that had fallen earlier had stopped long before, but the air felt as if another storm was lingering. She sat there until it was dark. Despite her peaceful surroundings, she couldn't quite burn the fury from her veins. How dare he make her feel this way about herself. She was better than that.

She'd give anything to escape her own head. She thought of Mitchell and the fun they'd found when they went hunting. She thought of his smile, void of tension or fallacy. He was a relief. A breath of fresh air when she'd learned to live on smog. He eased the shattering rejection. She thought of his caramel-colored eyes and the hungry look they sometimes cast upon her. For the first time, she thought about the way Mitchell had kissed her in Denver. It had been fast, and shocking. His lips had been passionately unapologetic. The more she thought of him to escape her dejected feelings, the more an idea niggled at the back of her mind. And once such a thought took hold, it was all she could think about because it offered such a sweet and tempting release. Her own personal escape plan.

She jumped up and headed for Mitchell and Guist's room before she could change her mind. She tried to block out any thought of her actions potentially ruining an old easiness born of a relationship she'd built over half of her lifetime. Mitchell had probably done this a dozen times. He was well-versed in women. If anyone could be casual about this, Mitchell could. Picking up her pace, she made it to the row of cabins she thought they were housed in. She remembered Nick pointing it out on their map the first day, but had never actually been to their room.

Her knuckles made a hollow sound as she knocked on the door. *Please let him be home. Please let this be his cabin.* Or not. Whatever was meant to be would be.

Guist answered the door. "Laney?" He stood aside for her to come in.

Mitchell had his back to her at the washbasin and wore nothing but a towel. His hair was wet, and the broad muscles in his back worked as he washed the leftover shaving cream from his face. He caught her silhouette in the mirror and turned with a startled look on his face.

"Out," she clipped to Guist.

He hesitated only a moment. "Oh, shit. This is happening," he murmured as he grabbed his jacket and hurried out the door.

"What're you doing here?" Mitchell asked, holding his ground on the other side of the small room.

She took her jacket off and watched his concern turned to re-alization.

"Why?" he asked. "Why now?"

She didn't answer. She was on a mission and talking wasn't necessary to complete it. She pulled her shirt over her head and unfastened her bra. She undid the hook on her belt as he took a sharp inhalation of breath. It shook slightly and she smiled. *He* thought her womanly. *He* thought her attractive. Warmth grew in her and spread to her very fingertips. Mitchell was a catch, as she'd heard many a woman say. Never mind his well-sculpted body and toned musculature, or his dark and hungry eyes that sent shivers down her spine for reasons she couldn't herself explain. Mitchell was funny, and confident, and protective, and caring in his own way. She'd seen the adoration in the women he gave his affection to at other colonies. While they were there, he always treated them as if they mattered. She wanted to matter. Why had it taken so long for her to tell him what she needed? What her body needed?

She stood in front of him, bare of clothing. Vulnerable. Her heart pounded wildly. Other than gate checks, she hadn't been naked in front of a man since Adam. Since before the outbreak. Since before she'd become the person she was now. And never in a fashion where she was asking a man to enjoy her body.

Mitchell drank in the sight of her. His eyes widened, and in the candle light, they looked so dark, like a starless sky on a moonless night. If she looked long enough, she'd be able to see his soul in them. The thirsty look that she hadn't even known she longed for had returned to his face, and the firelight danced in the dark planes of his eyes. The corner of his mouth turned up in an irresistible smile.

"Laney," he whispered, shaking his head back and forth slowly, though never letting his eyes wander from the shape of her body.

It was enough. It was already enough. She could leave now and feel the effects of Mitchell's lingering gaze overshadow Sean's careless views of her worth. She knew it, but she couldn't pull herself any farther from Mitchell's body. It had been so long, and she needed more. The cool wood beneath her feet chilled her as the cool air met her bare skin. She tiptoed across the room, seeking his warmth. Every sensual step toward him brought her excitement and anticipation. She placed the palms of her hands on his chest and felt the rise and fall of his quaking breaths beneath them. The rhythm of his racing heart matched hers, and she gave him a slow smile. He seemed as terrified and excited as she was. He caressed her neck and reached for her nape, pulling gently on her hair band until the weight of her long hair fell loosely around her shoulders.

"I have a request," he said in a slow, deep voice.

"And what's that?" she asked through a lazy smile.

"Tonight I want you to call me by my name. Say it."

"Mitchell," she whispered stubbornly.

He leaned down and came within a breath of her lips. He twined his fingers through her hair. "Say it," he growled.

She pursed her lips and shook her head slightly.

He lowered his lips to hers and kissed her in the barest of ways. His touch was so light she'd swear she dreamed it in the morning. She wanted more. Needed more. He pulled back, teasing.

"Please," she whispered as an acute desperation to keep his body close to hers brimmed inside of her.

He ran a feather-soft finger down the side of her arm. She hadn't the strength to take her gaze away from his lips. The game was through.

"Derek," she said softly, the enunciation odd against her tongue.

He smiled for only a second before his lips were on hers. He didn't hesitate. He didn't ask her permission. He took her lips and demanded she kiss him back as she'd never before kissed a man. His arms wrapped around her waist, and he pulled her to him in a crushing embrace. The pain brought her pleasure, and she whispered his name again with a ragged breath.

He groaned deeply in his throat and picked her up with ease. When her back was against the wall, he crushed his weight against her and kissed her desperately. She was empowered. How could such an untamed and masculine creature want her so much? She bit his lip gently, and he responded by hugging her body even more tightly to himself.

Someone banged on the other side of the adjoining wall. "Pipe down!" an angry voice shouted.

They froze and looked at the wall in question for a split second before they started chuckling softly. She hadn't even considered the thin walls. She'd been too enthralled with the velvet touch of his skin and utterly lost in the moment.

Mitchell raked his fingers down her side, ever careful of her injuries, and leaned his forehead against hers. "Are you sure about this?" he asked, looking deeply into her eyes as if they would provide the answer.

For one of the first times in her life, she wasn't afraid. She didn't have to put on a brave face for anyone. He could've seen right through her if she had. "I need this. I need you."

A slow smile pulled at his lips. It was happy, and calm, and adoring. "Okay," he whispered.

He picked her up and set her gently on his bed. The covers were warm and soft, and the glow from the stove in the corner let off a soft light, tossing gently rolling shadows across his bare skin. He took his time, caressing her body and making an effort to adore every part of her. Only when she was completely satiated did he give in to his own needs.

Laney smiled lazily at Mitchell as he traced her peacock tattoo lightly with his finger. He was lying on his side and propped up on one elbow, and in the dim candlelight, she had an impeccable view of the muscular planes of his chest and stomach. She lay on her front with her arms serving as a pillow as he stroked her back.

"Do you remember the night you got this tattoo?" he asked in a quiet voice.

"How could I ever forget? It hurt like hell."

He chuckled, the sound deep and resonating. "Yeah, before the outbreak this tattoo would've taken three sittings. But after the outbreak people had to be tougher and more flexible. Plus your tattoo artist could've died the next day and then you'd be stuck with a half done peacock."

"Exactly."

He frowned thoughtfully as the candlelight flickered across his face. "Do you remember anything else about that night?"

Was he being shy with his words? She thought back to the night they'd found a tattoo artist in one of the colonies. It had been scary times back then, and she'd wanted something beautiful done in the midst of all of the suffering. She'd still believed beauty existed out there, and she chose the peacock to remind her of that. "I remember I wanted to drink before I had it done, but you and Jarren wouldn't let me. You said it would make me bleed easier."

The ghost of her brother wavered in his sad smile.

"I remember you and Guist got tattoos too. He got an outline of a dragon on his arm and you—" she squinted again at the small script tattoo on his ribcage, only partially visible "—probably just tattooed your own name on yourself."

He laughed. "Not quite."

She propped herself up and eyed the tattoo. She'd never seen it this close and was surprised when he rolled slightly toward her to let her have a better view. It was a set of numbers, and she squinted to read them in the shadows.

"06-03-18?" she asked him in confusion.

He nodded but didn't explain.

"June third," she mumbled to herself. "Eighteen was two years ago. What was so important two years ago?"

"It was the day we got the tattoos," he said seriously.

"You got a tattoo of the day you got a tattoo?" she asked. "Your name would've been less douchey than that."

"Do you remember anything else about that night?" he asked.

She shook her head. "Not anything big."

"It probably wasn't big to you, but it was kind of huge to me. Do you remember holding my hand when you were getting yours done?"

Her heart skittered uncomfortably, and she sat up. This conversation was headed nowhere good. She pulled the blanket over her chest and huddled into herself.

The corner of his mouth twitched and a slight frown came over his features, but he pushed on. "That was the first time you let me hold your hand without trying to slap me, or punch me, or curse me out. You held my hand for hours. You leaned on me. I'd liked you for years, but that was the first day I knew I was done for. You were it for me. It was the day I knew I would compare every woman in my life to you and none would match up."

"Mitchell, stop," she whispered in horror. "I can't do this right now. You've had years to tell me this, and you tell me now? Tonight?"

Panic seized her. She wanted to be casual about what had just happened between them. That idea seemed laughable to her after all was said and done. How could it be that the unmanageable Derek Mitchell was the one having trouble with a casual night together and she wasn't? She jumped up and bolted for her pile of clothes on the floor.

"I don't understand," he said softly. "What was this to you?"

"Mitchell—"

"Don't call me that!"

"It's your name."

"It's my last name! The guys call me that. Acquaintances call me that. You can't call me that after what we just did. Why do you think I'm trying to piss you off all the time? You only call me Derek when you're mad at me. I breathe for that stupid word on your lips."

"Look, I just wanted you to treat me like one of your other colony girls," she pleaded as she pulled her pants on.

Mitchell stood, completely unconcerned with his lack of clothing. His hand hung in the air between them. "What does that even mean?"

"It means I thought you could be unaffected by this like you are with every other woman you take to bed!"

"How many women do you think I've taken to bed?" His eyes flashed dangerously, and his cheeks grew redder by the second.

"Forget it," she said. *Backpedal. Backpedal!*

"No! I really am curious. How many?"

"I don't know. Two dozen? Give or take."

Mitchell shook his head slightly and pulled back like he'd been slapped. He laughed and then ran his hands through his hair until he could talk again. "Two. I've slept with two women since the outbreak, and that was just because I was so damned lonely watching you pine for Adam. I waited for years for you to see that what you wanted, what you needed, was right in front of you the whole time."

She shook her head in denial. How could he have been hiding all this emotion for so long? "I'm not even your type! I see the girls hanging all over you at the colonies. The only ones you give attention to are frail. Sweet. Weak. I'm none of those things!"

"And why is it, do you think, it's so easy for me to leave them when it is time? Hell, I even told most of them I belong to someone else. I know it's stupid. I know it is! But when I brought those girls around it was to see if you'd get jealous. And you never did—until Vanessa. And then you came in tonight." He paused, his voice softening. "You came in tonight and it was everything I've waited for and more than I could've imagined."

He held his hands out pleadingly, as if he were begging her to understand. Begging her to return his feelings. She couldn't. Her feelings were unreadable, a jumbled mass of hurt and disappointment and hope all rolled into three different men's names. Adam, Sean, Mitchell. It was too much. She needed time and space to sort everything out.

"I can't. I can't right now, Mitchell."

"Please don't call me that," he whispered.

Her heart was in her throat. It was too much information on top of her confused feelings for other men. How could she tell him what he wanted to hear when she'd come to him out of anger over another? He'd find out and never forgive her and she wouldn't expect him to.

"I need some time," she said, dragging her face away from the disappointment on his. She pulled on her shirt and walked out of his room, more broken than when she'd entered it.

Chapter Seventeen

A thunderous knock on her door woke her early.

"Laney!" Eloise shouted excitedly.

She opened the door, uncaring that she was in her underwear and tank top once again. Sooner rather than later, she really needed to get to the general store and spend some of her hard-earned money on flannel pajamas.

Eloise's bright eyes focused on Laney's hair, and with one side of her lip curled she said, "Ugh!"

Laney swung the door wider for her to enter and padded off toward the sink as Eloise danced into the room and plopped onto the bed.

Laney brushed her teeth at the sink as Eloise talked.

"I guess I have you to thank," she said.

At Laney's confused look, she continued. "Guist told me you and Mitchell needed some privacy so he came and spent the night in my room." Eloise waited with a frozen, open-mouthed grin. "Did you hear me? I said he spent the night in my room!"

Laney spit her toothpaste and rinsed her mouth. She wasn't responding well, but her own encounter of that nature had left her raw. Being reminded of it first thing in the morning hadn't been on her to-do list for the day. Time to rally. She smiled in apology and sat on the bed. She hadn't had a close girlfriend in so long and was rusty at girl talk. "How was it?" she asked, hoping the question wasn't too weird. Apparently it wasn't.

"Amazing," Eloise sang. "He was so sweet and gentle with me. And he told me he loved me. Not even before or during. He said it afterward, when he could have just left instead."

Laney tried to maintain an interested smile. The same thing had basically happened to her the night before too.

"So, Mitchell, huh?" Eloise said, elbowing her smartly in the arm and waggling her eyebrows. "We're some very lucky girls." Eloise must've read something worrisome in her face because she stopped mid-elbow. "Oh, sweetie. What happened?"

"El, I messed up so bad with him." Laney told her what had happened, and about her mixed-up feelings with Sean. She told her what Mitchell had said to her and how she'd panicked and hadn't been able to sleep for hours thinking about him and his unexpected confession.

"I'm sure he understands about you needing time. That was a lot to put on you when you didn't expect it. How are you feeling about everything this morning?"

"I don't know. I haven't even really processed it all. It's like, this relationship I thought I knew for all of these years wasn't what I thought at all. I used to be infatuated with him when I was in high school. Every girl was, and he was older, and hung out with my brother, and all of that made him really attractive to me. But then I met Adam and my heart hasn't been open since. Not until recently when I threw it at Sean." She fidgeted with the edge of her blanket. "I have no idea how to handle this. I know I feel something for Mitchell. Something bigger than I'd like to admit, but is it partly because of this perfect night we spent together? Intimacy is so new and confusing to me. And even if it isn't only that, how can I tell him about any of what I'm feeling for him until I get all of my feelings sorted out with Sean?"

Eloise shrugged sympathetically. "I don't know. Probably sorting this Sean issue out first would help. Come on. Let's hit the showers. Who knows? Maybe Mitchell will be totally normal to you this morning at breakfast."

"Maybe." The sinking feeling in her gut said otherwise. She'd hurt him, and the thought of the disappointment on his face the night before was a knife in her.

She left her hair down, but the reasons she did were confounding. She kept messing with the dark, damp tresses with nervous fingers. Did she leave it down because Mitchell had seemed to like it that way the night before? What was wrong with her? She bit her lip in frustration and pointed her breakfast tray toward the table the group was sitting at.

Guist's face lit up like the morning sun when he saw Eloise trailing behind. Speeding around her, Eloise plopped down beside him before they started chattering happily. Finn waved a greeting, Vanessa glared at her as per usual, and Mitchell looked glumly at his food as he stabbed at some eggs with his fork.

She sighed and sat on the other side of him. "Hey," she said as cheerily as she could manage. When he didn't respond, she bumped him gently with her arm.

"Don't," he said quietly.

"Come on. Please don't be mad at me," she begged in a whisper.

Vanessa put a protective hand through his arm and leaned over him. "I think he just told you to piss off."

In a burst of fury, Laney stabbed her metal fork forcefully into the wooden table right beside Vanessa's hand. She felt bad, and wondered what had possessed her instincts to want to press fear into the little she-weasel, but her regret was quickly overshadowed by jubilation as Vanessa paled and pulled her hand away with a gasp.

Mitchell stood and left without another word. The sinking in her gut grew into a physical ache.

Heavy silence blanketed the table. Eloise recovered first and shoved a giant bite of eggs into her mouth before nodding toward the exit. Around her breakfast, she said, "Let's get you out of here before you maim someone, hmm?"

She didn't have to ask twice. With a lost appetite and time to spare before their shift started, Laney followed Eloise through the door and up a winding path, past a sign with an arrow and the words "General Store" painted in drippy white letters. "Store" was an overstatement. It was more like a booth she'd seen at a flea market or one of those stands people used to sell firecrackers out of during the fourth of July—back before the end of the world. Every square inch of wall space was taken up with goods to trade or buy. There were canteens, sweatshirts, homemade jars of jams and salsas, bag chairs, binoculars, and beadwork necklaces sitting on shelves. Rows of clothes and winter shoes filled two tables out front. A gangly, redheaded man sat behind an old-timey cash register and tipped his baseball cap at them before he went back to reading a battered paperback.

Laney purchased a dark gray long-sleeved T-shirt with a light pink moose on the back, a nicely fitting pair of blue jeans, a light blue hoodie with a Breckenridge ski logo on it, and a pair of flannel pajama pants. As a last-minute decision, she purchased a deep purple fitted cotton shirt with silver and gold sequins around the low cut neckline. She couldn't explain why she'd suddenly wanted it so badly, nor did she want to delve into the list of possible reasons. There was no time to go back to their rooms to store their loot, so she and Eloise carried cloth bags of clothing along with their sack lunches to the gardens.

She grew excited at the possibility of Mitchell guarding the garden gates, but when they arrived, two guards she'd never met before stood watch.

Nelson waved after they received their gardening assignments from a woman named Athelda.

"Where's your sister?" Laney asked, failing to muster any actual interest.

"It's her day off. She's probably hanging out with her new boyfriend."

The warmth drained from her face. When was Mitchell's other day off? Was it on Saturday?

The boy gave her a quizzical look. "Hey, thanks for the other day."

"Huh?" she asked, not even pretending she'd been paying attention.

"You know. For saving our lives from that Dead and all. That was pretty intense. You were kind of amazing."

"Oh, sure, sure," she said. She muttered a goodbye and went to work by herself preparing another piece of land for winter.

She worked at a feverish pace. It was in her makeup to work hard, but that day she was also desperate to escape thoughts of Mitchell and Vanessa together doing goodness knows what. Unfortunately, she had a very creative imagination when it came to matters of the heart. The light snowfall that came down at lunchtime only served to add to her melancholy mood. As she and Eloise ate their lunch, the girl seemed to know Laney didn't feel like talking. She didn't seem to mind either. Instead she happily ate in silence and gave small smiles to faraway places. Probably thinking about her night with Guist.

Laney squinted at a figure approaching from the gates. Was it him? She groaned internally as the man came close enough to reveal Sean The-Last-Person-She-Wanted-To-See-On-Earth Daniels. His eyes landed on her, and he headed in her direction.

"Perfect," she grumbled.

Eloise looked up from her daydream. "Good luck," she said as she scurried off.

"Hey. You got a minute?" he asked.

She chewed a huge bite of sandwich slowly. He didn't seem quite as attractive to her any more. He was still an extraordinarily handsome man, but she suspected he had disappointed her too many times and her heart had reached for something besides him. Something more fulfilling. She squinted up at his face. Dark eyes really did have a much more subtle sexiness than crystal blue ones.

"What do you want?" she asked, gulping the last of her meal down.

Sean sat beside her. "To apologize."

"Again?"

"What do you mean again?"

"I mean, you're always apologizing. Isn't that exhausting?"

He stared at her, his brows drawn together in question.

"Blech, apology accepted. You know what I've decided?" Honesty was the best policy. "We should just be friends."

Sean chuckled. "Oh you've decided this? All on your own?"

"Yeah. I think you stood me up one too many times. I want a man who wants me back, you know?"

Sean nodded thoughtfully. "You deserve that."

He was quiet for a while, and she leaned back against the building.

"What if I could be better for you later?" he asked.

"I think that is a crafty way of trying to keep me hooked. There's something about me that scares you, Sean. And if you add that on to not being well matched in the first place, I don't think it would ever work."

"But you don't know that. What if I worked through that stuff and realized you're the one for me? Would you give me another chance?"

She dipped her head and sighed. "I don't think so. You're a good man, Sean, but you aren't a good man for me. I need more."

An air of disappointment lingered in his hesitation. "Why the change? Is there someone else?"

She kicked a small rock with the toe of her boot and nodded. "Mitchell?"

She nodded again.

"I thought so. His feelings for you are kind of obvious."

"Not to me. It may be too late anyway. He's really upset with me. But he showed me how someone could treat me. I don't think I want any more mean boys," she said, rocking her weight enough to bump his side slightly.

Sean walked away, and where she'd expected sadness, relief comforted her instead. Her heart was ready to let someone in; it had simply latched on to the wrong person for a time. And that attachment had been a poison in her veins she hadn't realized. She'd tell Mitchell how she felt after work. They could start slow and build up together. The more she thought about his confession, the more of a mystery he became. How could he have bottled up all of that feeling for so long? Only the strongest could do something so chronically painstaking, and he'd done it for her. He hadn't forced her, or sheltered her. He waited patiently for her to mourn her loss. To realize how it could be between them.

He'd helped her tirelessly search for Adam without hesitation, despite his feelings for her. He hadn't done it to suck up to her. She hadn't even found out he cared until it was finished. He helped because he wanted her to be happy. Where Sean smothered her to keep her safe, Mitchell had always trusted her to handle her own fights and ask for help when needed. Though he'd stood up for her countless times, Mitchell found her capable of protecting herself and he had no problem taking orders from her in the field. She couldn't deny how he made her feel when he touched her body. Being with him was unlike any experience she'd ever had before. He made her feel as if she were the only woman that mattered, and though she was strong and capable on her own, leaning on a man such as him was intoxicating. She marveled at how drastically her feelings had changed for him since their hunting trip the day before. The strange sequence of events that had plucked her heart strings neatly from Sean and placed them onto a man more deserving was dizzying.

When the day came to an end, her impatience to find Mitchell had her wound tighter than a bow string. Eloise caught up at the gate. She was chugging breath to try to keep up.

"Are you going to talk to him?" she asked excitedly.

"Yep."

"So you've decided?"

"Yep."

"Sean's out?"

"Yep."

Eloise squealed.

She smelled Deads as soon as they left the gate. She put a hand in front of Eloise and sniffed at the air to track a direction. She pulled her Mini around to the front and readied her weapon. The scent was faint. The Deads were farther off, but she wasn't taking any chances.

She turned to the guards who held the garden gate open for them. "There're Deads out here. Can you call it in?"

"I don't see any," the guard said primly.

Laney growled and grabbed the walkie from his hand.

"We've got Deads near the garden gates. Advise."

"Laney?" Guist's voice crackled over the small speaker.

"Guist? I tried to tell this guy there are Deads out here." Laney sniffed the air again. "Smells like they're getting closer."

"Is Eloise with you?"

She smiled. "Yeah, I got your girl."

"Good. Put Klein back on."

She handed the guard the walkie.

"If Laney says there are Deads, there's a hundred percent chance there're Deads. Mark is calling it in to Mel. Laney, do you think it's worth a run for it?"

She considered it. She was so ready to find Mitchell. A look at the scared faces of Eloise, Nelson, and Athelda had her shaking her head. "Nope. Not worth it," she said into the offered walkie.

Guist sighed. "I don't like this."

"I don't either, but you know I'll take care of her," she promised. His worry wasn't for Laney. Not this time.

"I know. Lock up the gates until we get rid of them, okay?"

Laney herded everyone back inside the safety of the gardens, and three hours later the gunfire that signified the final ending for the large herd of gathered Deads rang out. She felt sure she was going to lose her mind before they cleared them to run for the safety of the colony gates. She used the time to teach Eloise and Nelson how to load, aim, and fire her nine millimeter, but it still wasn't enough to keep her racing mind off thoughts of Mitchell. All the safety obstacle had managed to do was give Vanessa more time with him. Fury pounded her blood at the thought of them together.

When the gates finally opened, she dragged Eloise by the hand, ignoring the piles of Deads a handful of the guards were loading into the back of a flatbed trailer. Eloise couldn't seem to keep her eyes off of the carnage.

"Don't look," Laney advised.

Back at the colony gates they had to do a quick bite check, which she didn't even mind in her haste, and when Eloise was safe and sound in Guist's embrace, she scurried off to find Mitchell.

She checked the mess hall first, but dinner had long since ended and only a few stragglers were still chatting at one of the tables. She tried Mitchell and Guist's cabin, but no one answered her incessant knocking. She even tried the showers, but he wasn't there. Puzzled, frustrated, and out of ideas, she headed for her own room. A lot of people were bustling about at that time of the night, and she had to dodge a few rambunctious groups of kids horsing around. She stepped up onto the porch, and a teenaged boy ran into her by accident. Grunting, she dropped her bag of new clothes onto the wooden floorboards. As she stooped to pick them up, a familiar grating giggle rang out and she looked up. Vanessa was placed delicately between Mitchell's legs as he leaned against the railing in front of her room, and she was laughing obnoxiously loud at something he was saying.

"What are you staring at, Landry?" Vanessa said, throwing her an ugly look.

Her disappointment was so acute she couldn't say anything. She couldn't even move from her squatting position. Had he been in Vanessa's room? Was he coming or going?

Mitchell straightened up and walked over to help her pick up the clothes that had tumbled out of the bag.

"I didn't realize you lived so close to Vanessa," he told her.

"Yeah, we're neighbors." She stood and cleared her throat. She'd thought about what she would tell him all day long, but now that the time had come she was scrambling. "I'm—I was actually looking for you."

Mitchell sighed and looked around. "Look, Laney. We really don't have to do this."

"No, I think we do. I have something important to say."

"Ew, is it about Sean?" Vanessa asked viciously. She seemed to find heart in the horror on her face. "You were going to tell him about hooking up with Sean, no?" She grinned toothily and turned to Mitchell who had fixed a confused gaze on her. "I'll tell him, then."

"Vanessa—" Laney tried to stop her.

"No, really. I don't mind."

Laney looked at Mitchell and bit her lip as Vanessa launched into her story.

"Adam caught our little skank here hooking up with Sean Daniels on his desk at the saw mill a few days ago. Isn't that right, skank?"

Mitchell glared at her with an unbridled fury and waited.

"He kissed me. We weren't hooking up."

"Same thing," Vanessa argued.

"No. You make it sound worse than it was."

Mitchell turned to leave, but Laney grabbed his arm. "Wait. It isn't like that. Adam was saying horrible things about me, and Sean was just trying to make it seem like we weren't listening. Ugh, it doesn't sound right. Just give me a minute to explain this. Please."

He grabbed her shoulders with both of his large, strong hands. "Laney, I don't ask you for much, but I'm asking you to tell me the truth now. Tell me you didn't come to me last night because of what Sean said about you being the cure yesterday. Tell me it wasn't because you were mad at him. Tell me!"

She opened her mouth to speak but couldn't find the words. She tried again. "It's not the only reason."

He released his hold on her. His eyes burned with shock and disappointment. "It's the only reason I care about. Forget everything I told you last night." The words ground out of his mouth like they had an acrid taste.

She watched him go, bitterly defeated. The weight of her despair was enough to lock her into place until he disappeared into the woods.

Vanessa laughed as she looked after him. "Landry, you're making this way too easy for me."

Laney retreated to her room to escape, but as she was shutting the door Vanessa's cruel voice sang out. "Mitchell really is a great kisser, isn't he?"

She shut the door behind her and leaned her forehead against the rough wood grain. The staggering weight of Mitchell's anger left her emotionally exhausted. The bitter sting of betrayal washed over her at the thought of his lips touching Vanessa's right after he'd caressed her own body with them. She really shouldn't let it hurt so badly. She had no claim on the man, but she burned just the same.

Chapter Eighteen

Laney found solace in the routine of daily life at Dead Run River. The heaviest part of that routine, unfortunately, was Mitchell ignoring and avoiding her. She tried for the first week to talk to him, but he'd have none of it. He seemed to be detaching himself from her as her heart had detached from Sean. The awareness was debilitating.

She looked for him everywhere. Even just a simple glimpse of him would soothe her for a minute or so. He'd be with Vanessa from time to time, but mostly he seemed to be throwing himself into work, picking up extra shifts.

Her heartache became a part of her, like an uninvited friend who, though she didn't want to hear it, told her she was still alive. At least she felt something. It was more than most could hope for.

In the two weeks since she'd graced Mitchell's doorstep, the gardens had closed for the snowy winter and Mel had promised to reassign her.

"Where do you think Mel will put us?" Eloise asked as they hiked farther up the trail to the leader's house.

"I have no idea." Mel probably hadn't had a change of heart about assigning her to guard duty. Sillier hopes had been rewarded though.

Not to her, but surely out there in the universe somewhere. More likely kitchen duty would be her lot in life.

"Has Mitchell forgiven you yet?" Eloise asked.

"I don't think it's a matter of forgiveness. Mitchell doesn't hold a grudge like this. He's always been fast to get over an argument. I think he's scared of getting close to me." She shrugged miserably. "Or he's trying to get over me. It's the only thing I can think of." Talking about him didn't relieve any of the hurt. She was tired of thinking about him, of pining for what could have been. "How are you and Guist doing?"

"Aw, Laney. I don't want to talk about that when you're so upset over Mitchell."

"El, distract me! I need a love story. I'll live vicariously through you and your happy ending. It is kind of weird that your knight in shining armor is Guist, though."

"Why's that?"

"I've just known him forever. It's kind of crazy to see him this happy and considerate after being so robotic for so many years. He even asked me if I wanted him to talk to Mitchell on my behalf, like some sort of matchmaker."

Eloise's eyes grew wide. "What did you say?"

"I said no. Well, what I actually said was 'Hell no, but thanks for the offer.' I don't want Mitchell to get mad at him too. I've caused enough tension in our team." She led the way up Mel's front steps and knocked on the door. "Jarren would roll over in his grave if he knew I seduced his best friend."

"Your brother?"

"Yeah. Sometimes I wonder if he knew how Mitchell felt all this time. I'll wake up in the middle of the night and remember things he said, and I think he might have."

Mel opened the door. "Ladies. Come on in." She stood to the side and let them pass. "Laney, you have an appointment with Dr. Mackey this morning, don't you?"

"Yep. The highlight of my week."

"How has that been going?" The statuesque woman opened the door to her office for them.

"I look like a patchwork quilt, but Doc says they're making progress."

"Very good. Well, I know you have an appointment to keep so I won't take up much of your time." She motioned to the chairs in front of her desk and they took a seat. "Laney, I know you want guard duty, but Sean would have my head on a platter if I okayed it. I tried for you, but that man has a stubborn streak much wider than mine. The best I could do was put you on livestock."

"Livestock? Like horses and cleaning barns?"

"Mostly cattle. We have a herd we maintain and they provide the beef for the kitchen. We have a barn where we keep pigs, horses, and other animals, but it's separate. The cattle need more room and are located farther down the mountain where grass grows a little easier in the spring. I know it doesn't sound that exciting, but our cattle are fenced in, which satisfies Sean. The compromise for you is that you get to leave the colony every day to go to work."

The tiny consolation still didn't come close to getting assigned guard duty. Maybe Mel would miss the disappointment in her voice. "Thanks for trying."

Mel turned to Eloise. "I'm going to give you an option. I know you two have become friends, so I'll extend the same offer to you. You can be assigned to livestock with Laney or you can do kitchen."

Eloise didn't hesitate. "I'll do livestock. Someone has to keep you safe," she said to Laney with a wink.

"Guist is going to freak out," Laney warned.

"Good thing you've been working with me on weapons."

Mel gave them directions to work for the next morning. They'd meet a team, two guards and three other cattle workers at the front gates of the colony. They were to take an SUV together down the mountain to work the herd. If they didn't run into any Deads, it was only a fifteen minute drive down. Mel dismissed them, and Eloise chattered happily down the trail to Dr. Mackey's office. Though the assignment wasn't exactly what she'd hoped for, Eloise's excitement over a new adventure was infectious.

"Doc," she called as she and Eloise opened the door to his office. "You in?"

"In here," came his muffled reply.

She followed the sound to the very back room but came to a dead halt.

"What's *she* doing here, Adam?" Sabrina asked angrily. She was lying in a medical bed holding a very tiny baby.

"How should I know? I'll get rid of her."

Adam grabbed onto Laney's arm and jerked her painfully from the room.

"Let go of me!" She wrenched her arm from his iron grip.

Adam's face had gone a very dark shade of red. "Laney, what the hell are you doing here? Is this some sort of game to you? Surely you can understand we need a moment of peace from you."

"I have an appointment," she growled. She lifted the edge of her shirt to reveal three small rows of cuts in different stages of healing. "I didn't know you had your baby. Congratulations, by the way." She made her voice as sarcastic as she could.

Adam hadn't taken his eyes from the bloodied butterfly bandages. "What's going on?"

"Doc is running some tests on me. It's the reason we came to Dead Run River. Contrary to popular belief, I didn't actually come here to ruin your life."

"What's happened?" Dr. Mackey asked as he approached from the lab room.

"Does she really have an appointment?" Adam asked the doctor.

"Yes, she does," he said testily. "Laney, you're late."

"Meeting with Mel," she snapped.

"All right. Thomas is going to be doing your blood draw today. I think you need a break on the skin samples. He's in the lab. I'll be in there after I check on the new mom."

Eloise gave her a wide-eyed look and led Laney into the lab room. Her friend knew her way around the doctor's office by now. She'd been coming to all of her recent appointments for moral support. If she couldn't have Mitchell to hold her hand through it, Eloise was the next best thing.

When they left Dr. Mackey's office, she made sure to refuse even a glance in the direction of Adam and Sabrina's room. She was well over him, but she didn't need their happy little family moment thrown in her face. Eloise burst into laughter as soon as they exited the front porch. Laney tried to glare, but Eloise was doubled over, gasping between giggles.

"Good grief, Laney. You have the worst luck!"

Laney stifled a giggle of her own. "Thanks a lot."

A few minutes later, Laney wiped tears of laughter from the corners of her eyes. It was a situation that shouldn't have been funny in any way, but if she couldn't laugh at herself and the unfortunate circumstances that had taken over her life, she'd cry buckets instead. And from the horrified looks people gave her when she actually shed tears, it was likely she was an ugly crier.

"What are you doing for the rest of the day?" Eloise asked when she'd recovered enough to speak coherently.

"I told Sean I'd take care of Adrianna today. Finn had a late guard shift and Sean has a bunch of work to do at the mill. The weather has been slowing them down out there. I'll probably take her ice skating on that little pond at the back of the colony or something. What about you?"

"Guist," they both chanted in unison.

"You eating dinner at mess hall?" Eloise asked.

"Yep. I'll see you guys there."

They said goodbye, and Laney headed straight for Finn's trailer. He was hanging out with Adrianna while Sean worked, but she knew Finn needed as much sleep as he could get. Those night shifts were grueling on the guards.

Finn had propped a lawn chair in the snow in front of his trailer. He laughed as he watched Adrianna try unsuccessfully to throw snowballs in his direction. The child was bundled with so many layers she looked like a pink marshmallow. Laney pressed her finger to her lips and slunk behind Adrianna. She scooped up a handful of snow and lobbed it at the child's feet.

"Laney!" Adrianna exclaimed, giggling with the challenge of try-ing to hit a moving target.

Finn waved and disappeared into his trailer. When Adrianna tired herself out, Laney took her into Sean's house to warm up. She was accustomed to Sean's cabin. In the two weeks since she had decided he would make horrible boyfriend material, the tension had eased between them. She couldn't explain what had caused it in the first place, but after they both accepted each other in a platonic way, they simply didn't argue as much. Sean still had a way of getting under her skin from time to time, but he wasn't offensive anymore. It was just part of who he was and his douchebaggery failed to offend her. She shook her head at his behavior, sighed in frustration, and moved on, grateful it wasn't her job to condition him to be more supportive and sensitive in a relationship. Whoever he ended up with could undertake that endeavor. She had been over to Sean's house on several occasions for meals and to watch Adrianna when she had down time. She enjoyed spending time with the child, and she knew Sean was busy trying to earn a living for them.

She toasted a grilled cheese for Adrianna's lunch and stoked the fire in the wood burning stove in the living room while she ate. "What do you want to do today?"

"Can we go fishing?"

"I wish. The river is covered in ice though. It would be pretty hard to get the fly to the fish. I think they are probably sleeping and not very hungry anyway. What about ice skating?"

"What's ice skating?"

"I'll show you. It'll be a new adventure, but your daddy said before we do anything today he wants you to take a nap. He said you're a monster in the evening if you don't get a nap," she said through a grin.

The little girl jumped up and started to pretend to take bites on her arm. Laney grabbed her up and made chomping sounds while she tickled her. It might have been inappropriate, but there wasn't a game in existence more fun than zombie attack. Besides, after what the child had seen and been through, the lighter they could make the subject, the better.

She snuggled Adrianna on the couch in the living room closest to the fire. Pulling a thick blanket over them, she sang to the girl until her eyes became heavy.

> *"Hush-a-by, don't you cry,*
> *Go to sleep little baby,*
> *When you wake, you shall have,*
> *All the pretty little horses.*
> *Paint and Bay, Sorrel and Gray,*
> *All the pretty little horses.*
> *Hush-a-by, don't you cry,*
> *Go to sleep, little baby."*

It was Adrianna's favorite lullaby. That suited Laney just fine because it was the only one she remembered her own mother singing to her when she was little. When Adrianna had fallen asleep and was breathing deeply, Laney relaxed beside her and watched the slow falling snow out of the window.

She thought of her lost family: Mom, Dad, and Jarren. She wished they could have made it long enough to find such a peaceful place amidst the tragedy of the outbreak. Maybe it would have made their violent passing easier.

After Adrianna woke, she took her to the frozen pond in the back of the colony. She strapped two ill-fitting pairs of ice skates she'd borrowed from Mel to their feet and pulled Adrianna around in slow, careful circles. They weren't the only ones with the idea. Other colony members came to skate or to socialize in small groups. She recognized a few of them and joined in their conversation while Adrianna skated with two little boys around her age.

She pulled her jacket more tightly around herself. "Come on, Adrianna. It's getting close to dinner and we need to get you in some dry clothes."

Adrianna came surprisingly easily. She must have been exhausted from all the physical exertion to come so obediently. Laney took her hand and led her through the gray haze of early evening, only to be pulled up short by Mitchell's approach. An unavoidable smile lit her face, but when he looked up, he halted and searched the woods with frantic eyes like he sought an escape. The gesture hurt more than she thought it could have.

"Hey, Mitchell," she greeted him.

"Hey," he sighed.

"Adrianna, do you remember Mitchell?"

The girl waved shyly from behind her leg, and Mitchell smiled at her.

"Did you go ice skating?" he asked.

"Yes, I went around and around."

"Good, that means you warmed up the pond for me," he said, showing her the skates dangling from his hands. "You girls have a good day." He eased around Laney.

She waved to his receding back as regret pulled at her like a strong current.

Sean met her and Adrianna at dinner in the mess hall.

"You're actually eating with the rest of us peasants tonight?" Laney teased.

"Shut up," he said around a bite of scalloped potatoes just as Eloise and Guist joined them. She knew the exact moment when Mitchell walked through the door to mess hall. She knew because she'd been looking for him. Guist waved him over to their table, but Mitchell stayed only long enough to gulp down his food before he left with a mumbled goodbye. His aloofness toward her was like a dagger. On top of that pain, she was the cause of all of this tension and unhappiness for Guist, who tried to remain neutral. "I'm Switzerland!" he'd say.

Eloise consoled her, but it wasn't enough and she left soon after.

The crisp and snowy morning came early to Dead Run River. Laney shivered as she tumbled into the clothes she had left warming by the wood burning stove. A hot shower felt good, but it was only a momentary relief from the bitter cold. Eloise met her at breakfast and they headed to the front gates together.

As they approached, Guist's booming laugh could be heard at a distance. Eloise squeaked and ran for him. He was barely able to catch her as she rushed into his arms. Realization dawned on a surprised Mitchell's face that she was there for livestock duty.

He rounded on Guist. "Did you know?" he demanded. "Is that why you were so gung ho to volunteer for livestock today?"

Guist shrugged. "Laney and Eloise were assigned to livestock yesterday. I had nothing to do with that."

"You could have told me," he snapped angrily. "I'm driving. Everyone's here now so let's go."

She looked longingly in the direction she had come from. Was it too late to change her mind? She frowned. Probably. She hopped into a four-wheel-drive SUV with Eloise and three other cattle workers. Fifteen terrifying minutes later, Mitchell pulled the vehicle up to the gates of their destination. Guist jumped out and opened the gate, chatting with two guards stationed there while the rest climbed out of the SUV and into the frosty morning air. Mitchell tossed one of the guards the keys and took his post near the entrance to the gate. The guards pulled away, taking the getaway vehicle with them until the next shift would bring it back.

Laney hung back as the others headed for a barn off to the left.

"Mitchell?" she asked quietly.

"Laney, I have to work. This isn't the place."

"Well, you won't talk to me anywhere else and you have to be here so I'm going to say my piece. I'm sorry. Damn it, I'm so sorry I don't know what to do with myself. I'll do anything. Just talk to me again. Please, just don't hate me anymore."

He had been doing a stellar job of avoiding her eyes, but on her last pleading sentence he looked at her as if he couldn't help himself. "I don't hate you. I wish I could, but I can't. I just need time," he finished, using her own words to burn her.

"Fine. I can wait." She left for the barn without a backward glance.

He wouldn't be watching her go as he used to. He was changing. Not the natural sort of change that came with growth or maturity. Mitchell was forcing the change to protect himself from something she couldn't understand or control.

Livestock proved to be much more physically demanding than she had expected. They each had ATVs to drive the cattle with, but the day proved long. After feeding them and leading them to part of the river that snaked inside of the gates, they had to break through the ice for the cattle to drink. Two calves had been born late in the summer and one had died in the night. The cold had overcome his ability to survive. The other calf's mother was nowhere to be found, so they had to use a technique called grafting to ensure the mother of the deceased calf would accept the orphaned one. It was a brutal process of skinning the dead calf and placing its hide onto the living one so the mother would adopt its new smell. Eloise had to leave the barn while a man named Unger coached Laney through the process. Eloise's stomach couldn't take it, or so the retching sound that came from the front of the barn suggested. When the cow and her new calf were settled into a bed of thick straw in a stall, they brought the rest of the herd in from the river to the shelter of a huge covered area. The thickly furred cattle huddled together for warmth, mouths moving rhythmically as they bellowed and chewed. The day had come to an end, but they still had to wait for the next shift of guards to bring the SUV back for them. Unger kept them busy in preparation for the next day, but at the sound of a smattering of gunfire and then a second, Laney rushed from the barn toward the livestock gates. She already had her Mini readied when she reached Mitchell and Guist. They had climbed sturdy wooden stepladders secured on either side of the gates. She could smell the Deads as soon as she was clear of the barn. There was nothing for her to do by the time she reached the team. They searched the woods with scopes, but finding no remaining walking corpses, Guist lowered his weapon.

"Clear," Mitchell said as they relaxed their stance but remained alert on the ladders.

"So this is why you have been hiding out here, huh? More action?" she asked Mitchell.

He spared her a glance. Progress. "It's one of the reasons," he admitted. "The cattle make a lot of noise and attract a lot of the Deads' attention. It's slowed down, though, with the snow. They can't move around in it very well."

"Where is Eloise?" Guist asked her, sounding concerned.

"Not feeling well. They made us skin a dead calf."

"Can you do me a favor?" Mitchell asked her.

"Will it get me out of the doghouse?"

He rolled his eyes. "Go grab an ATV. Tell Unger you need a trailer hooked up to it. We need to dispose of these Deads before the snow covers them."

"Sure." She jogged off, reveling in being needed.

She rode with Mitchell and loaded the Deads onto the trailer while Guist kept his post. When they were finished they drove a good distance to a deep ravine and dropped the bodies in one by one. Mitchell explained that it was their go-to Dead drop zone. When they returned, the new shift of guards still hadn't arrived. Eloise was leaning up against the fence, huddled into herself to keep warm, while the other workers had opted to stay in the warmth of the barn until the shift change came. Laney plopped down beside Eloise and washed her hands as well as she could with snow. The cold prickled her raw skin, but she was desperate to rid herself of the rotten smell.

"When are you leaving?" Guist asked.

Laney looked up to see who he was talking to. He was waiting on an answer from Mitchell. What a frightening question. Her mind raced with the implications.

"Tomorrow," Mitchell said in a deep, tired voice. "Dr. Mackey said the baby will be okay to travel tomorrow. I think Adam is ready to get away from Laney so he's rushing their departure."

"You're leaving with Adam?" she asked, unable to control the fear-filled curiosity in her voice.

"Yes," he answered shortly.

She pushed. "But why?"

Mitchell sighed. "Because they need armed escorts to get them to Fairplay safely. So I volunteered."

He was leaving. He was leaving. Mitchell was leaving her. She jolted upright and then groaned as her skin protested. Her hands found her waist and she placed a gentle pressure on the wounds Dr. Mackey had been whittling into her flesh. She forgot about them sometimes, but her quick movement made the injuries scream for attention.

She rocked forward in an attempt to ease the stretching of her skin, as if it would push her open cuts back together again and provide relief. Mitchell hopped off the ladder and kneeled beside her.

"Don't," he said softly. "Let me see."

He pulled her hands away from the tender area and unzipped her jacket. Lifting her shirt and hoodie, he grimaced when he saw the rows of injured flesh.

"Some of these look infected, Laney. I'm taking you to see Dr. Mackey when we get back to the colony. This has to stop." He gestured to the cuts angrily. "You aren't dying for their tests. They've taken enough from you."

She tried to smile. "If they are infected it's no wonder. Mel keeps assigning me to jobs that involve cow crap."

Mitchell snorted and looked up at the sound of the returning SUV. He turned toward the barn and let out a shrill whistle to the other workers. Then he drove them back to the colony and took her to the doctor's office as soon as bite checks were finished. As she climbed the porch steps, the first symptoms of an infection manifested. She wiped her moist forehead with the back of her shaking hand and sat up on the table. Mitchell talked to Dr. Mackey and the older man lifted her shirt to see for himself. He pressed his hand firmly on the side of her stomach and amber fluid dribbled out from under one of the butterfly bandages. Mitchell cursed softly under his breath.

Adam charged into the waiting room. "Laney, if you think—"

Before he could utter another word, Mitchell jabbed a finger at him. "No," he said furiously. "Leave."

Laney lay down as Dr. Mackey started the painstaking process of removing all the bandages. To take her mind off the pain, she focused on Mitchell: on the set of his serious jaw and the attractive stubble on his face. Her fingers itched to feel it. "If you hate him so much, why did you volunteer to escort him?"

He pursed his lips into a grim line. His caramel eyes were reserved. "I need a change."

"Are you leaving forever?" she asked bravely.

He looked out the window and shook his head slightly. "Not yet."

She winced as another bandage pulled one of the fresher wounds. "Will you hold my hand?" she whispered.

He hesitated. "Who has been coming with you to these appointments?"

"Eloise."

"I'm going to get her for you." He stood and turned for the door.

"Mitchell, please don't leave."

The look he gave her was tortured, haunted, like the ghost of the man he wanted to be stood within the pleading glance she gave to him. "I can't do this, Laney."

"Not just now," she pleaded. "Don't leave."

Mitchell rubbed a hand over his face and opened his mouth to respond. His teeth clicked as he shut his mouth and left without another word.

Eloise came in a few minutes later, but the damage had already been done. To her body and to her heart.

Mitchell left early the next morning with the young family and three other guards. He didn't come to say goodbye and Laney wasn't able to see him off. Instead she was stuck in the deep throes of a raging fever that had scorched through her body and landed in her mind. *You'll never see him again,* it screamed. The small part of her that was still sane was afraid the fever was right.

Chapter Nineteen

Laney healed, but slowly. Much slower than she was used to mending. Dr. Mackey had opted to leave some of her wounds open so they could drain as needed. For three days he kept her in the infirmary, watching her until a small wrinkle of worry etched itself into the bridge of his nose and threatened to become a permanent fixture on his face. The attention had been exhausting, though necessary. She knew how sick she was. She hadn't felt that bad in years.

Guist knocked lightly on the door to the small recovery room.

"We're here to bust you out," he said with a grin.

Eloise helped to put her jacket on as they received a list of strict instructions from Dr. Mackey.

"She shouldn't be alone," he told them firmly.

"Don't worry. I've borrowed a cot and I'll be staying in her room until you give us the okay."

When Dr. Mackey was satisfied she was in good hands, the three of them made the tiresome hike to her cabin. Leaning on them heavily, she waved weakly to a group of passersby who gave her well wishes. Her arms weighed a hundred pounds.

"Any news?" she asked Guist.

"Not yet. They're supposed to be gone for five days though, so no news doesn't mean anything." He held the cabin door open for her.

Home sweet home. She'd missed her room. It looked especially nice with all of the colorful scarves hanging from the ceiling and the hand drawn "welcome home" sign strung across her back wall.

"I was only gone a few days," Laney murmured.

Eloise shrugged unapologetically. After showing Laney all of the board games she'd smuggled in, she proudly pointed to the tin of brightly colored nail polishes by the washbasin. Eloise had obviously tried to think of everything to keep them occupied while she finished her recovery.

"I'm going to get us some dinner," Guist offered as Eloise helped her to the bed. Frigid air blasted through the room when he opened the door and left.

When the fire was stoked and the room comfortably warm, she dressed in her flannel pajama pants and tank top, which she rolled above her injuries so the fabric wouldn't irritate them anymore. Eloise cleaned them thoroughly and put away the first aid supplies. The door opened, letting a bone-chilling draft in as Guist stomped the snow off his boots on the mat out front.

"Look who I found out there," he said.

Mel stepped lightly into the room and pulled the chair up by the bed. "I made you chicken noodle soup. I know you don't have a cold, but I figured you could go for some comfort food."

Laney looked at it hungrily. Soup sounded divine.

"So I wanted to thank you for everything you've been doing for us," Mel said quietly as Laney dug into her meal. "You have been working so hard, and you haven't complained even once about all of the samples Dr. Mackey has had to take. And you risked your life to save some of our people without hesitating." She nodded at Eloise. "I didn't know what to expect when you came here, but I've been pleasantly surprised. You and your team have a home here as long as you want it."

The offer was a first for her. "Thanks, Mel. This place is kind of growing on me."

Mel squeezed her leg and left her to the rest of her meal. "Do you guys have a schedule worked out with who is taking care of her or do you need some days off from livestock?" she asked Eloise.

"We worked out a schedule. Sean has a day off tomorrow so he is coming by first thing in the morning until we get off for dinner."

A worried look flitted across Mel's face, but no one seemed to catch it but Laney. "Mel, could I talk to you for a minute?" she asked the leader before she could get all the way out the door. "Guist and Eloise, could you excuse us?"

"Sure. I'm going to go get my overnight stuff. I'll be right back," Eloise said.

Mel sat back down in the chair beside her bed.

"I just wanted you to know you don't have anything to worry about with Sean and me."

Mel looked taken aback. "I would never suppose—"

"No, it's okay. I know you guys have history, and I don't know your feelings toward him, but if ever you think of hanging back on my behalf, don't. Mitchell's my man." She smiled sadly. "Even if he doesn't know it."

"I don't really know what to do about Sean," Mel admitted.

"Well, I wish you luck with that. Arguing with that man is like trying to manage a lion with a sparkler."

"Don't tell him," Mel said shyly. "I'll work up the nerve eventually."

"Your secret is safe with me."

Laney woke the next day fervently wanting a shower. Sean and Adrianna had shown up just in time to help Eloise drag her weakened carcass up the mountain to douse it with hot water. Eloise showered too and waited patiently for her to finish. Laney had to stop frequently and take rests, since the simple task of shampooing her hair proved draining. Eloise left for work after their trek down the hill, and Laney lay in bed with her hair dangling down the side of it. Her dark locks dried quickly in front of the heat of the stove. Sean had taken a seat on Eloise's cot with a book, and Adrianna was playing quietly with the checkerboard on the floor. Laney was drifting in an out when someone banged on the door so soundly the walls shuddered.

"Come in," she called, not bothering to get up.

The door rocked open, and Vanessa stood there, leaning against the doorframe with a feline smile that didn't quite reach her eyes.

"Mitchell's going to be pissed when I tell him how much time Sean Daniels is spending in your room."

Laney propped herself up on her elbows and glared at her tiredly.

Vanessa's eyes dropped to the still red and enflamed injuries across her hip and stomach. "Ew, you look awful."

Did the woman not have a censor? "Um, thanks?" she said with an arched eyebrow.

Sean apparently found no interest in Vanessa and leaned back against the wall, continuing to read as if she hadn't just let the cold air in and accused him of diddling the injured.

Vanessa closed the door behind her and plopped down onto the chair beside the bed. She stared unapologetically at Laney's exposed and bruised stomach, her nose crinkled up in disgust. "What happened to you?"

Laney sighed and lay back down to dangle her hair in front of the stove once again. The heat was heaven against her scalp. "Doc had to run some tests and they got infected. Now I can't be alone for a couple of days and Sean is the only one who has a day off today to make sure I don't keel over." She turned her head and smiled cheerily. "Since you seem so concerned about him being in my room, you could do Sean a solid and watch me for him until dinner. I'm sure he has better things to do on his day off."

"No. I mean what happened there?" She pointed to the angry red puckered scar.

Laney gave a quick glance where she was pointing and plopped her head back onto the bed again. "A Dead bit me."

Vanessa's laugh dripped with sarcasm. "Funny, Landry."

Laney shrugged. What did she care if Vanessa believed her or not? "Hey, while you're here, can you paint my toes?"

Sean chuckled from the other side of the room.

"And maybe do a manicure on me and Adrianna?"

Vanessa glared at her. "Why would I do that?"

"Because you owe me. You know, for saving you and your brother's life and all." She was bored, and annoying Vanessa was proving to be very entertaining.

Vanessa groaned unhappily. "What color?" she asked, making her way to the tin of nail polishes.

"Adrianna, you pick," Laney said.

One impressive and scandalously red manicure and pedicure later, Vanessa left the room grumbling about her "worst day off ever."

The rest of the day consisted of napping, board games, and visitors. Finn, Eloise, and Guist came by and brought dinner for everyone. They all stayed crammed in the small room and ate amid easy laughter. It was late when everyone left and Laney was completely taxed, though happy, after entertaining for so long. She and Eloise got ready for bed and fell asleep to the sound of the wind picking up.

By the next morning, she was on the mend. Not a hundred percent quite yet, as she was still weak, but the redness and swelling had gone down and her belly didn't feel like a basket full of hungry wolverines anymore. Credit went to Eloise, who'd cleaned the wounds every forty-five seconds. Or that's what it felt like, at least.

She managed to get up the hill with only Eloise's assistance, and she even mustered the energy to shave her legs. If that wasn't a small victory, she didn't know what was. Back in her room, she stared at her smooth limbs which tapered into an eye-pleasing pedicure and smiled. It had been a while since she felt feminine and pretty. Eloise had the day off, so she braided Laney's hair and let it dry into cascading waves down her back. After lunch Laney decided she felt up to a short hike. The small room was stifling, and Eloise had Dr. Mackey check on her and okay a trip to the general store. With the absence of actual antibiotics, retail therapy was the next best thing. Being quite accustomed to living on very little, Laney hadn't spent much of her earnings. She bought more warm clothes, including a pair of gently used snow boots. She picked out an array of sweaters that Eloise had assured her looked nice on her physique. She purchased two more small bottles of shampoo and another disposable razor, along with a new toothbrush and a bar of rose scented soap.

"Those are all things you need," Eloise pointed out. "You just had a near death experience. You should pick out something you want."

An old guitar sat in the corner of the store. Mitchell had played before the outbreak, actually quite well. The past three years hadn't given him time or resources to do things he liked. The guitar would take the rest of her earnings, but he would love it. She hoped.

Breathing heavily, she trudged to Mitchell and Guist's room. Guist was at work, so they let themselves in. Laney laid the guitar on

Mitchell's bed with a small hand scribbled note that read, "Hopefully you remember how."

Mitchell's bed still smelled of him, and a pang of worry shot through her for the thousandth time.

She and Eloise made it back to their room, and Guist and Finn showed up soon after to stomp them in a team game of Battleship. Just as she opened her mouth to declare the need for a rematch, the door swung open wide.

"Hey," she exclaimed as the cold air blasted through the room.

One look at Sean's face quieted them down instantly.

"What's happened?" Dread snaked down her spine and settled in her stomach. It had to be about him.

"Mel sent me. It's Mitchell."

She flew into action, throwing her jacket on without even bothering to zip it and pulling on her new snow boots. Her jeans were still tucked into them and they weren't laced properly, but she didn't care enough to fix it. The others were a flurry of chaos, as they tossed each other jackets and pulled shoes on. She left for the trail up the mountain before they were even finished readying for the tumultuous weather.

"Where?" she asked, terror seizing her voice.

"Mel's cabin. She has them on the radio."

She flew as fast as her weakened legs could carry her up the steep trail to Mel's cabin, but it wasn't fast enough. The others caught up easily, and Finn pulled her neatly into his arms and raced up the hill after the others. She covered her face with her hands to protect it from the whipping wind. Was he dead? Bitten? Was he on the radio to say goodbye?

When they reached Mel's cabin, Finn set her down onto the porch and she followed the others into the office. Mel, Nick, and a handful of other people were already there, huddled around the desk. Adrianna held tightly to the somber colony leader's legs, and with a flick of her wrist, Mel ushered Laney over to stand beside her.

Laney couldn't make out what the voices on the radio were saying. It was chaos and confusion, laced with static and yelling and screaming and gunfire. She tried to pick Mitchell's voice out of the noise, but was disappointingly unable to.

"They've been ambushed," Mel said shakily. "The first reports came in at over thirty Deads. They aren't reporting anymore. Someone has pushed his walkie against something. It's holding the button down so we can hear everything." Mel shook her head. "From what we've heard, it doesn't sound good."

"Guist, we have to go get him," Laney snapped.

"Where are they?" he asked stonily.

"It's too late. You'd never make it to them on time. We sent a rescue team out as soon as the ambush was reported. They are en route to look for survivors."

Laney grabbed the radio, unsure if they would even be able to hear her. "Mitchell. Mitchell! Come back to me. Come back!" There was a catch in her voice, but so what? He was dead or dying and she hadn't even been able to say goodbye. She wasn't there to cover him.

The radio went silent. The only noise that came from the small speaker was the continuous hum of static.

"No, no, no," she chanted, shaking her head in denial.

Sean touched her shoulder gently.

"Don't touch me!" she screamed. "I know what you're thinking, but he's not dead. He's smart. He climbed a tree. He got out of there." She left the shocked house and skidded her way down the snowy trail to the front gates to wait.

Guist showed up within minutes and wrapped a huge blanket around her shoulders. A truck was sitting to the side of the gates, and Guist lowered the tailgate and lifted her into it. She shared her blanket with him and huddled into his warmth. Her long, loose hair whipped in the wind and snow swirled around them as they waited in silence. There were three guards at the gate who were scanning the road in front of them with binoculars. Every time a radio sounded, she jumped.

Finn, Sean, and Eloise walked slowly out of the woods. They didn't say a word. They didn't need to. Their presence was enough. They piled in the back of the pickup truck and waited in agony with her and Guist.

At long last, one of the guards signaled to another. He saw something through his binoculars. She scrambled out of the truck bed and ran to the gate, careful not to touch the electrified wire.

"Do you see anything?" she asked Guist.

"Not yet," he answered as they strained their eyes for any movement.

Finally, after excruciating minutes of waiting, a black SUV limped slowly up the mountain road toward them. It had taken damage. Its mirrors were ripped off and the dents in it were so deep it looked as if someone had catapulted bowling balls onto it. Pieces of piping and metal were hanging from beneath the undercarriage, and the front right window had been smashed. Laney looked desperately but couldn't tell who was in the exposed passenger seat.

The vehicle came to a stop at the gate and the doors opened. She searched each face twice for any sign of familiarity, but none of them were Mitchell. Two of the guards started performing bite checks on the arrivals, and her heart sank to the space where her feet met the earth.

She held her hand over her mouth to contain the sobs that wracked her body. Someone moved in the SUV and two more men exited the car, one on the other side where she couldn't see anything but the top of his dark hair. *Please, please, please.*

"He saved my life," the other man said shakily. "He saved me. He dragged me up a tree. He saved my life." One of the guards tried to soothe the shaken man with comforting words and he quieted, his mouth still forming the words but lending no voice to them.

The man on the other side of the SUV limped slowly around to the front of the car and revealed a face she had feared she would never see again.

"Let me out," she told the guard at the gate excitedly. "Let me out, let me out!"

"Do it," Guist warned him.

She edged out of the opening gate and flew at Mitchell. He turned in surprise and caught her. He lost his balance and landed hard up against the car, but he didn't seem to mind. "Laney," he rasped, holding her so tightly she thought she would suffocate and die happily. He clenched her shirt in his hands and rocked her gently. "I'm okay. I'm all right," he said.

"Bite check," one of the guards snapped.

Mitchell drew away from her just enough to take his jacket off and pull his shirt over his head. Guards tugged him and yanked him but she didn't care. She couldn't take her eyes off of his face. It was bleeding. His nose had been split by a branch or something, and the way he favored his leg said he had messed it up pretty badly. But he was alive. She put her hand over his chest and felt the strong and steady drum of his heartbeat. Such an all-consuming, important little cadence.

"I was so scared," she whispered.

He searched her face and ran his hand through her long, whipping hair.

"Bite check cleared," the guard told him mechanically.

Mitchell looked at the man, distracted, and nodded his thanks. Then he took Laney's hand and pulled her through the gate. Guist hugged him tightly, pounding on his back, and Mitchell said something quietly that elicited a laugh from his friend. Sean, Finn, and Eloise were grinning broadly. The latter wiped tears away from her puffy eyes and laughed with embarrassed relief.

Mitchell pulled her into the woods toward the colony center.

Gooseflesh come up in waves across his bare back. "You are going to freeze to death," she worried.

"Do you have a fire going in your room?" he asked, picking his way over snow-covered trails.

"Yeah, but—"

He cut her short and switched directions, heading down the mountain. When they reached her room, he threw the door open and shoved the cot against it as a make-shift lock. They didn't make it to the bed. The cold wooden floor would have to do. He turned on her with such fierceness that for a split second a little part of her was scared.

His kiss was violent, without reserve or uncertainty. He forced her lips open and explored her mouth with his own. She groaned, and the tiny noise of pleasure seemed to make him even more frantic. He pulled at his belt with quick, jerky motions as if frustrated by the obstacle. He didn't even bother to remove their pants all the way before he was inside of her. Mitchell wrapped his hands tightly in her hair as she clutched desperately onto his back. It only took a few strokes before they were riding the wave of climax together. Her body pulsated to encourage his own fulfillment and his breath shuddered as she dug her nails deeply into his back, breaking the skin in long, thin lines.

He cursed softly. "I shouldn't have done that," he said before the warmth of her climax had even worn off.

"Don't," she pleaded. "Don't treat me like that. Not like I'm just some girl."

He pushed off her. Leaning back against the cot, he ran his hands through his hair. Without meeting her eyes, he said, "Laney, I'm leaving."

The wind caressed the cabin, whistling low as it brushed the roof. If only she could pretend he hadn't said it. "When?"

"Two days."

"Why?"

"Because I can't keep going the way I have been, Laney. I'm unhappy. I think it's the first time in my life I've ever been really unhappy. It's like I told you how I felt and now I can't plug it up again. It's leaking out onto every part of my life here. Leaving for Fairplay? It was hard going, but I got a break from seeing you with him. From watching you with his kid. Like one big happy family. I can't get over you if I stay here."

"But I don't want you to get over me. And it's not like that with Sean."

Mitchell shook his head and held his hand up. "I know what I see and it rips my guts out. I've waited all this time for you to be ready, and you gave yourself to another man."

"But it's not like that, Mitchell."

He stood abruptly and fastened his pants. "What would you have me do? Stay unhappy? Stay hurt?"

"Of course not, but—"

"I have to watch you day in and day out with him and his daughter. Would you have me stay here so I can guard your family with another man? I should be protecting you and *our* children. I need relief from this. From breathing and living for you. It's suffocating me. I can't just be the man who watches you move on. I want you happy, Laney, but I don't have to watch you find your happiness with another man."

He kicked the cot out of the way and threw the door open. He turned abruptly. "I'm sorry," he said before he closed the door behind him.

Chapter Twenty

"Laney. Laney? Have you heard anything I've said?" Dr. Mackey asked.

She puffed air into her cheeks and let it out slowly before she shook her head. "Sorry, Doc."

"I asked you how you were feeling."

"Oh! I'm fine. I'm great actually. Couldn't be better. I mean, I had my heart ripped out but, you know, time will heal and all."

Dr. Mackey looked at her as if she had suddenly sprung a unibrow. "I was talking about how your injuries felt."

"Oh," she laughed nervously. "Those little things." She looked down at her stomach as he palpated each cut for tenderness. They really did look a lot better. "Think they are close to tip-top shape. I'll be wearing a bikini again in no time."

Dr. Mackey pulled up a chair and looked at her with sympathetic curiosity. "Laney, are you doing all right here? In Dead Run River, I mean."

She bit her lip and nodded but found herself unable to say more.

"One of your team members came in early this morning to get a pretty nasty leg injury patched up."

She perked up. She couldn't help herself, and from the slow smile on the doctor's face, her movement hadn't been lost on him either.

"Was he okay?" she asked, trying to sound nonchalant about it.

"The leg will mend in time, but he told me something that was quite disturbing. He is planning on leaving tomorrow morning. Said he wanted to get out before he got snowed in for winter. On his own, I'm afraid that injury will get him into trouble with no one to assist him. I tried to advise against it, but he seems determined. Now if I didn't know better, I'd guess he is running from something. Or someone?" His eyebrows arched questioningly.

"Dr. Mackey? Hypothetically speaking, would you say you have taken enough samples from me to extract a vaccine?"

He seemed to think on her question before answering. "I would say you've given more than anyone could have ever expected from you. We have already made headway, but with the limited technology at our disposal it will take some time, I'm afraid. The skin samples and blood are excellent specimens and should hold us for some time. Hypothetically speaking, of course."

Promise to Jarren: kept.

She hopped off the table and pulled her shirt down. "Well, Doc. Now it's up to you to save the world. I'll see you when I see you."

"Hmmm," Doc said. "You still have to take care of yourself, you know. Keep the wounds clean. Eat and sleep when you can. You are still important, and not just because of all of this." Dr. Mackey gestured to the lab.

She smiled at the thought that she had almost let someone convince her differently. "Thanks, Doc."

Stepping outside, she pulled her jacket more tightly around herself. She pulled clean, cold air into her lungs and looked up at the snow-covered pines. Dead Run River was a paradise, but it still wasn't enough to bring her happiness.

She spent the next hour looking for Mitchell, but the man had simply disappeared. When she found Guist guarding the garden gates, she questioned him on his roommate's whereabouts.

"If I had to guess, I'd say he's hiding from you. Probably swindled a shift over at livestock when he figured out you were on sick leave for a while."

"Did he tell you?"

"Yeah. He told me this morning."

"You going, too?" she asked, unsure of his answer for the first time since the outbreak.

"I've been thinking about it all day, but every time I imagine how it would be to leave this place, to leave Eloise, nothing in me wants to go. I don't want to fight blindly anymore. I want to protect a life that means something to me. I didn't know how badly I wanted to settle down until the moment we drove through these gates." His look pleaded for understanding. "I think this is where I get off."

She understood. If her heart wasn't wholly in charge, it would be her choice as well.

"What about you?" he asked.

She sighed regretfully. Guist was like family and she would miss him terribly. "Mitchell is my home."

He smiled sadly. "I'll come over and grab your pack after my shift. I'll refill it for you one last time. For old time's sake."

Dinner brought a sense of peace to a confused part of her. The peacock tattoo that snaked across her back had been painstakingly drawn into her flesh to remind her of a belief that something beautiful and vital and worthwhile still existed somewhere on this broken planet. As she watched her friends' laughing faces in the warmth of the mess hall, shielded from the whipping wind and stinging snow flurries outside, she knew she had found it. And that beauty was something to be protected.

She couldn't find it in herself to ruin such a lighthearted mood with somber news. The tinkle of Adrianna's laughter was enough to make her choose to savor the moment instead of darken it. So she listened to Sean, Finn, and Eloise joke and laugh until tiny tears stained the corners of her smiling eyes, trying desperately to capture every moment. To put it away in her mind like a picture of her personal paradise. Someday, when the end of her life came, she would need a happy thought. Something that would make all of the hurt and sacrifice of her nomadic life worth it. Someday she would draw on this moment to bring her peace where none existed around her physical form.

Guist caught her eye. "You okay?" he mouthed.

She nodded. He would understand her need to say her good-byes later.

She checked the door for the millionth time to find that Mitchell wasn't there. She wasn't surprised that he was skipping a public meal, but she continued searching for him nonetheless. He was trying to get out under the radar. Less emotion involved that way.

After she parted ways with everyone, she tramped through a layer of snow to Mitchell's cabin. She didn't know what she would say, but why sweat the details? She climbed the simple porch quietly and raised her hand to knock. A noise stopped her fist's advance and she stood there stunned and listening. A strum of notes drifted through the cabin, barely discernible through the thick song of the woods, but still audible to a listening ear. Mitchell was playing the guitar she had given him.

She lowered her hand slowly and stepped back to lean against the railing of the porch. The notes engulfed her completely. It was a sad melody, as lonely as a wolf howling unanswered into a sliver of a moon. She couldn't talk to him. He was stubborn, and though he was wrong and confused about her feelings for another, if she tried to explain herself and failed, he would run in the middle of the night and she would never again be able to find him. She had no doubt a man as cunning as he was could disappear and never be found if he didn't desire it. Like smoke. Like he'd never even existed at all. The thought felt heavy on her heart. She turned and climbed silently back down the porch steps and was startled to find a man's figure contrasting against the steady snowfall.

"You're leaving, aren't you?" Sean asked.

She pulled her jacket more tightly around her and nodded slightly. "Walk me to my cabin?" she invited.

"Why now?" he asked as their boots crunched with a satisfying sound on the snow-covered trail.

"Mitchell's leaving at first light," she answered.

"Did he ask you to go with him?"

Her silence was answer enough.

There was a pregnant pause. "Do you love him?"

"More than anything," she said honestly. "It just took me a really long time to figure it out."

"I guess that means there really is no chance of a future for us," he said quietly.

She slid a smile around the edge of her fur-lined jacket hood. "Sean, you and I would go nowhere fast. I will always be a fighter. I'll always pine for adventure. I'll never want to stay safe and confined. I'll bring out the worst of your protective instincts and you will resent both of us for it. You need a partner who is more like yourself." She turned back to the trail. "Someone like Mel."

"Mel?"

"Oh, come on, Sean. You guys get along great. I've never once seen you fight. We fight every time we talk. And you can't honestly tell me you haven't noticed that Mel is a stone cold fox. I mean, anyone with eyes in their head can see she is a ten." She stepped up onto the porch in front of her room.

"Will you ever come back?" Sean asked, peering at her in the dim light.

"I don't know. I have to try to find a place Mitchell and I can both feel at home. Maybe someday. Take care of Adrianna." She headed for her door before turning back. "Teach her to use a gun when she gets older."

Sean chuckled. "Will do."

He pulled his hands out of his warm jacket pocket and waved as she shut the door gently.

A knock before dawn had Laney up and hustling to the door across the cold wooden floorboards. Guist stood outside. The air he breathed puffed like steam from a train.

"He just left for the front gate. He did most of his packing yesterday, so you'd better be quick about it."

She jerked her head as a silent invite out of the cold. Scrambling into her warmest layers, she handed Guist a handwritten goodbye for Eloise. He traded her for her pack, newly stuffed with supplies the way only he could do it. She shoved what clothes she could into the already full pockets and strapped into her weapons. When she was done she looked at him. Here it was. The moment she had dreaded and would forever remember.

"Stay safe," he told her. He gathered her into a tight hug and patted her back roughly. "Keep your nose to the wind. Take care of our boy. Promise?"

Her throat tightened. "I promise."

He let her go, and she stepped through the door. She looked back once and could have sworn his eyes were watering. A first. She blinked hard and cleared her throat to keep her own sadness at bay.

She jogged down the trail to the front gates. The fear that Mitchell would leave without her spurred her heart into an erratic pace. She saw a figure on the trail up ahead and slowed. She squinted through the early morning light. Vanessa. The emotional tidal wave emanating from the girl was almost tangible.

"Ugh," she grumbled and high-kneed her way off the path and behind a large tree.

Vanessa could have easily seen her escape route through her obvious boot prints in the snow, but the girl was immersed in her own private misery. As Vanessa walked by, she muttered something that sounded like "that stupid skank witch," but maybe Laney was mistaken. Vanessa was far too sweet to mutter such unbecoming things.

When she had passed and disappeared up the trail, Laney started to run to make up for lost time, and by the time she came to the clearing that encased the front gates, her heart was fit to jump right out of her chest.

Mitchell was there. He waved to the guards who were opening the gates and limped around the back of the truck they had driven into Dead Run River. Apparently he was still okay with grand theft auto.

"Mitchell," she said, hurrying toward him. Her backpack jangled with her movement.

He opened the driver side door to get in, but didn't turn at his name.

"Derek!"

He paused and turned his head slowly in her direction. She ran for him, her pack heavy and restraining against her back.

"Derek," she said again, reaching the bed of the truck. "I thought I was going to be too late. I thought you would leave without me."

His face was a mix of shock and disbelief.

"You called me Derek," he observed in a low voice. "What are you doing here?"

"Going with you."

He looked heavenward as if his patience were being tried. "I can't do this. This is why I didn't want to see you before I left. This is why—"

She threw her pack down and covered the small remaining distance between them. Throwing her arms around his neck, she kissed him. His surprise only lasted for a moment before his powerful arms snaked slowly around her waist. He pulled her into his warm body as his lips softened and moved gently against her own.

Pulling back to lean her forehead against his, she said, "It was always you. I'm sorry it took me so long to realize it."

She opened her eyes to find him smiling. She hadn't realized how very much she had missed his smile until that moment. He looked as if the weight of the world had been lifted from his shoulders.

"Did you say your goodbyes?" he asked gruffly.

She nodded slowly and ran her fingers through the back of his hair. "I'm driving," she whispered.

He snorted. "No. We'll be dead in two miles." He gave her bottom a firm squeeze and sidled around her to throw her pack into the back seat of the truck.

"Oh, so you think it's safer for you to drive with a bum leg?" she argued happily.

He groaned, but his eyes said he didn't mind a scuffle with her. "Is this what I have to look forward to, Landry?"

"It's Laney to you, and yes." She hopped in the driver's seat and pulled the door closed with a thud. "Besides," she said as he climbed into the passenger's seat, "your driving is terrifying."

"Not as terrifying as you in the mornings."

"Pfffffft, there's nothing more serene than me in the mornings."

"I was talking about your hair."

She rolled her eyes, and they both waved to the guards at the gate as she pulled the truck out of the colony.

Mitchell reached over and held her hand to his mouth. "Are you sure about this?"

She squeezed his hand in her own. "Do you love me?"

"Yes," he said without hesitation.

"Well, I love you too, and I don't want to waste any more time being apart."

"Okay," he said. His light brown eyes danced with affection. "No more wasting time, then."

She looked in the rearview mirror as the gates of Dead Run River slowly faded out of sight behind them. She wouldn't ever forget the place where she had chanced upon everything that meant anything. She had found where the Deads had gathered at the water's edge in the mountains of old. She had found the place where peace could still be found in simple acts of valor and happiness.

She had found her asylum from the damned.

Epilogue

Derek took his eyes off the road long enough to look worriedly at Laney in the passenger seat of the truck. "You've been quiet for a long time. What are you thinking about?"

She smiled at the concern in his voice and pulled her attention from the passing woods outside her window. "I was just thinking about our time at Dead Run River."

"Good memories?"

"Most of them." She bit her lip and shook her head in disbelief. "I still can't believe it's been a year."

"A lot has changed since then," he said.

"A lot has changed," she agreed softly before she turned her attention inward again.

She had been doing a lot of internal searching as of late. It probably had something to do with the swell in her belly that Derek couldn't seem to keep a protective hand away from. She squeezed his hand gently as it cradled the roundness of her stomach.

They had tried to settle down. They had agreed early on that they were both tired of the constant motion and uncertainty that came with living as fighters. They had headed south after their stay at Dead Run River in search of a warmer climate, but had only managed to compare every colony along the way to the place they had come closest to calling home. They'd stayed in two separate colonies for a time before growing restless and leaving to search for something that would hold them. Each was missing something crucial that neither of them could quite put their finger on. When she had grown suspicious that she was with child, they started moving north, to the Rocky Mountains, before either of them was conscious of where they intended to end up.

"Does Guist know we're coming today?" she asked.

Derek's slow smile, the one she adored so much, spread across his face. He wasn't one to complain, but it was pretty obvious he had missed Guist terribly.

"He knows it's today or tomorrow. I bet he'll be working the front gates. You feeling okay?" he asked for the tenth time in an hour.

She chuckled. "I feel fine. We're all right."

"A few more miles and we'll be there. You sure you want to go back to Dead Run River? What if things aren't the way we remember them?"

"You know as well as I from the correspondence with Guist that things haven't changed that much." She intertwined her fingers in his. "I want to go back. I miss having our little family together."

So Aaron Guist and Derek Mitchell weren't blood. They had been through more together than most families ever would, though. Losing Jarren had been hard, and bitterly so. But she had been lucky to have Derek and Guist there to keep her sure in the knowledge of who she was and where she came from.

"Besides," she said flippantly, "everybody around here says Dr. Mackey is the best if you're expecting."

"So I've heard," Derek said as he turned the truck onto the familiar winding road that led to the colony.

She leaned forward. The finished wooden gate loomed ahead. She squinted at the guards who were standing at the entry, searching for a familiar face. They had a very big job to do. They had to protect the colony and the important assets it boasted. Rumor had it that Dead Run River held the beginnings of a vaccine against the Dead virus. Such a medical breakthrough had to be protected in its infant state until it could be perfected, tested, and dispersed.

They were still too far away for her to tell if one of the guards was Guist or not, but as she and Derek drew closer, she began to suspect the one on the right was in fact the last member of their trio. The gaping grin on his face gave him away.

Derek hopped out almost before the truck was in park to greet him. She took a little more time. Though she was only a little over halfway through her pregnancy, she seemed to ache more and more after long trips. She zipped her jacket closed against the frosty air, effectively hiding the small bump that protruded tellingly.

"Laney!" Guist bellowed as he picked her up in an uncharacteristically affectionate hug. Eloise had obviously been rubbing off on him. And for the better.

Derek looked at her in panic.

"I'm fine!" she mouthed, unable to stifle her giggles at Guist's oblivious happiness.

He put her down and pulled a radio to his lips. "Mel?"

"Yep," came the answer from the other end, followed by static.

"Can you and Sean bring Eloise down? Tell her I have a present for her at the front gates."

"Are they here?"

"Yep," he replied excitedly.

There was a pause on the other line. "Be there in a minute."

Laney looked at him accusingly. "You didn't tell her we were coming?"

"She likes surprises," he said remorselessly. "You want to know what housing assignment Mel gave you?"

She grinned. "Lay it on us."

"Well, Mel moved us to a roomy trailer farther up the mountain, and since you guys got a noise complaint last time you stayed in Dead Run River—" he winked "—you aren't okayed to stay in the connected cabins, so we're going to be neighbors. Sort of. You guys will be a few trailers down from us, but on the same row."

"Noise complaint?" Derek laughed as he put his arm around her. "Blame that one on Laney."

"What?" she said in mock anger. "He complains, but I got us upgraded."

"Laney?" a familiar voice called.

She spun around with a ready grin. Eloise had changed drastically in the past year, mostly due to the huge swell of her belly that led the way as she waddled quickly toward her.

"Eloise? What happened to you? You look like you swallowed a basketball!" Laney laughed with amazement. No jacket could hide how far along she was.

Laney jogged over and hugged her tearful friend, careful not to knock her own belly.

"Oh, Aaron." Eloise sniffed. "This is the best surprise ever!"

Laney pulled away and wiped her own eyes. "I have another surprise for you." She unzipped her jacket and turned to the side. She couldn't contain her grin as Eloise stared in wonderment at a matching pregnancy only a few months behind her own.

Guist recovered first—likely because Derek was clapping him on the back and congratulating him.

"Laney, you're pregnant?" he asked in shock.

She giggled and nodded. The look on his face was priceless. Like he had just realized his little brother could bear children.

"Why didn't you tell me?" he asked Derek, the first signs of a smile tugging at the corners of his mouth. "You dog! Why didn't you tell me?"

"We wanted to surprise you. Why didn't you tell us?" Derek gestured to Eloise, who had gone completely rosy in the cheeks.

"Same reason. And I figured from the way you were sounding that you were headed back here sooner or later. I was just banking on sooner so you wouldn't miss everything."

Guist grabbed Derek's shoulder and shook it slowly as their news set in. Laney rolled her eyes at their laughter and turned to Eloise.

"You'd think they were the ones having the babies from the way they're congratulating each other."

Eloise snorted. "Well, it was a very important thirty seconds of work those boys did."

Movement caught Laney's eye. The woods were just as she remembered. Dark, safe, inviting. Magic. Sean, Mel, Adrianna, and Finn all smiled from the edge of the tree line. Sean had his arm around Mel's shoulders, resting on her comfortably, and Mel was talking quietly with the most relaxed expression she'd ever seen on the woman's face.

Laney's heart welled with happiness that those two had found each other. She waved and headed for them while the others followed.

It felt better than she could ever have imagined, having her family and friends back together in one place again. She slid her hand into Derek's and smiled happily at him. She knew she was glowing with contentment. She could see it reflected in his eyes.

They were home.

Acknowledgments

It takes village to write a book. A heartfelt thanks to my husband, Anthony, for supporting me through all the crazy late nights of clicking away in the corner of our room, and for giving me a romantic life to draw inspiration from. My parents for hearing me say, "I'm stressed about a deadline," and interpreting it as a need to take my kiddos on a surprise library adventure to give me time to work. To Grammy, success cheerleader and bear-hugger extraordinaire. I'm thankful to my dear all-weather friend, Amy Vesper, for not blinking when I admitted I wanted to go on this crazy adventure called a writing career and plopped a giant first draft manuscript and a red pen into her outstretched arms. To the editors at Omnific Publishing for using their magical abilities on a book that means so much to me. To Traci Olsen for her unwavering dedication to marketing the pen-and-ink renderings of the voices in my head. And lastly, the sharing of the story of *Love in the Time of the Dead* wouldn't be possible without Omnific Publishing, who took a chance on a hopeful author with an apocalyptic love story to tell.

About the Author

Tera Shanley has completed twelve romance novels of different sub-genres. A self-proclaimed bookworm, she was raised in small town Texas and could often be found decorating a table at the local library. She currently lives in Dallas with her husband and two young children, and when she isn't busy running around after her family, she's writing a new story or devouring a good book. Any spare time is dedicated to chocolate licking, rifle slinging, friend hugging, and the great outdoors. For more information about Tera and her work, visit:

www.terashanley.com

Erotic Romance

The Keyhole Series: Becoming sage (book one) by Kasi Alexander
The Keyhole Series: Saving sunni (book two) by Kasi & Reggie Alexander
The Winemaker's Dinner: Appetizers & Entrée by Dr. Ivan Rusilko &
Everly Drummond
The Winemaker's Dinner: Dessert by Dr. Ivan Rusilko

Paranormal Romance

The Light Series: Seers of Light, Whisper of Light, and Circle of Light
by Jennifer DeLucy
The Hanaford Park Series: Eve of Samhain & Pleasures Untold by Lisa Sanchez
Immortal Awakening by KC Randall
Crushed Seraphim and *Bittersweet Seraphim* by Debra Anastasia
The Guardian's Wild Child by Feather Stone
Grave Refrain by Sarah M. Glover
Divinity by Patricia Leever
Blood Vine and *Blood Entangled* by Amber Belldene
Divine Temptation by Nicki Elson
Love in the Time of the Dead by Tera Shanley

Historical Romance

Cat O' Nine Tails by Patricia Leever
Burning Embers by Hannah Fielding
Good Ground by Tracy Winegar

Romantic Suspense

Whirlwind by Robin DeJarnett
The CONduct Series: With Good Behavior & Bad Behavior & On Best Behavior
by Jennifer Lane
Indivisible by Jessica McQuinn
Between the Lies by Alison Oburia

Anthologies

A Valentine Anthology including short stories by Alice Clayton,
Jennifer DeLucy, Nicki Elson, Jessica McQuinn, Victoria Michaels,
and Alison Oburia